NIGHT and other
Short Stories

to Michel
L.

13/4/75

to Emma
the shopping
is in the
kitchen

portrait of M.S. by Laura Ford.

NIGHT and other Short Stories

Michele Spina

Habet mundus iste
Noctes suas et non paucas.
St Bernard of Clairvaux

COLIN SMYTHE
Gerrards Cross, Buckinghamshire

THE WOLFHOUND PRESS
Dublin

First published in 1998 by Colin Smythe Limited
Gerrards Cross, Buckinghamshire SL9 8XA

British Library Cataloguing in Publication Data

A catalogue record for this book is available
from the British Library

ISBN 0-86140-393-2 Colin Smythe Ltd

First published in Ireland by Wolfhound Press, 1998
Wolfhound Press, 68 Mountjoy Square, Dublin 1

ISBN 0-86327-629-6 Wolfhound Press

Printed in Great Britain
by Guernsey Press Company, Vale, Guernsey GY1 3BW

Contents

INTRODUCTION

Michele Spina died in 1990 aged sixty-seven. He is one of those writers whose fate, as Maria Corti of the University of Pavia has remarked, is 'to achieve posthumous fame'. In fact, even if 'his work did not pass unrecognised by Elio Vittorini', one of Italy's leading intellectuals in the Forties (some of it appeared in Vittorini's *Politecnico* in 1946), it did pass unrecognised by the majority of Italian readers. One reason may be found in Spina's reserve, his disinclination to draw public attention to himself or, in general, to appear in public. His long absence from his native country may also be responsible for this undeserved neglect; in fact he spent most of his adult life in England where he taught at Leeds Polytechnic, absorbing the English way of life. He published sparingly in Italy, Great Britain and the USA. His manuscripts belong to the *Manuscript Fund* of Pavia University.

Only in 1981 were three of his stories published in Milan by Scheiwiller under the title of *Passo Doppio* with an introduction by Guido Almansi. More recently (1991) the Sicilian publisher Sellerio issued his *A occidente della luna* ('West of the Moon') with an introduction by Maria Corti; a novella very well received by the Italian press; an English translation by Ann Colcord appeared in 1994, published by Peter Owen.

The six stories collected here under the title Night give a coherent overview of the most relevant and interesting aspects of the Sicilian writer's style and main themes. Five, translated in English by Ann Colcord (Last Hotel, 1946; Fortune, 1972–1983; Angela, 1989; Intermezzo, 1986; Night, 1948–1989) are still unpublished in Italian. All these are no plain tales from any hill; they are for no easy consumption, even in Italian. Yet the reader is soon enthralled by the compressed energy he can perceive through the lucidity of a fully controlled, rich style. Only after going through them several times can one fully appreciate their

1

multi-layered narrative qualities, their iconic and symbolic force and the inexhaustible variety of rhythm and tone.

What all of the stories share is a deeply-felt preoccupation with what can be considered real in man's life, and with what relationships can be drawn or discovered between man's idea of reality and the wider, more comprehensive reality of the universe. At bottom there is a profound distrust of man's capacity to conceive of any stable, substantial idea of reality. Like the monk of 'Fortune', unceasingly 'after the essential, whatever this essential might prove to be', the stories are continually concerned with the questions which have troubled man's mind from time immemorial: what are we, why are we here, what is our final fate, what sense can we make of our actions?

The protagonist of 'Night', for instance, is a man who – like Gregor Samsa in Kafka's *The Metamorphosis* or Joseph K in *The Trial* – is constantly trying to find a logical explanation for what is illogical, viciously iniquitous, and humiliating for the individual; a man who – more through silent, never-ending brooding and reasoning than through actions – tries to take a stand against the alienating absurdity of a nocturnal world whose outlines soon fade into the vast chasm of nothingness, and where silence and obscurity conceal menace, betrayal, and the promise of annihilation. But like the actions, claims and expostulations of Joseph K and Samsa, the man's efforts in 'Night' are doomed to be swallowed in the unsympathetic silence of a tragically meaningless universe. In the same way every thought expressed, resolution suggested, and hypothesis framed peter out in the ineluctable slowing down of action, and in the deterioration of speech finally leading to stillness and silence.

Setting about finding some meaning or sense in whatever happens or is accomplished is a typically human activity; yet it is apparently also futile, and the male protagonist of 'Night', with his strong disposition to excess, emphasizes man's metaphysical condition midway between tragedy and farce, a grotesque condition we obstinately pretend not to see or try to conceal behind more or less noble actions. The corridors and the narrow, nocturnal streets in the story seem to lead us into the dark world of a psyche in which a whimsical, capricious network of haphazard mental connections fails to reveal any logic or coherence. Walking up a country lane or a town alley – notwithstanding the accurate and realistic description of all physical details – soon becomes a descent into the nether world of the unconscious, a darkness which envelops everything, creeping into every nook and corner of the natural or human world. The result of this search is not insight, but a disquieting awareness that reason is fated to be finally consigned to oblivion in a bottomless sea of primitive forces which keep dragging down whatever tries to ascend. Logic, the ordering and classifying device of reality, cannot hold sway or find any room of its own in the vast abyss of the unconscious dominated by violent, elementary impulses, which rule over social life and the diurnal world more than is commonly thought or accepted. Spina's writing describes the triumph of the arbitrary even if this victory is kept concealed under the forms of necessary social pretence.

Thought, as it 'disposes random and disconnected things in any gender or class of possibilities' ('Paso Doble', p.196) seems to possess a certain degree of certitude, but 'Ideas . . . are perhaps as indifferent to men as they are to chickens or scorpions' ('Paso Doble', p.193). Human life seems to be made up of moments, intervals, bits and pieces jumbled together in a way which, contrary to all appearance, has nothing of the inevitability and consequentiality of logic, and which is only slightly determined by man's decisions, either individual or collective. In fact, these bits and pieces could easily be manipulated, rearranged in 'as many combinations as can be mathematically derived from three terms', the beginning, the middle and the end, so that they would be 'continually rehearsing sameness after sameness'. ('Paso Doble, p.192).

The world 'occurs': the excess of occurrences is at the same time evidence of freedom and confusion, giving rise both to exhilaration and perplexity. Human thought tries to give some temporary order to the world of occurrences, but it becomes unreliable when it tries to govern that world or when it suggests there are such things as order and reason. The universe is actually incomprehensible: only words allow us to confer a meaning to it, and the more powerful words are no longer those which helped us to survive in the civilisation of orality, but rather those which have acquired a new, disturbing power in the relatively recent civilisation of literacy.

By writing down experience, past or present, we confer a different sort of reality on experience itself, or rather we just 'confer reality' with no further specifications: 'writing restores a slower movement to the passing of the past, taking the slowness from the passing of the present'. Writing thus creates a new past as well as a new present which contradict the passing of objective time: the only real paths open to man are those which find their justification in the mind. In one of his moments of extreme tiredness and dejection, the monk in 'Fortune' feels that the present is becoming 'always more of a struggle' for him to live in 'and at the same time always less governed by thought'. ('Fortune', p.32). When this happens, when we cannot cast the blanket of our thought onto the ever-shifting world of sensation, the world seems to elude us while still bearing down upon us. Outside ourselves, in our absence, reality seems to have a chance to exist in stones, branches and other natural objects: 'to let things be what they are', cogitates the monk, 'one must grant them a sort of consciousness, a form of awareness that is not like ours' ('Fortune', p.53). In other words, nature is and will ever be incomprehensible to man in its essence.

The only meaning which may inhere in events arises from that particular type of logic which we seem to find in orderly arrangements of words, particularly in their written form. The act of writing – a fundamentally 'human' activity, as it is something entirely conceived and carried out by man – brings back the absurdity of life to the domain of intelligibility and sensibleness: if we can find any meaning at all in the universe, it is only, paradoxically, 'the effect of grammar' ('Night', p.154). Reality is therefore synonymous with textuality: its rules are the same as the ones which make a piece of fiction coherent and readable.

And yet, when the last word has been said or written, the only perceptible truth is that behind the castle of words there lies a dense, unfathomable mystery, which is best expressed through silence. All the stories collected here end with a sense of amazement, almost stupefaction – in the original meaning of the Latin word 'stupor' – before the unbearable awareness of the futility of any search for a final and satisfactory explanation of the mystery of existence. At that point, words seem to be 'no more than the falsifications of silence, or, perhaps, if daughters of silence, bastards' ('Paso Doble', p.172). The sound of words is only a mask on the face of aphasia, the impossibility of establishing real contact between individuals through speech acts. Behind the sound of human words there is only silence, or rather a terrible resonance which is inaudible to human ears, solemn and at the same time powerfully sonorous: 'the thundering of the unknown' ('Fortune', p.32).

All the stories are without a conclusion, perhaps even without a real beginning, suggestive of the entire history of man after the Fall.

Spina testifies to the creative function of language. By resorting to strict reasoning and skilful rhetorical devices, he is able to make general statements (or rather he makes his characters or the narrator make those statements) out of trifles or events of little or no relevance; in this way he can show ironically how our knowledge of the universe and ourselves has been constructed on false analogies and other tricks of the thinking mind. In 'Paso Doble', for instance, the villagers, 'quite naturally' refer the effect back to the cause and recognise 'the continuation of the mother in the son'. This is of course quite arbitrary, but this casual connection affects the future course of events and the world view of the Sharrock child as well as the villagers' own outlook. Spina is fully aware of the socio-political implications of this conduct and draws upon them to formulate a mocking judgement on the self-cheating quality of all human certitudes. In addition, if human life, as it seems, is pre-arranged by language, there is also a strong possibility that it may be regulated by the manipulators of language, that is by the holders of power and social control: the Church, the State, public opinion, tradition. Here lies the other side of Spina the sceptic: he does not accept that any man should be cheated by any other man or institution through the exploitation of his inner fragility, a fragility which is found in everyone. A humane indignation prevents his scepticism from turning into cynicism, changing it instead into satire and social criticism.

All this complicated musing on the nature of reality, on the meaning of time and the functions of language in the shaping of our world view could easily make these stories into something

other than works of fiction. Of course any form of fiction,
including the short story, allows the incorporation of other
literary genres, such as verse and the essay into its texture, yet it
is necessary for those other genres to be kept within certain
boundaries so that they do not interfere with the distinctive
features of the text or cause an incongruous mixture of too many
styles. Michele Spina knows these boundaries very well and
never allows the philosophical reasoning to interfere with the
narrative quality of the main text; indeed, reasoning itself
becomes a narrative through quick and sudden changes of
rhythm and language patterns. Through stylistic devices, which
do not rely too much on plot, astounding images of beauty and
eternity suddenly emerge out of some strict, abstract, apparently
essay-like reasoning. Unexpected lyrical or dramatic intervals
reveal that the main texture of the writing is still that of the tale,
and that there is as much concern with establishing an emotional
and aesthetic connection with the reader as with proving a
theory or making a political or philosophical point: 'In the curve
of waves, infinitely grey, travelling over the ancient wreck
beneath, the molecule, in its clinamen pirouettes, and suddenly,
then, ends in silence'. ('Paso Doble'.) His descriptions of places,
things, and human features are never generic: on the contrary
they are always analytical and precise. Indeterminacy may be a
trait of human existence, and there may well be puzzlement as to
where to place the boundaries of reality, but Spina never lets that
indeterminacy affect his style; indeed, it is his often obsessively
meticulous style that gives – so to say – a body, a substance to
incertitude and the conundrums of human life. See for example
the description of the landscape the monk goes through in
'Fortune' and that of the interior of a tavern, also in 'Fortune',
reminiscent of certain masterpieces of Baroque oil painting, in
which even the mysteries of faith, the spiritual and symbolic
qualities of the subjects, are portrayed through the solid, dense
contrasting of colours, the interplay of light and shade, and
accuracy of line, pattern and shape, as, for example, in
Caravaggio's 'Calling of Saint Matthew' in the Roman church of
San Luigi dei Francesi.

On the other hand, the maze of thoughts and the tight line of
reasoning which characterise Spina's style do not imply that
there is no story, no plot; the story is simply not given right

away: it comes in bits and pieces, like the fragments of a broken mirror, reflecting both the tiny details of an image and, gradually, the whole image itself as all the fragments come together. The plot is usually like a knotted and tangled skein of thread beyond any hope of unravelling, which finally unwinds itself all at once straight and free, ready to be neatly rewound.

Also the main and lesser characters which Spina introduces are not at all sketchy and unpolished. Quite the contrary; all have their own vigorous and full-bodied distinctiveness, which makes them memorable. The women have the fleshly sensual appeal of certain sixteenth or seventeenth-century allegorical or emblematic images – like, for instance, H. Goltzius's engravings representing Fame and History or those of Lucas von Leyden depicting Cardinal and Theological Virtues. Each of these visual oxymorons, in which flesh and spirit, libido and intellect coexist in one figure, highlights the function and meaning of the opposing qualities which it embraces by their very contradictory conjunction. The languid, soft postures of their bodies, the tender, melancholy, and distant look in their eyes point to the metaphysical remoteness of those female figures, whose voluptuousness paradoxically makes abstract virtue more desirable. Yet the rights of the flesh keep calling loudly from the exuberance of tangled hair or the bulk of female nakedness with the massive build of the hips and thighs strongly contrasting with the tiny size of almost adolescent breasts. The woman whom the monk discerns walking on the other bank of the river in 'Fortune' and whom he kept following as in a dream or hallucination has this oxymoron like quality; the same can be said of Edi or the director's wife in 'Night'; nor is the poor girl, who is constantly assaulted by young and old men alike from the age of eleven and who finally dies on a dungheap, too different from the others.

The male characters likewise have a distinctiveness of their own which makes them unforgettable, whether they be small peevish old men or children combining in themselves the gracefulness and the natural curiosity of adolescence on the one hand, or, on the other, the compressed potentiality for immense and wild violence. There are recklessly intemperate big fellows as in 'Night' and 'The Last Hotel', or troubled monks puzzled by the ever-changing facets of what we keep calling truth, as in 'Fortune'.

But perhaps the most pleasant special trait of these stories for Italian readers – which can certainly also apply to English-speaking readers, given the excellent quality of Robert Welch's and Ann Colcord's translations – is their peculiar comic flair, which gives them that special touch of originality, which is likely to be associated, in the long run, with Michele Spina's singular style. It is a comic power which does not easily fit in with the Italian comic tradition. It is a sense of humour much closer to English, or even Irish, wit: cold and pitiless, it can cut and dissect like a knife or scalpel rather than smash and crush like a stone. It is an unsettling sort of humour, which disturbs and calls in doubt even the most stable social and moral values. The description of Mary Magdalen in 'Fortune', for example, reverses the traditional iconography, going back to Renaissance and Baroque models, which represent the saint as sexually attractive yet averse to sexual desire, and in the monk's bizarre imagining, she decides 'to wash her arse too' after she has started 'to wash her breasts at a fountain in the shade' (p.33).

There is yet another facet to Spina's comic disposition, which is not exactly either Italian or Northern European: this is a cruel and brutal kind of humour which delights in extravagant and inordinate situations and in an exuberant, savage idiom reminiscent of Rabelais. The frequent accounts of totally unjustified and abrupt kicks, and of people being thrown out of the window; or absurd situations, like the main character's attempt, in 'Night', to get hold of the little man in the post office and drag him in through the narrow opening of a window: these scenes are related with the utmost casualness as if they were absolutely natural or insignificant. One is shocked and amused by the terrible contrast between the situation itself and the language through which it is narrated. There is an exhilarating feeling that the narrator is regarding as quite natural what is far from natural; that he does not see the infringement of social law implicit in the bland and deadpan style. Laughter here, as often with comedy, accompanies the breaking up of all social or cultural norms. Litotes and hyperbole are two common devices of comic discourse and Spina avails himself of both in all the stories, often shifting abruptly from one excess to the other with very pleasing results. Yes, 'pleasing', for all great works of literature find their final justification precisely in the pleasure of reading as such, which may result from the intellectual content or the moral insight of the story, but also from textual characteristics and the inner coherence which derives from each part being harmoniously connected with all other parts.

This quality is everywhere evident in Michele Spina's work. The stories published here are just a small sample, but a significant one, of the artistic qualities of a contemporary Italian writer who definitely deserves to be discovered by English-speaking readers; and, much more so, by readers who speak his own Mother tongue.

GIUSEPPE SERPILLO

SASSARI UNIVERSITY, ITALY

THE LAST HOTEL (1946)

This winter is endless, more rainy than cold, and particularly gloomy. It seems to be less a season than a special epoch, extremely long and drab, in which one moves blindly first one way and then another only to find oneself apparently back where one started, because this perpetually dreary light makes everything look so much alike. But this doesn't surprise me. Winter has always been a bad time for an out of work actor, without money, even without baggage and without friends, since friends are either working or pretending to work in other cities. After I had heard there was a possibility of some work I arrived one morning to find there was no basis for those rumours and that I didn't have the return fare. So I started to walk through the town, first one way and then another, trying to protect myself as best I could from the incessant rain by taking shelter in porticos, doorways and porches. Finally, I was so overcome with weariness, having almost forgotten hunger, that I could think of nothing but bed: a dry place where I could lie down to sleep. But I needed to keep thinking in order to stay awake and so I began to consider how ugly the place looked, and how sullen and sloppy the men and women there appeared, and in general concluded that the entire world was getting more and more squalid and bleak, and also more shameful and dangerous. It was a criminal world, I thought. And this thought seemed right to me, so I resolved to use force with people, since I could see I was taller and bulkier than most of the others there. In other words, I intensified the wicked nature of reality and the impossibility of acting out of good purposes or even merely decent ones, and tried to console myself with vague ideas of that violence of which I knew I was physically capable. At a certain point I realised that this consoling function of evil was only apparent and provisional, since it did not alleviate the disgust that was my dominant state of mind but actually increased it.

What is the purpose of living in a world which is not only wicked spontaneously, but also wicked from this moment on because I so wished it? And also: since it was so difficult for me to do any sort of good at all, would it not be more reasonable to dedicate myself entirely to avoiding evil?

It was at this point that the idea of suicide came to mind, and immediately attracted me for its very function of consolation which the idea of robbing someone, one of the ideas which I had previously had, also had. But this time the consolation appeared more resistant in me: For one thing killing myself appeared to me more immediately practical and more final than assaulting a stranger to get some money off him: this action would certainly have to be repeated, even in the course of a single day, to be somewhat useful; besides, the gloominess of the idea of suicide accorded with the dreary but solemn misery of the season and was also so dignified that it encouraged thoughts to linger on it calmly.

Perhaps my style as an actor, which is more drawn to the spontaneous and natural than the artificial, to the repetitive and wearying, also had a bearing on the easy and immediate contentment this idea gave me. For suicide is certainly an intrinsically dramatic action; and I do not like rehearsals or discussions about why one turned one's eyes up or to the side or raised an arm. Of course this is also a part of work, but in this case, no rehearsal would be possible and the performance would necessarily be entirely spontaneous. The scene in itself and for itself, that is, winter and, as I have said, the world deprived of good, the world *sub ratione ardui*, would have suggested at the last minute, I believed, every particular still unconsidered. Above all, there would be no audience or critic whose judgement I would fear, because I would be the only spectator or at least a hypothetical spectator.

However this is not the story of my suicide, but rather the story of a friendship that grew in the space of a few hours out of the most obscure recesses of a world I believed populated only by faithless, hostile individuals who were basically insignificant. This friendship – which I would call exemplary – or even affection, at the last moment brought my part to perfection but also rendered it difficult when I'd thought it would be simple. Actually this almost fraternal affection could not conceal my fear that I would show myself unworthy of such an example in rehearsal and, in fact, only a mediocre version of myself, or as some say, an out of work ham without art or a part.

But let's proceed in an orderly fashion: at about 11 o'clock at night I came to the end of a very long street, with the wall of a factory or warehouse on one side and houses three or four stories tall on the other. I had never been in this area before and I thought I would go back, until I saw the name of a hotel gleaming red in the rain. I had no money, no luggage, as I have already said, but although I had discounted violence on principle, I thought this time I would profit from my imposing height to acquire the sleep I needed. I intended to kill myself the following day, when I was rested and cool-headed. So I went in. As soon as the man at the desk looked at me he shook his head, with a gesture of refusal and disapproval, and said the hotel was full. I grabbed him by the collar.

'Then take me to *your* bed!' I said, banging him against the stairs. No one wants to call the police in hotels of the lowest category like this, so bullying brings favourable results: the man moved instantly and began to climb the stairs without saying a word.

'There is a double bed' – he explained to me while we were climbing – 'with a little man, actually very little, who doesn't take up much room.'

In my line of work, especially touring small towns, I have occasionally had to share my room with strangers. I was very tired that evening, what's more, and had decided to make an early start the next morning, so I did not want to lose any more time. I accepted his proposal. I had no reason to be irritated with the man sharing my room, the man I intend to talk about. Certainly I was the one in the wrong: bullying someone so frail is something I can't explain; actually, before, I would have considered it an act of true and thorough cowardice.

He got up from the bed where he had perhaps already been sleeping, and began to walk about in his nightshirt: a strange very long flannel shirt. His face was tiny, but dignified: his eyes were a shiny yellowish colour, like old pottery. I barely saw him. Perhaps I noted this detail only the following morning; his eyes were unforgettable. I didn't pay much attention to his nightshirt at first. I know that men who live alone often have strange habits and the nightshirt could have been one of these oddities.

I paid no attention to him: I was doing this deliberately. If only I had been a bit more aware of him, I would certainly have been aware of the similarities in our situation from the very beginning, but that was not how it was. The fact that he was walking around the bed irritated me; at a certain point I remember actually threatening to make him sleep on the floor, if he didn't stop. He seemed unable to be still: he sighed and tossed and turned all night. He switched on the lights several times, although I shouted at him harshly about it; once I even hit him, but not very hard: just a mild slap and a punch.

Only then did he actually catch my attention: he whispered that we shared a problem that needed to be resolved and that I should think about it too.

At first I thought he wanted to communicate the secret of some hidden treasure. For however strange my interpretation of his restlessness may seem, it is important to keep in mind how tired and sleepy I was and the way sleepiness often bestows a strange logic on the most absurd suppositions. At that time this absurdity seemed probable to me: I truly believed that he was talking to me about buried treasure, particularly since he mentioned something about a garden. I then struck him to get him to be quiet; on the thread of that mistaken logic, I concluded that the treasure was of no interest to me at all in my present state. I was trying to sleep.

But he began to write, when he could not speak, and I stopped insisting that he turn out the light: I had already hit him, and I couldn't keep on all night. Then he took a notebook out of his little suitcase: a notebook slightly bigger than this one I am now using: a writing pad perhaps that he should have known would end up in the hands of the police. Nevertheless he was writing for me, he told me. He had guessed the nature of my engagement the following day and actually seemed to be alluding to it, using this same word of mine.

These events of the night have a relative importance. The man caused me great irritation, but I still managed to sleep most of the time. I woke up not very late: the day was cold, and bright foggy light came in through the window. He was sitting next to this window, in full light, still wearing his dreary white nightshirt. His appearance was vaguely lugubrious: his wrists were too big for his body, as if deformed, and also his knees under the nightshirt looked out of proportion and made of too much bulging bone.

'He must have rickets,' I thought, considering these deformities and his build which in the light of day, or rather the fog, looked more miserable than it had the night before. When he noticed I was watching him he smiled several times, and pointed to his nightshirt: 'It's a flannel!' he explained, believing I was interested in his nightshirt. I didn't even answer.

I must confess that at the beginning his presence in the opaque and blinding brightness of the fog was repulsive to me. What's more, although I had decided the night before on my engagement, in the morning, at a certain place on the outskirts of town, I wanted to linger in the shelter of the room a bit longer when I saw it was such a wet day.

'Why aren't you going?' I asked. I slowly dressed myself in silence. Looking at myself in the small oval mirror above the washbasin, I took a very long time to comb my hair. The resolution I had made the previous evening now seemed precipitous to me. I kept looking at myself in the mirror: in the faint early light I barely recognised my own face, as if it was not part of me, so unimpressive it looked to me. I was still very tired.

In the meantime the little man spoke softly, as if he were whispering to himself. At first I paid no attention to what he was saying. Then his voice became louder. He apparently wanted to make himself heard, and that is probably why I started to listen to him.

'No way!' – he was saying. 'At the basis of this "engagement" of ours there is an idea we cannot manage to discard: it is as if we had to go into a garden, perhaps a bit hard to reach, but still a garden. And yet at the point we have now reached we should also clearly understand that, first, it is quite different . . . that it is not merely a pleasure trip.'

When he alluded to our complicity in something, although there was no justification for it, I was persuaded he was right. I actually felt he was speaking more about me than himself. So I sat crossways on a chair in front of him: 'Let's hear all about it' – I said. 'Make me laugh!' Then after all, I listened to him with full attention.

I don't know what kind of work he did, but he certainly showed he was familiar with religious observances and sermons: his talk was full of quotations that sounded Biblical to me, and impressively solemn. He used his arms to make magnificent gestures, and this made a great impression on me. He was standing as he spoke with his back to the light that came from the window. I observed him silently without missing any of his gestures, no matter how ridiculous some of them were.

'Yes, sir' – he was saying – 'it is true! We are both mortal, shut up in a room that looks even more ugly by day than at night,' and then he went on: 'Faith is a clumsy reasoning that says more or less this: "If it is bad now, it will get better later. If it is winter now, spring will come. This seems certain."'

He paused and seemed to be listening to vague city sounds. 'Yes, but what is this nausea?' he asked. 'We don't know, but this time it is not the detailed and sophisticated way of reasoning which replaces the elementary reasoning of faith, but it is the non-faith, the not knowing that springs up like an interval right in the middle of the concise security of faith. It is fear, nauseating fear. *Ut qui? . . . Ut qui? . . .*'

After this last question, he leaned forward, bending towards the floor as if some answer would come out of the cracks. This gesture embarrassed me. So instead of continuing to look at him, I stood up and went back to the washbasin to look at my face in the mirror.

At this point his conversation became direct: 'My friend' – he was saying – 'you are a man of faith like me, rather than a person of subtle reason. You are above all courageous. But, even without denying you have an engagement, you could put it off, postpone it *sine die*, for another time. Why don't you admit that it is not an easy undertaking? That there are some doubts? You see' – he said, coming a few steps closer – 'I admit that I am afraid. I myself am not courageous! But if we are together, with your courage and my determination it would all be much easier!'

'What do you intend to do?' I asked, without turning to look at him. To such a pointless question I didn't expect an answer. My own face appeared more unrecognisable and lacking in sense than before; actually crazy this time. 'That fool is me!' I said without managing to convince myself, because even my suspected folly had vanished from the face I saw reflected. I tried to remind myself of a different me: desperate, actually angry with everyone and everything, despising everything: this despising in retrospect seemed desirable and noble in comparison with the cold and tiredness I now felt.

'Basically men are all alike!' the voice said to my back, becoming even nearer, from the little man in his nightshirt. And suddenly everything seemed to dilute itself into universal likeness. I was no longer desperate, nor angry, nor tired, but merely indifferent, without malaise however and also without nostalgia.

'And what do you want?' I asked rudely.

'Nothing' – the voice replied after a moment of hesitation. 'I wanted to thank you for having shortened for me the malaise of the interval. The room has been paid until next Tuesday' – he continued in a tone almost of excuse. 'If you want to stay on, I would not want you to have to pay again. It's not worth the trouble.'

These were his last words. After a certain time, I realised he had left, but I didn't mind. I didn't know anything more until late in the evening, when the police came to annoy me, and also to inform me that they had found he'd hung himself by an electric cord from the pipe of the toilet. But then, independent of this news, my dialogue with him had already begun: a dialogue, I mean, completely confidential, without reservations. And it is for this that I spoke of affection and actually of love, not only for making the readers of the police station laugh.

Let me explain myself better: now it is clear that the situation in which I find myself is an exact repetition of his. Now I don't need to be reserved or even discourteous with him. He no longer irritates me, actually his voice (or probable voice, I should say) is something I like, and also like his nightshirt, and his un-forgettable yellowish eyes. I no longer need to turn my back on him, but I can, without any more embarrassment, imagine I hear his magniloquent propositions not only with curiosity, but even with respect. But so be it. Perhaps this story of affection is only something I made up: a cleverness even; but whether it be affection respect or trick, it is now necessary for me. I could waste time in doubts, thinking for example that there is nothing better to come, and that actually all the good possible has already gone by, somewhere, without my knowing it. On the other hand, if, to alleviate loneliness, I look at myself in the mirror, the face I see is indifferent and extraneous to me. But his face, as I remember it, or the way I actually see it again is not extraneous, but by now familiar, not indifferent, but kind. And above all serious, engaged, because the two of us have no more time to waste in silliness.

FORTUNE

To John McDade

A monk making his way along the banks of a river somewhere northwest of London rounded a bend and found his path blocked by a thick hedge. The spot was quiet and remote, even secret: and yet there was a pleasing appearance everywhere beneath the pale sky. To gain the attention of his learned brother monks, he might have said that one could almost observe the triumph of imminence in the luminous haze that all but veiled the landscape. That is, the meaning of each visible thing came neither before nor after that thing, but with it: appearance and meaning were joined in the same instant.

'What meaning?' the brothers would have asked.

'Any one of the possible meanings,' he might have replied, to keep up appearances. What he meant, leaving speculation aside, was that these appearances, kept up or somehow secured, definitely presented themselves as a form of actual happiness. Uncertainty, doubt, confusion, when they occurred, no longer came about because of the things or the world, but because of him. So who was this monk? 'Who am I?' he asked himself; and, taking his habit into account, concluded he was no better and no worse than many another: a religious man of uncertain religion, with a reputation just as uncertain even if in a moment of indulgence he could extol some of his merits without needing to blush, but with actual pleasure. So he was not lacking in doctrine, but actually quite knowledgeable; and, if one were to be so indiscreet as to ask fastidiously in how many areas he was knowledgeable, the reply would emerge spontaneously and with an almost joyous simplicity: 'A great many things!' And so rather evasively setting aside any enquiries as to his wisdom, comforted by the number of different notions he possessed, one could go on to consider his many other praiseworthy virtues. In the light of this benignity, suddenly descended from the heavens, he could proceed to summarise, or rather make a

19

confused listing, which in the last analysis appeared to be not so much a list as the repetition of a single virtue: the virtue, if it could be called such, or possessing the virtue, of being alive: *hic et nunc*, that is at five o'clock in the afternoon.

Fortune, therefore, rather than virtue. And so what? If he had to talk about himself, would it be no more than modest to acknowledge the generosity of fate? In any case, fate gives, and fate takes away, without regard for merit; but no fortune, however ill, could take away more than it had already bestowed, and therefore the nature of fortune should be shown by giving, in this its almost inexorable generosity.

This thought aroused such anxious happiness and such impatient anticipation that he started to hop on his good leg, towards the edge of the thicket which kept him from moving forward. Why go on? Why should he go on, after all?

'Who can say what I'm in for!' he mumbled, grinning sarcastically and unrestrainedly; then he took another leap and started to sing: 'I am glad it's come to pass/I've two balls and an excellent arse' while he was aware that neither balls nor an excellent arse nor the world were in themselves causes for being glad; that, on the contrary, being glad was the reason for the world, the balls, the arse and countless other things as well, which were present in it, just as he himself was present, but perhaps indifferent, or hidden in indifference, until a certain contentment, any kind of joy or grace or fortune might draw them onto the scene in the full light of the instant.

So here you are with your balls and arse and world; and because it wasn't altogether satisfying to stay there contemplating his balls, fortune the great rescuer, when summoned, swiftly responded from the height of the heavens: 'Coming, coming!'

With that promise still sounding in his ears, gazing idly at the river, beyond the sluggish muddy water, the monk noticed on the other side a figure stationed under a tree at the edge of a field, which sloped gently towards the stony bank.

'Oh,' he said to himself, somewhat ashamed of the hops and leaps he had been making a few minutes before, 'I thought I was on my own!' and as he spoke, he felt his embarrassment at being somehow discovered, spied upon and judged, turn into irritation and regret for his vanished solitude.

After all, in company, or in the eyes of other people, he was just an ordinary monk: Cucullatus ('cowl head'), some called him scornfully, thereby robbing him of his own personal identity and reducing him to a label. A monk. What fate or fortune could ever touch anyone in his category? What unforeseen circumstances, what hazards and risks? What pleasures, or triumphs or surprises? Aside from the hypothetical delights of good luck, the same expectation of fortune to which he had just abandoned himself unrestrainedly, for him really started with solitude, or, perhaps even better, from a direct confrontation with nature: trees, stones, natural objects which were as undeniable as they were silent (with a silence that could therefore be definitive and present), to which one could speak without fear of being contradicted, or of being accused of madness like those who argue with nothing. Adam probably found that all that silence in the earthly Paradise made him think that only a peace pact stood between that alien silence and his own voice or the rustling of thoughts that controlled the quiet exterior difference from within: *Herba virens et silva silens et spiritus aurae – lenis et festivus* etc., of the same sort.

Then things changed, probably because of another voice in addition to his, one more voice. It's always possible to nudge a woman to be quiet, but no amount of kicking could put an end to the rustling of taciturn thoughts, that flow or rather trickle of other words, of extra words, words on words, in another interior, in another soul. Anyway, before the voice was added, all was silent: not just any tree or rock but the universe itself, insomuch as it started from the silence of a tree. But what started from another voice? He was uncertain: if a woman is silent, while she is still thinking or meditating on what to say, everything could also begin with her. A woman is truly the taciturn dignity on the threshold of the future, the still illegible silence before prophecy. But he, as a monk, had always had little to do with women in the full sense of prophecy: figures through whom might be glimpsed the calmness of the world, destiny and perhaps the promise of everything. The other voices for him were futile and graceless masculine voices suggesting only uncertainty, anxiety, distress. Everything seemed interrupted, disturbed, imprecise, as if the smooth and apparently serene voices of monks seeded shadows onto the surface of the day,

with vocal signs of strife and black syllables. For example: it was
an imprecise autumn. He remembered that the leaves on most
trees were already brown or yellow. It was evening; the
mountain, lit by the red glare from the sun that was already
hidden, loomed with its ridges emphatic against the bluish
shadow of the valley and greyer shadow of the cloister like a
blazing stone candelabra. Birds seeking a destination exchanged
information on the good and the bad in their beaky language;
then they fled from the valley screeching towards the cold light
in the sky, and in the opposite direction they plummeted down
from the sky like stones, their wings closed inside the foggy dark
that loomed over the river. It was a sunset like many others, one
might have said, but there were too many different kinds of
things mixed up and superabundance can sometimes poison.
There were tiny blue and red and yellow fragments suddenly
shining; then a wind of ashes snuffed out every colour. The red
of the maple leaves was already blackened by the shadow rising
at the side of the church.

'Too many things!' he said, shaking his head. It was late and
many things would have to be left; but where to begin?

Renunciation is always a process with an uncertain and
difficult beginning as if one were at a banquet table after a long
fast. When one is not feeling able to swallow it all, one becomes
aware of negative choice, that is of choosing to renounce
something: the lamb? the quail?

'Renounce, renounce!' a litany of neutral voices proclaimed.

All right, renouncing is a convent practice; but even outside
the convents, aren't there many things that have to be given up
in comparison with those that may be kept! These summers,
these autumns, these fleeting lights: all fleeting, changing things
that vanish almost before memory has fully taken hold of them.
Maybe women manage to hold onto things more: they are the
custodians of cupboards and closets and storerooms.

He closed his eyes: he imagined housewives and also nuns
moving around, keys at their belts, their evening-like movement
calling forth light at dusk: going through the motions of the
contemplative life, that is, withdrawn from the service of the day-
to-day and suited for meditation and for memory instead. What
did these cupboards and closets of theirs actually contain? When
the doors were open the shelves revealed things that were old, no

longer used, documents rather than objects: the now peaceful residue of past life . . . some jugs, an onion, chestnuts, even a pomegranate. But who would eat a withered pomegranate with whitened seeds? Who would drink from a yellowed jug in the dark? These are no longer useful objects, but offerings to the silence, more like words than things. But words like fleeting shadows. What onion for example? The white? The red? An imaginary onion? The one already seen at the market? Now he understood with some approximation that these onions and jugs which were hard to define no longer belonged to the world of trade, but to that of contemplation. In a certain sense women also belonged to this second world, despite their contemptible and generic feminine being. In fact one could watch them, scrutinise them with greatest care, without ever reaching a reasonable classification. Nun? for example. Or: Whore? or even: Saint? Each of them, on the contrary, being indefinable according to the gender, difference and species was also impalpable. Certainly whether she was a woman or a nun, he would have certainly palpated her: the impossibility of touch did not dissuade him from an interminable attempt that at least in his imagination seemed to change the intangible into almost tangible, through the very slowest possible approach or imperceptible drawing near, almost by virtue of a long voyage of desire towards nothing other than the inexhaustible continuity of itself.

'And after all this,' he said, 'at least with nuns, it's better that way.' His voyages of approach, with their comings and goings, were so rooted in improbability that sometimes, losing himself for hours along the way, at the end he no longer knew what was occupying his mind, whether dream or madness. Sometimes in the middle of the night, he imagined seeing himself deep in the country and wandering around orchards and vineyards, in the darkness of night without bodily substance, finally slipping into the nuns' dormitories, and making only a slight disturbance as he passed through, like a puff of wind coming up at night.

That was how he entered the room of the prettiest and there began his long study, there his uncertainties began, and his silent ploys for getting as close to the sleeping woman as possible: her sleep was like the sleep of trees in the orchard below the remote watch of the stars, it seemed to him: solitude, watched over and made safe, a protected silence.

'Whether asleep or awake,' they told him, 'these fantasies are certainly temptations by the devil, that is, female apparitions, even nuns. Well, what were these devilesses doing?'

'Nothing! They weren't doing anything. Not even moving. It was only the mind which caused them to change position. Sometimes it almost swooped a reclining figure to her feet, but without weight and it was more out of geometry than transport.' In fact it could be said that the mind's eye saw the figures standing, because of the equilateral triangle formed by the points of the breasts and the navel, as if the principle of the verticality came from the triangle and not from the woman's body.

'And her belly, what was her belly like?'

'Geometry wasn't helpful for her belly. Roundness and the smoothness that one imagined were somewhat helpful, not like a solid surface, immediately tangible, but rather like a remote, almost lunar gleam.'

'What does the moon have to do with it?'

'A vagueness of colour in which white predominates.'

'But what sort of belly are you talking about? Hard? Soft? Swollen? Flat?'

'A belly like a tummy,' he babbled at random.

'And her legs?' the prior persisted. 'What sort of legs did she have?' And when he received no reply he continued with a menacing haughtiness: *'Venient autem dies quando dicant: beatae steriles et ventres qui non genuerunt.'*

'Ventres qui non genuerunt!' he repeated to himself, seized by irresistible laughter, because thinking about it now, against the greyness of the river, these cold bellies in their pallor seemed to have finally acquired a formal clarity for him. In other words even if their outline was still feeble and uncertain, their name at least was quite distinct, without possibility of mistake. Ventres-bellies! Certainly not tummies! But in this case, why laugh? The joy that he felt, futile as it was, was a signal to himself, to his own ego. The Cuclato caught in the act, even an imaginary one, with all those bellies! Certainly in his nocturnal impudence the word belly was far from pleasant or ridiculous, and actually seemed to be a sign of decadence and ruin. If there is smoke, there's fire, it's said. But because it is hard to detect smoke at night, these phantoms of bulging feminine bellies advanced. Or,

to spare the imagination any effort, one could think that these pallid women became solemn bearers of a great prophecy to compensate for their nudity: without a screech, they fly through the dark sky at dawn, one after the other, each actually bearing a 'silence' placard.

'Damn them!' he exclaimed. 'What prophecy could this be?'

The tender nordic whiteness of the summer sky suddenly looked severe and sad to him: *Multiplicabo, inquit mulieri, tristitias tuas et gemitos tuos.*

'That's their business,' he commented; irritated. But it was not their business. These women actually recognised him and called out to him using a familiar idiom, more a matter of complicity than of voices. Putting aside the solemnity of the curse, the procession through the air and the sign 'silence' were transformed into a melancholy walk in the country, like one along the banks of the river, and every step they took along the way, every movement of their hands and tilt of their head made a confident reference to something exclusive, to a knowledge they alone shared and all others were kept in the dark. That sort of silence now seemed to be wisdom and protection, rather than commandment or condemnation.

He shook his head: 'All the folly that passes through the minds of men!' he commented. He had to admit that in the mind, or if you will, in the shadow of the soul, woman and folly looked very much alike, especially because of the exclusive and tyrannical character of their inner understanding. There are certainly few things that are contemplated only from within, aside from the virtues, which are notoriously interior monuments. There are gardens, trees, clouds and even the same women: all are best seen outside themselves. Women, however, unlike apples, seem to be on the one hand objects of vision, and on the other objects of the soul. Because of their dual appearance they reveal the insufficiency of the internal universe which is not big enough to contain them. Therefore instead of madness, it was better to talk of meagreness of the soul, of a minor infinite or of evil infinity, so to speak, or at least for his own soul, of a miserable modest infinite, for which narrowness and distress seemed the most fitting attributes.

'Let's think about something else!' he decided, moving forward more forcefully amidst the low branches that continually intertwined at the edge of the path, blocking his way. Seen from above, the river showed long dark streaks: black stones and gravel were along the banks in some places. At a certain point on the riverbank he thought he saw a cow's bladder or intestines gleaming white.

'Perhaps there's a slaughterhouse upstream,' he thought. But the air smelled so good the simple purity of the countryside prevailed. So the place was delightful and even exciting because of the woman on the other side of the river, who now had started to walk in the same direction. Certainly, given the haze and the distance (in that part the river had become quite broad), he managed to see very little of that figure. Using the process of exclusion (she was not a cow) as well as the process of interpretation (the fact that she was walking in the same direction as he indicated docility), he decided she was no longer young, but flourishing, even – flowering in middle-age. 'And middle-aged women like that,' he said to himself, rubbing his hands, 'are often better in the flesh than young ones!'

'Well, all right!' they would have said. 'Let's hear the rest of this.'

'If I talk about women occasionally,' he justified himself, 'I do it in order to talk about uncertainty. Sometimes before falling asleep, while the imagination is following one line of thought, another entirely different one happens to come in without impeding the first, so that actually the propositions show a parallel virtue one with the other, although there are no similarities or even vague analogies.'

'Let it be,' they warned him. 'What about this woman you were mentioning . . .'

'I am talking about her like any other woman,' he continued. 'I am saying that women can be looked at in two different ways, or at least once a certain amount of time has passed, they can be considered in an entirely different way than before without any disturbing contradictions. Just one gesture, the slightest change in the voice, and the second way establishes itself alongside the first . . .'

'Nothing, she did nothing,' he began patiently. 'It was night time, or nearly. The road upstream had caved in, so I had to knock at the door of the last house in the valley on the way to the pass . . .'

The woman who opened the door, from what I could see in the misty shadow that is frequent at dusk in those places hemmed in by high mountains, had red hair and a bulging belly, covered with coarse and shiny embroidery. Later I learned that she embroidered cushion covers, and the bulge was only a pillow. She was a widow who lived alone with a very old female dog who was also very ill.

'But how can I offer you refuge?' she asked with hesitation. 'I have offered only hospitality to people passing if they were women and preferably nuns.'

But because the rain had turned to snow and the swollen river had already flooded the road lower down the valley, they decided in good faith that the Lord God would have seen and provided. So he was allowed into the house and offered an abundant supper with a big bowl of gruel and pork boiled in milk, which would have been very good if the grunts and the stink of the sick dog and the banging of the doors and windows in the storm had not saddened the evening. Then he went into a tidy room with a good bed and fire in the fireplace and closed the door. Although he was very tired, sometimes he was disturbed by the sound of the widow speaking kindly to her bitch and weeping in her room on the other side of the wall.

'Well?'

It was nearly dawn when the dog died. The fire was out, but there were still some glowing coals and perhaps some light already slipped through the cracks of the shutters. She said she had come for some coal and told me in tears how she had brought the bitch into her bed to comfort it. At the point of death the bitch had managed to get its piss and shit all over the bed, and had also vomited as it yielded up its soul. If she had a few pieces of coal she could start to dry the sheets.

'Oh, no!' he had said. 'You must sleep in this bed!'

'Why, what sort of story is this! The disgusting death of a miserable dog, an unclean beast as there ever was?'

'A story of death and resurrection,' he had explained, becoming fierce. 'Resurrection of the flesh.' But immediately repentant, he had added that he had no idea what sort of story it was, or whether he was speaking out of a need for confession or justification, and he was even uncertain whether the story he was telling was his own or someone else's. In a certain sense telling a tale to justify oneself is always about someone else or another story and even the same memory is perhaps the memory of something else, because memory also tends to justify.

Besides, sometimes the mouth adds things of its own accord that the mind does not mean, like his mention of the resurrection: *In resurrectione autem neque nubent neque nubentur, et erunt sicut angeli.*

Get on with it, he chided himself crossly. And so he went on, panting and puffing with the effort. He did not proceed more rapidly, but with more impetus, shoving the branches aside vigorously, sometimes even breaking them; he stuck his whole head through the leafy branches to look at the road ahead and also to try to see the woman on the other side of the river again. A great part of this excess, he admitted, was to distract himself from nagging memories, because certain memories provoked an anger with himself that overwhelmed all reason. Perhaps it wasn't only anger but also shame. Or fear? he asked himself. He was even uncertain about that. If one had permitted him to express his opinion about uncertainty, he would have begun with a survey of uncertain topics, to distinguish them from doubt. Women, he would have said, are in the first place a source of uncertainty in that passion for females is desolately poor in form (every carnal act is rudimentary and inarticulate) but superabundant in the content: fear and hope, shame and desire, grief and grace, the most diverse feelings become this passion and blend triumphantly in it in great confusion, thus separating themselves from thought, if not from life.

'Oh, that's a good one! What theory is this?' they would have asked him, starting to sneer.

'It is a sketch,' he would have excused himself. 'Just a sketch for a theory.'

He shook his head. Fortunately he had never ventured to formulate such a theory. Instead he had spoken, in a feeble manner, of his undecidedness as a fundamental defect, from which perhaps other defects derived: a generative nucleus of sin.

They had warned him, reproached, and in the end also tranquillised him. He spoke of himself, glorifying his deeds to irritate the others, they said, and advised him to practice calmness, humility and especially detachment: to forget about himself, to distract himself, and for the time being to forget himself would be of help.

'Oh, yes?' he would have said. And after a pause for internal reasoning he would have asked: 'Perhaps the situation of any sort of cowl-head, is that of being always distanced in respect to myself?'

Their only answer would have been to turn their backs and go away, and some would have lifted their arms up to heaven.

The fact is, he thought, that distracting himself, ignoring himself or hypothetically being someone else was a way for fortune or the anticipation of fortune to come out of the same uncertainty and in the meantime, as they had suggested to him, it brought calm and a vague interior rejoicing, which allowed him to make occasional leaps in celebration. For the time being, of course, because the questioning would soon return: what should he say about himself?

He was tired! This he could say with certainty and for good reason, also considering his bad leg. But would a declaration as futile as that have contented the Lord? In his hope, a bit grumpily but with implicit benevolence, the Lord Himself would have replied: 'If you are tired, go to bed.' And so he would have gone off to bed happily and with little leaps, because, aside from the good fortune mentioned before of being or hoping to be other, there is no better fortune, in being oneself, than a good night's sleep. Unfortunately he didn't manage to keep this hope very long: he knew he had no faith in it, because he knew of the power of divine judgement.

He shrugged his shoulders in resignation: 'There is no remedy for the wrath of God,' he thought. So he might just as well distract himself: to go blindly on, knowing the worst, but foolishly hoping for the best: 'I was not the same man that now stands in front of you!' he would have excused himself, meaning that he had been, in respect to the being and even imagining himself now in judgement, as if in a lie with respect to the truth. Certainly memory remained: a lying, artificial memory, like limbo, estranged from himself, like the memory of another. Seeing things through a filter of lies, the past could be considered with a certain liking, with even some vague sense of participation, almost as if he were watching a play (one of those plays in which things of a reproachable and sinful sort happen with females), without feeling either grief or harm: in other words the lie seemed to him one and the same thing as the artifice which allowed him to entertain himself with things that were not part of his experience. And moreover this lack of experience, whether make-believe or actual, is what allows one to enjoy idle chatting. Often he had happily listened to discussions without beginning or end, laughing at the most absurd statements circulating at the time: rumours about people's malaise, robberies by the powerful, simony and so forth. And recently he had listened to many silly predictions, some of them amusing. The worst concerned armed groups that had escaped control by the authorities and decided to overpower the Holy Father and impale him. But putting aside any silliness, that is without indulging in entirely unfounded desires, just wanting to be amusing, what would he have said, returning to Milan?

'I was walking along the river, and then saw a woman stationed in the shade of a tree on the other side.'

'What was she doing?' they would have asked.

'Nothing, she wasn't doing anything. She wasn't moving.' To say any more he would have needed to see more, or even vaguely imagine more the way one imagines a story not yet read or a play one had not yet seen just from the title. This story about the woman he had met or just happened to see did not require any experience: it was a story about something else, like the ones you tell just for amusement. One may amuse oneself by telling a story about anything that one has seen that does not touch us in any way: innocent things like: 'I saw a worm.'

'How disgusting!' the interlocutor commented. 'Did you squash it?'

'Not me,' the narrator defended himself. 'Others did that.'

So, without grief or harm, the story of the worm was complete. And similarly he could also say he'd seen a woman.

'How splendid!' the same indiscreet interlocutor added. 'Did you fuck her?'

'Not me. Others did that!' one could reply. Or, to spare feminine dignity one could say the woman was not fuckable because she was old or ugly or because she was a saint.

'And if she was really a saint?' the monk asked himself, sharpening his eyes in the haze.

Actually sanctity could be the title or some placard for a story not yet read or a play not yet seen; or a sign, an emblem, moral resolution and at the same time a project for a story ready to be told, no longer, this time, as justification or confession on his own account, but in the most general sense for edification and purgation of the many.

FORTUNE II

Countless offences to God's honour are perpetrated every day, including swearing, heresies, and misguided beliefs. He retaliates instantly, and releases famine, war, floods and earthquakes on this earth; wholesale on those wicked people who deserve death. *Ad hominem* on the contrary, that is retail, divine punishment in this world is more intermittent: God, it's said, doesn't pay Saturdays. And so many, religious people among them, live in this momentary suspension of punishment, actually enjoying the good of the world to whatever extent they can, instead of passing their time in penitence. It is not that they have no fear; but actually, at least for the religious ones, this gift of the Holy Spirit, that is, the terror of God, was generously given at a very early age. For example, when he was a novice his fear of God was so great that he sometimes pissed himself during divine services. Later on, in order to prevent any disagreeable incontinence, since the moment for punishment was yet to come, he adapted himself for living in this provisional absence of vengeance, in this gratuitous void of the wrath of God, almost pacifically, knowing full well that beyond there was nothing but damnation. In other words, in the long run his desperation had settled down in his soul, naturally and almost happily, or at least disposed for humour, merry rather than whining.

Not that he was always laughing or saying amusing things; he was so oppressed by fear of God's imminent punishment that he was often speechless, in the sense of deprived of both his voice and his thinking. This was an interior void, which perhaps corresponds with God taking time off as avenger: to dissimulate he said lewd and irreverent things or simple silliness, the way monks do. This was not all. In order to dissimulate this silence or void, he sometimes fell more deeply into sin with women, as well: occasionally whores, occasionally not whores, or less whores than the first ones; but even going to whores, crazed and serious, sinful and happy as it can be, didn't manage to remove the sadness of this recurrent aphasia of his. He certainly wouldn't have known how to describe his loss of words, if not in just a vague approximation, because he was uncertain if he (subject) was the one to lose the words or rather the words lost their speaker. He imagined this aphasia to be a momentary loss of contact between the speaker and the spoken. The conversation or chatter might well continue; but the aphasia persisted behind the sound of the words, not always and not only silence, but sometimes also a great resonance: an inaudible sound, a thought, perhaps, but as solemn and noisy as it was unknown. On one side, therefore, this thundering of the unknown, on the other the so called chatter of humour, or, more precisely, stupidity. His life in flesh and bone was stuck in the middle and flattened, even with his bad leg that was more of a nuisance every day. What was this unmentionable affliction that impelled him to hobble along with increasing difficulty, if not a subtle, almost invisible, strand of amazement, sometimes called solitude or weariness?

'It's better not to think about it!' he said to himself. As usual others would have ended up finding one or more ambiguities also in this reasoning. They said logic was not his strong point. But, he objected, he didn't want to speak of logic or with logic: only of a thought that was confused and yet utterly serious. Couldn't serious ideas and momentous thoughts sometimes present themselves in an uncertain way?

They almost never deemed him worthy of response. Once they established that he was being silly as usual, they silently shook their heads. Or sometimes one of the kinder ones gave him a smile and a wink, and then turned away and went on with what he was doing. In other words, any time he hinted at his confusion, they left him alone: and so he took his solitude as an aspect of that unknown thought of which he had tried to speak. That thought, in other words, that seemed to be an event for him alone, not so much indecipherable as impossible to communicate.

Looking at it more closely, he was drawn first to one side and then to another; towards solemnity or at least a pompous and solitary dignity or towards being gregarious and stupid and incidentally, since it was there, fornications. Intervals that were neither solemn nor entirely stupid, but fragile and vague, like marks in the sand at the water's edge undulated in the midst of this oscillation. They were mostly memories, or fantasies or inventions or a mixture, but never enough of one of these sorts to be defined as something with a coherent unity; usually it was a fragment and then another and perhaps a third and even a forth: of a feminine profile, for example, and a light.

What was the relationship between these two things? He supposed the light illuminated the outline and came from the window, touching and just glancing off the surface of a mirror and perhaps the outline was reflected in the mirror. So, aside from the uncertain placement of this figure in profile, there was a window, with a mirror on the side. This mirror was actually dark: even black, shining in malice. This fact could not be passed over in silence, although not mentioned at the beginning. Certainly if one stopped at this point, without going on, this mirror episode, named because of the importance of that piece of furniture, could not be called a memory, in the sense of full memory, the way one remembers a woman from the beginning to the end. Perhaps these memory flashes that came into his mind without warning were not part of the interval or the neutral stupor of life, but the contents of the so-called emptiness or the supposedly serious thoughts he didn't want to think about.

'No!' he said, shaking his head. It is useless to quibble: even in fragments his memories were only of sin. Faced with the wrath of God there was no protection for him in dissimulation. All he could do was to huddle behind some saint and hope for the best. To what saint could he turn?

'A female saint would be best!' he thought. Then with an involuntary sneer and without being able to stop it, he saw Saint Mary of the Egyptians negotiating her passage by sea, or alternatively Mary Magdalene in the desert. He had just opted for the latter, when Mary Magdalene began to wash her breasts at a fountain in the shade.

'All right! There's no harm in a bit of cleanliness!' Then, however, without a moment's pause the Magdalene decided to wash her arse too. 'Oh, no, not that!' he protested, barely managing to look away. Besides, he asked himself, why turn away suddenly and act almost scandalized? After all that arse of hers was unreal, not only imaginary but also bearing or bringing no consequence or real effect. As far as looking, no one could detect any implication, but perhaps an idea that had settled down, so to speak, next to a sentiment or emotion. It was all part of the heraldic device in which the arse, considering the desert also *en abyme*, only means the sanctity of silence.

But this was also a confused way of putting things because rather than having meaning, this combination of figures was the end product of meanings. In other words, the problem with allegories, symbols or mottos of this very special sort lies in their terminal character. They are always the final image, the final idea, the final phrase. Nothing follows. From there, what's more, one can look towards this practically infinite *non sequitur* as if looking at nothingness. But looking backwards, that is taking apart or breaking up the result into those things that, out of love for brevity and clarity could be supposed to be highly general premises (therefore good for other allegories or mottos as well as for this) he only found his anxieties or more constant pre-occupations and above all two of these: his love of women and his fear of God. Perhaps these two preoccupations were somehow proportional or symmetrical after all. Otherwise, he told himself, even admitting the sanctity of silence, in what way could this bare-arsed silence defend him from divine fury?

So should he flee? But then *quo ibit iste fugiens a facie dei?* Probably it's best to pretend nothing has happened and slip away without saying goodbye. Besides, he was going where they sent him, out of obedience, that is without asking why, even if he then knew that the decision to send him to the four corners of the earth was often taken merely to keep him away from certain women towards whom he had showed an excessive inclination. So one couldn't talk about flight or hiding: his wandering was not voluntary and so it didn't seem to be even an attempt to remove himself from the wrath of God. On the contrary, aside from this divine wrath which rested in suspension as before, often it happened or he was offered an occasion for distance, an alibi, a being somewhere else which, it appeared, could also be construed as being someone else. This alternative then was not merely a negative defence, because with his being other, even provisionally, came the promises of another life: a new life, in which fortune ultimately consists. With this hope of the new, he managed to leave every time without great regret, actually with joy, as if greener grass was waiting for him beyond the horizon, water more limpid and a cleaner sky. Even when he was on his way north he had fantasies of places that were sunny, or rather luminous, perhaps with feeble and melancholy light, but always promising clarity. Who knows what things he would see in that faint light! he told himself. Certainly the life behind him was lost in some way, but what was in front was stirring, calling him with the insistent gestures of leaves in the wind: Come, come!

Besides in this aura of renewal, even the past, lost as it might be, presented him with certain fleeting joys, barely signalled, like invitations that only now seemed about to reveal themselves: the tiny piazza, the fountain almost hidden in a corner, the great chestnut tree, dark and thick, the grey houses that held him in; above the July foliage a huge and silent sun sailed with tenacious slowness. Wasn't this also somehow fortune? Perhaps something had already been given, but so confusedly that he hadn't understood at the time, while now, perhaps for didactic reasons, the past sang again more clearly the old song of invitation: *Vieni meco, fior di rosa, sul paglion* . . . or Come with me, pretty rosebud, onto my bed of straw. . . .

'Oh no!' he exclaimed emphatically, covering his eyes with his hands to avoid seeing the appearance and disappearance of a slender and speedy arse, so speedy in fact to be confused with fruit, leaves, baskets in the scatter-brained movement of summers past.

'Tota mulier in utero!' he pronounced sternly.

He now had the strange feeling that 'the new' was more closely linked with the past than the future, that it was more hope of the memory than desire of the unheard. Perhaps if he had wanted to describe for himself what he expected under the name of fortune, he should have started by saying that the wait had been long and that to bring a happy ending it should have started not yesterday or the day before, but earlier, much earlier: from the beginning of hope and of memory. Things being as they are, at least for the time being, waiting for fortune as he did seemed only to bring out random items of the past: including legs, buttocks and breasts, flashing through the fog of regret. Her, in other words.

'Oh no!' he exclaimed with annoyance. 'Not her!' She was a

whore like all the others, even more malicious; only she dampened the broom to conjure up a cloudburst to drench him or put swallows' eyes into his sack-cloth to keep him from sleeping.

The path ascended, getting further away from the water, while the thicket had become almost a forest: not dense, however, but with some big trees amidst the stumps of trees that had just sent out new branches; and as he climbed he realised he was tired.

'After all,' he said, stopping and looking over at the woman on the other side of the river, 'it is not even certain I can catch up with her. But!' he shook his head and continued, 'What else can I do?' He knew that if he had stopped, tiredness would have risen from his legs to his head, colours would have started to lose their changing, almost volatile interweaving of light and would have looked opaque to him, as if drenched, with their edges sharply defined, disclosing the persistence of things. In other words, tiredness suggested a permanent world to him, enclosed in an interminable afternoon, or perhaps better, the time unmarked by hours when asleep. 'Let's say that my tiredness is like drowsiness,' he decided, to put an end to it, and at the same time tried to go forward more rapidly. 'What happens in these cases,' he thought, 'is that, already at the first sign of sleep, the *hic et nunc* become weaker, and at least in the first instance are replaced by his 'not now, not here', rather than by memory or regret for time past: the world as it would have been without him. 'And how was this world?' he asked himself.

Actually the present was still there. Only his own presence had vanished and with this a bit of hurry or urgency. Instead the residual present that he saw in dreams was calm and slow, and so everything that happened, happened slowly. Was it raining, for example? He felt it was raining calm, even serenity. Not only because of the clouds in the sky, the storms at sea, the hours of day and night, but also for human acts: killings, plagues, government raids, all happened with dignified slowness. And the appearance of things was so noble: wood, metals, pottery. Even the most lowly bowl showed the imperturbable thisness of what it was, with no trace of practical use.

'Ideal for the lazy!' they commented.

'That's how it is!' he admitted. In fact slowness interested him because he believed one can do a great deal without getting too tired if it is done slowly: even walking with a bad leg. And then this slowness was a sort of dream, that is, more supposition than deep sleep: a hypothesis with which one seeks to mix effort with the comfort of an imaginary repose. So everything becomes more bearable: evil, tiredness, walking in itself and for itself, the endless number of wasted steps.

He stopped dumbfounded: a short distance ahead the path levelled and widened. A boulder under a big leafy tree seemed to invite him to pause. He could not see her down there on her side of the river moving more quickly towards a wood. He thought he could see a thatched roof in the midst or perhaps just a haystack.

'I'll end up losing sight of her,' he said, and so he went on. 'I am tired,' he admitted. He was often tired! Once, two or three years before, he had tumbled down the embankment that flanked the trail he was following, waking up in the course of his fall. Lacking any external objects for attention, he had lost himself in one of his recurring dreams: one with an interminable walk. He had been walking also in his dream and on the right and the left, in a sort of luminous semi-dark, he distinctly saw pallets and shapes, most of them human, stretched out volubly now extending an arm, now a leg before going to sleep. Among the others a mule was also stretching out its hooves and farting to get ready to sleep; he was the only one proceeding along but was unable to tell whether it was a road or a path due to the way the play of light and shade was gleaming. 'What can this road be?' he had asked himself. And at this point he had slid down a long stretch of the embankment, coming to a stop against a stone at the edge of a forest.

'Oh yes!' he admitted. It was becoming more of a struggle to live in the present when thought held less sway; this situation bore down upon him and at the same time eluded him. The struggle among other things also came from a sort of quarrel with his own solitude or rather an interrupted discussion with his memory or with something that continually tried to suggest that he was truly the man he had been ten or twelve years before, almost as if the time that had passed since then were only a form of distancing or becoming absent from himself. What had he made out of all these years? How could he have lost them?

These questions didn't come to him as direct interrogation, but were occasioned by the motif of apparently innocuous distractions: the mirror, the profile, the light . . . or other such particulars, that moved forward out of the dark background to the foreground, and from an absence of words towards an uncertain attempt to use words, with the soft and oscillating ways of phantoms in sleep.

'Oh, yes!' he said, to return to reality. 'And today she should be fifty-four or fifty-six years old. An old woman,' he added. 'What would I do with an old woman?' he stopped as if lost in thought and then started to laugh. Then he continued his walk. 'You know,' he would have said, meeting her, 'they sent me away and we have lost sight of each other.' She would have nodded silently. Then she also knew. And suddenly faced with her knowing and silence, he felt that losing sight of her (or any other loss), instead of a damn shame, was an entire world that was lost, but tranquil: a garden or a terrace planted with little trees rounded off and resigned, and a handsome chequerboard pavement, where little animals, perhaps cats, moved with great slowness along the edges. Everything was calm and slow, even fear: fear of the sea, of ghosts, of God, were slow and calm with more the comportment of wisdom than terror.

'Certainly,' he said, contented, 'age or youth makes no difference if we limit ourselves to exchanging looks, or shaking hands, or even a kiss as a sign of recognition.' And a kiss also means a sign of peace and pardon, and understood in that way could free him from the burden of a feeling of restless distress without cause but unremitting.

'It's not my fault,' he would have said. She, believing him, would have kissed him; with no more rancour they would have set off together happy, whatever the road and the weather was like, because sometimes, we all know, a kiss works wonders. For example, about kisses, it is said that St John Chrysostom who was praying in front of a statue of the Madonna one day (probably to ask for help in making the most of his tiring studies) suddenly saw the statue move: 'John,' the statue said coming to life, 'don't be afraid, kiss my lips and I will fill you to the brim with learning.' The child hesitated out of fear, but then, perhaps more out of reverence than hope, he approached and placed his lips on those of the Madonna. Well! That kiss alone – it is said – gave him a boundless wisdom and an understanding of all the arts.

Certainly obtaining wisdom through kisses was another story altogether. His miracle was more modest. What he hoped to obtain was a clarification of memory. For example: what were her hands like, her arms, her legs? He only had a vague, foggy, memory of this, which was always on the point of becoming clear, through an imminent, but never attained illumination. It was the same as when one remembers or knows something, but this knowledge fails to reach verbal expression. 'I can't find the words for it!' one excuses oneself; and about words, this now seemed almost certain to him: her body was not made of names like legs, arms, lips, but rather of adjectives: so a kiss, he hoped, a simple kiss, would have been enough to catch hold of the top of the adjective chain.

'All right,' he continued, 'let's say that meeting her, old as she might be, he would have kissed her: with fear, certainly, for she was not the sort of woman for easy intimacy.' He would have approached, letting his desire show, and she with gracious condescension would have invited him to kiss her. 'Don't be afraid,' she would have said to him, 'come and kiss my lips!' All without speaking, naturally, but through her facial expression and the light in her eyes. Because there is a way of speaking that can be both imperious and mute. And then *maxime mulieres decet silentium!*

He realised that pain was making him drag his leg behind him, and lean forward.

'Oh, no!' he said straightening himself angrily. 'If she should see me like this!' He made a vague gesture with his hand, realising at the same time that the woman on the other side of the river had vanished. His eyes scanned the field from the road on the extreme left to the woods and beyond on the right several times without seeing her, but then shifting his glance he saw her stationed in the middle of a path where he hadn't managed to detect her an instant before.

'Well!' he said to himself, dumbfounded. 'Let her do what she pleases!' If he had to tell a story about this woman he would have said that instead of walking she moved in the same way a shadow moves. The shadow of clouds on a field, for example. But now there were no clouds in the sky: only a single covering from horizon to horizon, white and without shadows, so that without shadows only the woman seemed to move. Or perhaps only the point from which he saw her moved, slowly, while he went on searching for a hypothetical bridge, which he could then cross and finally meet her face to face.

'What a story!' they would have said. 'And suppose he had managed to meet her face to face, what would have happened?'

'Nothing!' he would have conceded. 'Absolutely nothing.' All his stories ended in nothing. So for a sudden lack of consequences the story utterly vanished in the void as if it had never been, leaving just the imprint or the shadow of what it could have been.

Certainly, telling it, he always had the possibility of falsifying, that is of adding some sort of conclusion or changing the antecedents. For example, if he had said that this woman, seen across the river, was someone he knew, perhaps that he had talked to her in a tavern, following her would have seemed more plausible to everyone and more worthy of interest. 'So, I was in a tavern . . .' he would have started to say, blandly smiling . . . 'and then a woman showing her breasts or almost showing her breasts approached me . . .'

At this point however he wouldn't have known what else to say, while they would have continued watching him silently with raised eyebrows, somewhere between stupor and indignation.

'All right,' he admitted, 'that did not happen!'

Actually a woman did once brush against his shoulders in a tavern, leaning over the table at which he was sitting. So doing, she had squeezed her breasts against the nape of his neck. He had considered the episode more ridiculous than humiliating at the time. When he was starting to tell the story however he had discovered every detail drowned in his own interior darkness, within his perpetual night, in which things, whatever they were on their own account, always became worse, progressively losing their clarity and sense. It wasn't really the decay or confusion of meanings (after all meanings are primarily pertinent for the listener), but it was the fading and degradation of the images that distressed him. What remedy could there be? This anxiety, or mania for remedy started to work from the first paragraphs of memory with candour, even with a special sincerity. So he sincerely felt for example that it was a great effort for the woman to bring her breasts out from her low neckline, first one breast and then the other. Forcefully squashed breasts therefore. He saw them clearly and almost out of necessity slimy and shiny, while he knew he had never actually seen these breasts either bare or covered with clothes, but had only felt them against the nape of his neck, just for an instant and certainly by accident. In other words he falsified things even in his memory in order to see better, perhaps to see more or to restore to what he remembered seeing and feeling a continuity in the possible and even in the risk, without which every memory seemed like a dead letter.

Then in the distance of time, how are details from memory distinguished from clarifying falsifications? For example, how was the servant in the tavern dressed? In a dress that was black, it seemed to him, and greasy. The woman on the other side of the river, for all he could see, wore a pleated skirt, quite full and coloured green, but dull and brownish like dried walnuts, while her shirt was more lively, perhaps yellow: pleasing colours in other words. He needed to remember them firmly, letting them be what they were. These were more or less the same colours she usually wore; one evening in autumn, perhaps in November, he had seen her go away towards the woods wearing a dress that he now remembered had exactly the same colours. But why were clothes important? Skirts and shirts? If he remembered something about them it was more to imagine removing them, until her strong and sleek hips were completely naked and smooth, and her body, breasts and neck as well.

'That's enough! It's well known,' he admitted, 'that the gate of impurity leads to the palace of the devil.' The sound of footsteps instead or in general sounds, pauses, silences, other different sounds and unexpected ones while she was going away towards the woods, that is the uncertain departure as it was the first time (protracted, even interminable) he could remember without showing malice, so much time had already passed. He had followed her with his gaze through the trees, and then when he could see her no longer, had attentively listened to the crunch of twigs and leaves under her feet until even that rustling became inaudible, at least to his ear.

The sound of a broken branch could also have been caused by

an animal, but it was the last sound he heard and he attributed it to her. Later, as he had already said, there was silence, but in the silence the departure continued almost as if in parenthesis or in an interval when one has no idea how long it will be. Everything, in a certain sense, looked like departure: the woods red and sparse, the wan rays of the low sun, which were sometimes dazzling, four small black and desolate clouds in the transparency of a sky that became ever more rigid, now almost nocturnal. In other words, he concluded, it was a beautiful vast silence; he had never heard such an abundant silence, so fluent and luminous, although night had almost arrived.

Water under the bridge, in any case. Now, he decided, if he didn't want to fall asleep again and trip, he should keep looking at the path: the stones and the branches. That silence was now lost. The silence that he now had around him in the woods was quite different: thick and opaque and despite the hour and the season, rather grey. There was a woman on the other side of the river, but at least until he caught up with her this silence was only his; even the landscape, looking at it closely, was only his: the sparse and vigorous trees, the fields, the grey and frothy water that he could occasionally see, were images only for him, and there was no point trying to talk about them. It meant that he walked and the things around him stayed almost equal, the tones equal, the sky equal after all; and even time seemed to stand still, despite the effort of his steps. It was time to keep moving, in other words; a lifeless and ashen time as if seen reflected in a mirror; this time as well for him alone.

FORTUNE III

'Isn't it absurd?' he said. 'When we feel lonely it is the world that appears alone to us, while on the contrary when we praise solitude, we talk about the need to return to ourselves: begin a dialogue with our own soul. Even in this second case, however, solitude never remains alone for long in the subject, but passes on to something else, and splits in two sharing the self and the soul, (rather than the self and the world) like standing in front of a mirror. It could even be that in this discussion with one's own soul or in private conversation with itself, that solitude is happy for one and sad for the other (that is for the soul). Certainly it could also be the opposite and perhaps, to simplify things, one could also say that there are two ways of being conscious: one happy and the other sad: two separate awarenesses, let's say: the awareness of the soul and the awareness of oneself, because the things happiness is aware of do not seem the same as the things of which sadness is aware. But perhaps the division lies elsewhere: one awareness is obvious, public, busy; it precipitates words, even stacks them up; the other is rather taciturn and if it tries to speak does so with extreme difficulty and with an exasperating slowness: once one has made this last distinction, it is no longer possible to relegate happiness and sadness clearly to one of these awarenesses or the other. One could actually think there are fractures and divisions of awareness in almost every direction; or even that awareness understood globally is entirely a fracture, a pile of fragments coexisting, but often not touching. These are certainly *figurae dictionis*, without rhyme or reason, which merely serve provisionally and somewhat at random to mark a difference between a consciousness overtly unhappy and a consciousness that is taciturnly, perhaps timorously joyful. But the distinction is still confused, on second thought, and the difference uncertain, so it is probably better to drop this subject of consciousness. What we can say, though, is that sometimes words, whether those of a dialogue with the conscience or those said out loud, seem to be reflected in a silence containing something of which we are obscurely, almost secretly conscious. In this last case therefore it is the words that split, and not awareness; as if one said or heard the word 'pear', construed in the normal way, but by reflection, or almost coming like an echo, another concept arrived. What need is there to say what this other concept is, from the moment it signifies, even inappropriately, the word 'pear?'

'Is this an example of one of your *pear-shaped* illogical ways of reasoning?'

'Perhaps!' he would admit. And yet sometimes it is possible to predicate any sort of thing according to any other and be satisfied; and it is certainly possible that the word pear can imply some sort of joy, even if quite by chance. There are in fact logical implications and others only possible, but whatever implications you please, in this case of the pear, it cannot be denied that at times one intentionally gives words and entire phrases at least two meanings. A talk or a conversation can be double in the sense in which one is speaking of the duplicity of an unfaithful man; certain other times doubleness can even be dual and without guile, given the case in which, through ingenuity or distraction, the doubleness of an interlocutor has nothing to do with the doubleness of the other.

Two (let's say he himself and another brother) are sitting facing each other; he, perhaps a bit sideways to not lose sight of the landscape through the window, which is obviously the subject of the dialogue.

For example, about pears: what quality does the orchard yield? Or: how much land is planted?

Beyond the window rain is falling calmly, blurring everything, and little by little the discussion lapses, confused by irrelevant details, but it continues; or, at least something continues, aside from the rain, that thing that he does not say and the other does not hear. Coincidentally the rain turns silvery and vibrant and he sees not only trees and fields through the window, but also imagines, almost deciphering the air between the strands of rain, her figure, her body glistening with water, just the way she has stepped out of a washtub after having a bath.

In what words could this fantasy or vision have ever lodged? Perhaps words that are intended to mean rain or autumn suddenly can jump over the edge of the discussion and fall right into the midst of a clandestine celebration. Or perhaps the express sound of the words falls silent, leaving in the foreground, well in sight, a verbal silence, more suited to imaginary figures. And this could be all, at least for now, because, he said to himself, this whole discussion is just an attempt to explain how at one time he had come to talk about flour and grain with another, when suddenly and in silence a woman with a naked arse had jumped into his mind. 'In this case,' he concluded, 'arse appears immanent to silence and what's more silence as far as an arse is concerned, makes good sense, as well as good taste. What is there to say about an arse, especially, an imaginary one?'

In the meantime, moving forward along the path that was now going down towards the water, and even more rocky, he realised the fog was getting thicker. The horizon was reduced; it actually seemed to rest in the field beyond the river, like a white curtain, vaporous but still, perhaps two hundred steps from the point in which he was standing. And within this enclosed zone, perfectly circular, the light did not diminish: in every direction things had become more defined and clearly visible. The woman had paused and was looking around. Now he could even see her eyes, which seemed to be blue, the line of her hair, and the scarf she was wearing, and her nose, mouth and the line of her chin. Such ordinary and commonplace nose, mouth, and eyes, he would have said, that looking at her without paying attention and almost distractedly, he could suspect he already knew her and was seeing her again.

'You can see women like that all the time,' he said, shrugging his shoulders. It was probable she had also seen him and was trying to catch up with him. She could also believe she recognised him or more probably, being a country whore as she appeared to be, she did not want to let one of the rare men passing through these parts get away without finding a way to offer her services to him.

So this story of the woman on the other bank of the river was accommodating itself to the typical, exchanging the strangeness and obscurity of the first appearance with a more clear, but banal probability: because of the incident it was possible now to recognise conventional indications of country tarts. But then why was it so hard to arrive at such an obvious insight? In his dream of walking he sometimes felt he was accomplishing some unheard-of feat, with a strangeness, obscure as it might be, which justified the exertion and discomfort. So he continued almost heroically, until his mind became clear with a sudden flash. 'But I am merely walking!' he said, 'Only dreaming about walking.' And so he woke up feeling greatly distressed at such wasted effort.

The revelation of the banality of his undertakings, though it happened later in his sleep, seemed to him to have retroactive bearing. And the preliminary judgement of banality, once accepted, then generalised itself, weighing on every instant, on every breath of his existence, even if he stubbornly persevered in his search for a new life. Perhaps the most livable of lives was not the most strange and adventurous, but a life that had some permanent or possibly true attributes, humble as it might be; in other words, about which it would be possible to be conscious, if not happily at least without distress. Because this was certain: false or weak attributes fell as soon as the light changed, leaving faint, dirty shadows in their place. Perhaps this story of unhappy consciousness as well, which he had devised for the bare arse, was only a story of unhappily placed attributes, of qualities manoeuvred in an awkward and depressing way. Improving the qualities and attributes posit, even an arse could appear shining and new.

And what qualities, he asked himself, could ever be said to pertain to the arse, supposing there is a wish for that talk? 'Here we are back with the unheard and unmentionable words again,' he thought with irritation. At this point it was worth being quiet in order to later say that silence was nothing other than the litany of unspeakable attributes of the arse; or that, however far-reaching the significance of the arse might be, there was always a residue to the word without significance and immanent which constituted its inexhaustible virtue.

'But,' he thought, changing the subject, 'there must be a bridge and probably near the bridge a tavern, an inn and who knows what else.' He was now thinking it didn't really matter about the woman; certainly if he had met her at the tavern he would have been happy; he would have seemed, at least at the moment, to have walked to some purpose, that is to see this woman who could also just as well be a whore. After all, what does one want from life? He felt that any motivation, even an invented one, could improve his lot, and lend a shadow of dignity to it. He saw his face, grey with weariness and beard, his eyes staring, like a portrait's painted eyes with the caption, 'He goes after whores,' certainly not a flattering label, but by virtue of which it seemed to him his journey had now ended in resignation and yet with the solemnity that definitive statements bring, worthy of inscription because in the rigidity of the words, carved or painted, could be seen, if not the essential in flesh and bone, at least the covering and apparel of the essential. What's more, if something could be said about him approximating truth it was about this journey: apparently going after whores, in reality he was going after the essential, whatever this essential might prove to be.

'Perhaps a whore is the essential?' they would have asked him.

'That may well be!' he would have been tempted to reply.

'And the arse?' they persisted.

'That may well be!' he replied obstinately, but then admitted that no, actually speaking of the essential he hadn't meant what the learned or the saints had already said, but in a much more superficial and imprecise way, an appearance of the essential, those inscriptions on tombs or scrolls to celebrate the dead: in other words those things one refers to that cannot be other than the way they already were.

'These thoughts come from tiredness!' he told himself, to find an explanation.

Tiredness and pain in his leg often made him see the world according to the perspective of the most recent glance. He looked at things around, in this case the bushes, the trees, the river up to the veil of fog that now had come nearer and was no more than fifty paces from him, with a glance of farewell and in reply things declared their having already been. Everything therefore seemed in the past; or at least, the past predominated; the past was the essential with respect to the present which could either be what the eyes could see or what was aroused by sleep or memory.

He stood dumbfounded for a moment. Now the fog appeared to have formed a courtyard or an ample well with a zone of distant sky rising above, showing the pale and already cold serenity of autumn. The woman had disappeared, lost within the thickness of cloud on his left. 'I'll never catch up with her!' he said to himself, discouraged, but continued along the path. Why was he following the essential, if the essential consisted of the predominance of the past? No, he decided, straightening up to give himself courage. Undoubtedly he went after whores, but he also went after the new, the unheard, after fortune. And fortune, whatever that meant, could only be festive and special, at least to compensate for the distance he had journeyed after her. So, just for a change, from now on there would be no more talk of arses. Well, why not talk about breasts instead? Udders! even in the sense in which *ubera ebiberant avidi lactantia nati*; or more generally, of whatever thing *profluens et uber*, as in Arcadia: clear fresh and sweet water; or in the land of plenty – where streams flowed with milk and rivers with wine – and perhaps there were even stewed breasts. Abundance of the easy and fluent sort induced by sated feelings rather than hunger, because (and this is certainly strange) it is easy to be sated by some things but not by others. Equally there are words that soon sound tiring, even though they are useful; so expressions like tripe and stew are tiresome and boring but a word like sleep never is. In the most sad or even irritating moments of existence no one who wants to get in a good mood would say 'I am going to bed', while the prospective of taverns, sausages and wine helps to banish melancholy. Abundance, therefore, is a better remedy than sleep. A tavern is certainly what it is, with whores and other people dedicated to dishonest trade: barbers, procurers . . . But a man pays no attention: he is tired, he goes in, and sits down.

'Where am I going in this fog?' he asked himself, realising that now, aside from no longer seeing the woman, he could no longer even see the river. He found himself in empty, flat terrain with furrows caused by wheels.

'In any case it is best for me to go on,' he said, starting to walk again. Returning to the idea of a tavern, one could say that what was interesting among the many things that the word tavern implied was not so much the food and the wine as the company: an unexpressed communion of intentions. Nothing clear is said: or rather what is said or shouted is almost indecipherable in the uproar. The things said and heard are equally indistinct and function in the surroundings as if they were 'the same things' as much heard as said. The sameness of the words therefore, their deafness and almost their internal silence is the principle of communion.

'And the whores?' they asked him.

He shrugged his shoulders. 'What I can say,' he replied 'is that one doesn't think about the sins of the world or, at least, doesn't think about them in terms of individual responsibility. Each one is submerged in the group; and so no one succeeds in judging or at least, even taking things as they are, one is not really grieved by them, but only mildly troubled, or occasionally disgusted. That's as true for sin as for poverty or even illness. Who would spit in the face of a beggar or kick a cripple in a tavern, as it happens in any other place? And how is it possible to judge and condemn if, as has been said, even what one says doesn't count? What everyone says is without exception all that it is humanly possible to say, not what the Church commands us to say or to not say. I have heard someone say the Creed backwards, trying to cure a cat of scabies.

'But then this is communion with the devil!' they would have shouted. 'That's no communion!'

'Certainly,' he admitted, 'if no one teaches, no one justifies, no one condemns to death, there is no more communion; yet the ego loses itself in the multitude just the same. One can however also think that words in this case are a way out towards perdition. Not magic, therefore, but hope without object. Or, to try to describe it more briefly, one could say that on the one hand there is the solitude of tiredness, and on the other the communion of rest and in this case tavern, tripe, titties and talk would be equivalent to rest and even of sleep. One could add that they stand for sleep in the sense that, in case of sleeplessness, they might be considered the best solace for one's tiredness.

'Why then,' he sighed, 'words that perhaps conceal nothing (what can a word like titty, stew or sausage actually conceal?), words even oiled, disarranged, words tossed out randomly into the void, are in certain circumstances the only ones that distract, sooth, console?'

He was shivering with cold, and suddenly stopped to sneeze into his hand. 'What a filthy person!' he said to himself, shaking his fingers. 'Yes! The void,' he started again. 'Especially on rainy days, one measures and gauges what one has lost: youth, of course, maturity as well, but above all one thinks of the lost thoughts. And, however cautiously and tentatively one proceeds, thinking about thoughts always enlarges the void of loss. What one once thought with conviction now appears unsuitable, faded in the sunset of memory: in the pale flood of forgetfulness that rises only words go adrift, little scatter phrases: 'the window . . . the mirror'. Or: 'Bend your knee . . .' The last phrase however, fortunately, was not ambiguous and uncertain, but explicit and still tendentiously persuasive.

'My leg,' she wailed, 'my leg is broken.'

'Move your knee,' he suggested to her.

But she was curled up in a corner with her knees drawn towards her chest weeping steadily, watched over by the dog. Or perhaps the dog whined steadily and she allowed herself only an occasional wail.

'Stretch out your leg. Move your knee. Move it!' he begged her, trying not to move her leg with his hands, but with every attempt she howled and the dog growled and bared his teeth.

'I must go,' he repeated. 'I can't stay.' And he reached over to slap the dog to make him stop growling.

'Broken!' she repeated every time. In the end he sat beside her on the floor, with his back against the wall, continuing to ask her almost mechanically why she had used such an wobbly ladder in the loft. His question was not a true question because he hadn't meant to ask what he was asking, but only behave in a practical manner seeing her immense sadness. This sadness as far as the eye could see sometimes disposed itself in a linear manner almost forming a thread; or like a barrier or insurmountable boundary. Beyond, a field of uncertain form and dimensions, but smooth and clean, could just as easily have been called the field of the past as the field of the future; but he understood that it was in reality the dominion of the possible, because it seemed to contain all the well-being possible, though it was lost. Therefore, beyond the border, there she was just as she had been: light, that is agile, (because she was large and bony, she could hardly be described as light). This side of the border however, or after his question about the wobbly ladder, here she was now in flesh and blood, that is, broken and lying in a corner of the room.

What was he to do with this large broken woman? The dog jumped up into the space between them and in the end was lying close to his foot. Time passed with the coming and going of hours all alike and the night seemed to turn in on itself many times. If one puts a foot on a stair in the dark, he reasoned, and goes down, because all the steps are equal, one will necessarily get all the way down, even if it is impossible to see where the stairway leads . . . into the cellars, perhaps, or worse into a dead end. Oppression is the word, he said to himself. But certainly he was saying, as a matter of speaking. Outside the cellar or other metaphors, even imagining himself outside in the fresh air, he felt desperately certain that everything was now going from bad to worse with an irresistible crescendo. A new panorama began to take shape in his fantasy: dismal from the beginning and uniformly dark, it then slowly levelled out into a swamp with shiny, harsh colours, but outlines that were indecipherable. At a certain point in this bitter imaginary metamorphosis, trying everything, he also started to wail. Perhaps at the beginning he was wailing in his sleep, because in the long run the inertia and mental block that comes from feeling that you are the prisoner of incessant images changes into sleepiness, if not into deep sleep, but in the end he was certainly awake. He was awake and was weeping; or rather he realised he was awake because he realised he was weeping.

At this point she had moved away from him, stood up and prepared some soup for them. Obviously her leg was not broken; she would not be a cripple, but the question why she used a wobbly ladder in the loft seemed to have been put once and for all and could neither be avoided or ignored. Nothing could ever be as it was before, for it was logically impossible to abolish the differentiating function which this question of the broken leg has been taking on in his mind during the night.

'I must make myself a walking stick,' he said, looking around. He had come to a clearing, from which two ways opened out: actually on the left what looked like a trail took off from the real road. Certainly the river was on the left; but, he reasoned, if there must be a bridge, it should be connected with the road, not with the track.

'Why not stop for a while?' he asked himself. The leg would certainly be swollen and stiff once he stopped, but he knew from experience that dragging a slightly rested swollen leg along is not much worse than dragging it along swollen, but aching. And what's more it was a nice spot. The woods had grown tall, and there was no way of seeing the river; the trees were big and beautiful, and amidst them the fog seemed no longer a wall or a boundary, but a vague whiteness that softened the brown of the trunks from a certain distance. On one side of the clearing were scattered pieces of wood, among them a log that he thought would be a good place to sit.

'Yes,' he said once he was seated, taking up the thread of his thoughts, 'to talk of logic in connection with the rungs of a ladder and legs, or even of thighs, now could seem irreverent, as well as improper; but then (he would have sworn) it seemed to him that it was as much about thighs as about logic and even ladders and grammar and buttocks as in the proposition 'if she had only landed on her buttocks!' Even the punctuation came to be sometimes drawn up into a ball to preserve the distinction between buttocks and thighs at least. He closed his eyes. He saw the cup again, the milk, bread, table, the leg on which she seemed to support herself with difficulty. He couldn't manage to take his eyes off the movement of that leg, so as he imagined them under her skirt, until almost out of pity she lifted her skirt and showed him a big bruise in the middle of her thigh.

'You were afraid I'd die!' she had said, caressing his face with the back of her hand. She had looked at him smiling, without losing sight of the beans she continued to shell. Now, she said, was the time for him to leave the convent. He had shaken his head without replying. They were both silent, she smiling, he from inertia. The longer they were silent the more the objects around them acquired strange colours with too much contrast. Due to those colours everything seemed different: from the battered leg to the death she had incongruously named. It was the world 'after': a world without return in which the violent white of milk and the yellow brown of bread were one near the other without mediations or transitions. Even their voices, his own and hers, no longer seemed to have anything in common. He heard her voice soft and mellow, like the rainy day that was starting to clear outside the window, charming, but without depth. Everything was on offer, but almost as if each thing came in sight for the first and last time: the bread, the milk in the cup, the leg under the skirt, the consoling gesture of her hand. They seemed to be hallucinations clipped out of the void; phenomena without antecedents or consequences. He felt no pleasure amidst these apparitions, as incoherent as they were surprising, but nevertheless was content with them as if to say: 'This is better than nothing', almost as if he had managed to swap nothingness for the fixed eternity of things.

'Yes!' he said, trying to find a more comfortable position on the log. It was a world without return, as if suddenly any participation on his part had come to an end.

'How did it come to an end?' they had asked him years later.

He had shrugged his shoulders: 'They sent me to another place.' In some way, like all stories that concerned him, this one had also ceased to be a story of his. The possessive had fallen, one could say. One could also say the subject, in this case himself, had fallen and what he remembered was only a story without conclusion like so many others, perhaps without even a beginning. Perhaps somehow she has also vanished, somehow forgotten; and what remained in his mind with so much precision was merely the void that memories have when they are finished, when what's essential in them is the past.

'No, it's not comfortable!' he said to himself about the log on which he was sitting. He looked around and discovered a big brown stone a short distance away at the foot of a tree. He moved with difficulty, almost crawling, towards the rock, and then sat leaning back against the tree. 'This is fine!' he said approvingly, closing his eyes.

When he opened them again, the fog had spread itself everywhere without truly being in any one place. There was a luminous and clear vapour or a powdery diffuse light, that made everything seem pallid: the pallor increased with distance up to an opaque and undifferentiated whiteness; near however, or at least up to the point the fog was transparent, the cold colour could suggest winter, but the trees full of faded leaves belied this impression without entirely contradicting it. The air had become almost cold and one was brought to think of a season special to that place, a product of the *genius loci* rather than the climate.

'What strange and graceful magic,' he thought. 'I shall certainly give an account of this.' In front of his eyes were fallen leaves, gravel, pebbles, brown and compact rich soil in places showing roots from the surrounding trees: some very big roots and other smaller, more slender ones, with a cautious delicately bestial appearance as they tried to burrow back into the ground. He could have said that everything seemed to know what it was about, or as they say, to be *compos sui*; every stone, every branch had a special shrewdness or awareness in putting itself into being in a persistent way that seemed almost stubborn, a stubbornness neither disturbed nor disturbing, but sure, patient, without uncertainties. 'Well,' he would have said, 'to let things be what they are, in our absence therefore, one must grant them a sort of consciousness; a form of awareness that is not like ours, unhappy or happy.'

Certainly they would have looked at him dumbfounded as usual: 'Well, well!' they would have responded, shrugging their shoulders.

'It's true!' he would have persisted. 'I found myself near the river, in the midst of the fog on a summer afternoon.'

'And what about the woman?' they would have asked, 'the one walking on the other side of the river. What did you do with the woman?'

'Well,' he would have excused himself, 'that woman was lost in the fog.'

'Before or after she broke her leg?' Others, more malicious, returned to the problem of the essential: 'How and when can a dirty arse be called essential?' And to stick with the subject, they suggested to him that perhaps the entire story wasn't even meant to be a story but a bad joke.

He shook his head in dismay. He admitted he probably drew things out a bit too much even to the point of weariness or boredom. Tediousness and effort sometimes seemed to him complementary qualities not only of the stories that he was trying to tell, but of all stories, however they were told. In the hum of the taverns, he sometimes felt that nausea, verbosity, tiredness were rooted directly in the words; in those that succeeded in surfacing out of the indistinct thickness of voices and in those submerged, murmured, inaudible, or only thought.

'Outside of silence there is only weariness!' he stated, but thinking about it again, added: 'Perhaps!'

Forsitan, fortasse, fors, fortuna . . . he continued, mildly grumbling. What he remembered, what he almost saw in his imagination and what he now saw fully face to face, the fog and its almost wintry whiteness, had always had a fortunate gleam for him, a moment of wondering revelation in which things no longer appeared, perhaps in one way, perhaps in another, but in a way more radically surprising, perhaps as nothing. Aside from these momentary exaltations of the present, of the wonder or of the fortune, everything was wobbling on tediously in a mediocre uncertainty. Perhaps tediousness is the quality of uncertainty that runs through a long coming and going of mistakes and corrections and more vaguely of proposals and amendments; an interminable voyage through night-time corridors of memory that persists not so much tireless as tired and stubborn, simply because tiredness is also in the nature of memory.

'Tediousness, tiredness, uncertainty!' he said to himself to summarise, and these expressions appeared like the sea with the rhythm and heavy thickness. 'I am falling asleep,' he said to himself. 'It is best for me to start walking again.' But when he said this he realised that perhaps he was already asleep and that this had no bearing on the intentions of memory, because now these kinds of sleep and of waking were memory time; a time without rest, but impartial, because now he no longer remembered going backwards starting from the present, but starting from his entire life.

'It's best to start walking again!' he repeated.

'Did you think I was dying?' she asked with a faint smile. Without answering her, he put his hand around her waist to support her, pressing his fingers into her flesh. This was an easier way for them to go together with their legs wobbly.

So, supporting each other they hobbled on, as a road opened in front of them boring as a litany, dark and with no shelter. *In habitationibus non ingredientur, sed vagantes errent dolentes semper et tristes ... videntes aliorum habitacula ab angelis conservari cum silentio magno. . . .*

ANGELA (1989)

To Lidia Vallino

'Of course – the police sergeant said to the attorney – as you see, this whole affair is somewhat embarrassing for me: the suicide note, its tone of intimacy which I must admit is not entirely unjustified. This familiarity might seem strange to you. But I must admit I would have paid something out of my own pocket to know that Nimando was settled once and for all, or else in prison. On the other hand, I must admit the man amused me; or rather he irritated and amused me at the same time.'

The attorney's office had been carved out of a previously much larger room, cut in four parts, that is split both in floor plan and elevation, so that the ceiling, not twenty centimetres above the head of the police sergeant who was the taller of the two, bisected the middle of the window. It was not so much light as interminable afternoon rain that streamed through this partial window in greyish streaks in the unreliable autumn of Lombardy. Since the police sergeant showed no sign of leaving, the attorney walked around his bulky desk and sat down, or sank into his shabby armchair, signalling almost rudely for the police sergeant to use the other chair.

'Please,' the attorney said, making a gesture with his left hand brusquely turned outwards. He had never liked this gesture, and yet from the time he went into this dreary office this very gesture became a stronger expression of inevitability and brutality. 'One time or another I'll end up dislocating my wrist' – the attorney thought. 'But what does this police sergeant want?' – he also thought. 'Philosophy? Psychology?' In any case, he himself had nothing to do, that is he didn't want to do anything nor did he want to get rid of the police sergeant.

'All right!' he said then. 'Let's even admit that it's a strange case, but nevertheless there's not much to it. What's more, aside from the suicide letter which is only a general lament about everything and everyone, there is nothing but vague indi-

cations, suspicions, and not even a criminal record con-
cerning Nimando.

'That's how it is, unfortunately!' the police sergeant admitted,
stretching out his arms.

They looked at each other for a few seconds without knowing
what to say until with an effort at courtesy the attorney smiled,
in the meantime deciding that he didn't like people from Naples,
including the police sergeant, although it was said in the family
that his maternal grandmother was a pure *napoletana*. He himself
had once spent time around Naples, at Castellammare di Stabbia
and at least the climate, if he remembered correctly, seemed
good.

'We can exclude that he was a terrorist,' the police sergeant
said in the meantime. 'And he was not a thief. I don't see
Nimando with a gun in his hand. And yet, if he should decide at
some time or other . . . See,' he explained, bending forward to
confide, 'the man is gentle, but, as I have already told you, I am
sure he is gentle only because he is undecided, because he lacks
courage: not because of his nature.'

The attorney objected: 'I think he's only ridiculous. You told
me that he dumps buckets of water over the public lavatory and
when those inside come out soaking wet, half drowned, he
consoles them and then steals their wallets. What is this? Theft?
Mere suspicion; no witnesses, only rumours. Also the story that
he was Von Stronzheim, a German film director . . . If there are
silly people at the German consulate, willing to believe him, too
bad for them: no charge has been reported even for this affair.
And now this suicide. This is undoubtedly a tragedy,' the
doubting attorney concluded. 'But then would this good woman
have thrown herself under the train because of Nimando? There
is a letter here addressed to you personally, Sergeant. And that
certainly is strange. Let us read it.'

Letter from the suicide.

Dear Sergeant, Now we three have known each other for three
years and all three of us have our fiftieth birthday on the same
day, September 12th, tomorrow. This is partly also a letter of best
wishes to you personally, and, when you happen to see him, for
my Matteo, or for Nimando, as you call him.

Do you remember? Last week, September 3rd, in one of your not infrequent visits, we realised we were born on the same day, although we are so different. 'Different?' Matteo asked. 'All three of us have the same kind of nose and are more or less the same size and height (although I am a woman). Our heads are the same shape and our hair the same colour and all three of us have double-jointed thumbs, which old Lombroso calls an indication of a criminal nature . . .' And he continued to list other similarities which are really there and so ridiculous that you yourself laughed about it, at least in part or only in part.

'On the one hand you make me laugh, Nimando,' you said. 'On the other hand you make me furious.' You were angry because of the credit cards, because you thought that Matteo was also guilty this time, but he managed to get out of it unharmed with his usual luck. Basically it was the same old story: 'I know everything about you,' you said. 'You can pretend you are German, French or Turkish, if you wish, but underneath it all you are still a chicken thief. Not much of anything: a cardboard hoodlum and a leaden babbler.'

'We may look alike,' Matteo said 'but with all respect, Sergeant, I can steal without being a thief, get drunk with you without being thirsty, laugh without being happy and weep without being afraid. So I can even speak without having anything to say. I have no motive: I am and do what each time I happen to be and do, while you, Sergeant, can only catch thieves. I live according to fortune, and you according to necessity. And here the resemblance between us ends.'

'And you don't want to be anything on the other hand!' you replied.

I am reminding you of all this because this confused story of similarities and dissimilarities, of fortune and will, seem to me the dominant motive. . . .

'But what motive would that ever be?' you might ask. 'A confused motive, a musical motif, one could say, like those motives that make one laugh or cry: a motif in my case that I fear is more about crying than laughing, although I hope that it is more funny than sad.

'If you feel like crying, go ahead and cry. If you want to laugh, laugh!' he said to me. But no, it isn't like that. Crying is somehow similar to laughing and vice versa. But there is something else. While I am myself, there is also something in me that would like to be like him to the point of actually being him; up to the point of believing me with his hands, his voice, and his own words inside that voice, but at the same time (the way one dreams of flying, while knowing one is falling) with the consciousness and the grief of a growing distance between that voice and those words. And as this distance increases I know I am reducing myself back to myself, although I had been him.

First however, before a resemblance starts, there is something that perhaps I would call a desire to laugh, and while laughing, a hope of being like something. And even before that, before wanting or hoping for anything, there is nothing: or nothing at least that could be like something in the sense of a similarity one truly wishes or wants.

When I was a little girl, sometimes in the country on a slope at the edge of a wood, I could see the valley in front of me full of fog almost touching my feet, and yet in this fog, knowing the places where I could look through, I could see almost everything, one farmhouse and then another. It was a faded view, a partial sight, since the eye cannot see through the fog, however slight it may be. This paling of things, due to the fog, which left them just as they were, each diverse from the other, also made them all equal.

'One man is worth any other,' my aunt said to me, when I was a bit older. And so it was then for the farmhouses trees and houses in town. I sat down and said: 'Nothing can be done about it. Here I am! Do you want to sing?' I asked myself. 'Do you want to throw a stone?'

But I didn't reply because it didn't seem worth the trouble until one day I saw, a short step away from the rock on which I was sitting, a cat with a lifted paw, looking at me with the blacks of his round eyes. To be brief, I put this cat in my basket of mushrooms. The blacks became vertical cracks in its green eyes when it watched me from the basket and stretched out a paw every so often to say something which, since cats cannot speak, was the same thing I thought the cat wanted to say.

So skipping and leaping, we went towards home, towards our little red farmhouse. In the courtyard near the woodshed we came upon my father. 'The cat, the beautiful little black cat!' I started to sing. He looked in the basket, grabbed the cat by its back, placed it on the ground and squashed its head with his foot.

'No cat' – he said. 'We have little chicks.'

I was singing before, and went on singing: 'No cat, we have little chicks,' until it was dark, when my mother knocked my head against the stove. Nothing could be done about it then; nothing can be done now, or ever. First with the cat in my basket I thought that what I couldn't do myself, it could do and vice versa. Everything seemed possible. If I so wished, I could be the cat and it could be me. With the cat dead, all the houses became the same again and all the trees, houses, chicks and fathers and mothers. More the same than they had been in the fog, because now, while without fog I could clearly see their differences, I knew that even this sameness was not the effect of visual confusion, but of truth, just the way the town the valley and life all fit together. When I was grown up, the way all men were the same, as my aunt said, with or without moustaches, red or dark-haired, drunken or sober, seemed clear to me, because like all things, they were never one thing alone: a single man or a single cat. If with the cat alive we could exchange places, it was because, being both of us alone, in solitude we wanted to be alike up to the point of being, in a single song, dance or laugh, as confused as drops of water. In other words, even if everything in general looks like everything else, there are also things that have a desire to be alike.

'But what does that have to do with it?' you'll say, as you usually do. – Of course cats are cats and people are people. But for example, let's stay with cats: one day I saw one walking on frost, on the big field in front of the bicycle factory that has been closed for ten years. The cat's paws were obviously cold, and it shook them one at a time; with three feet on the ice and one lifted, shaking the one it held up it seemed to be saying: 'And now what can I do in this miserable cold?' So I went up to it very gently, but as soon as it saw me it fled. I stayed there holding my shopping basket in the middle of the field, alone and so to speak abandoned.

'It is my little cat, I thought, my beautiful little cat has gone and left me: my poor little cat who was killed . . .' And thinking this I sat in the midst of the frost and started to weep.

A half hour went by, I think, or possibly longer. It was now almost dark; the only light, one of those violet streaks one can see across the rooftops in December evenings. At a certain point however, in the humming from the autostrada near the factory I heard the ground crunch behind me; I turned, still seated. And there he was. Wearing his handsome coat – that black one (he was a film director then) – he had come to find me in the middle of nowhere.

'He's come back' – I said to myself, weeping and embracing his legs. 'He's come back!' But what is most curious, Sergeant, is that I didn't know with any certainty who had come back: The cat? My lovely little cat? Nimando? All were alone and yet all together they seemed to have returned. 'Ah, you are here!' I said to myself, looking around the field. There they all were one by one: my mother, the cat, and also my father, changed for the better like a dream. He was so changed, that although he was familiar to me as a father, I recognised him but was doubtful: Is it someone else? My mother? The police sergeant?'

Alternatively, in fact I thought I also recognised you among those who had come back.

No, it was just himself alone. I saw him clearly but I also saw how everyone, being alone, can change their nature when they come back in that way: not only me, who if I wished, could believe I was almost he, almost in his place, or through love believe he was almost in my place, but everyone, if they wished, could almost exchange places with others, even men in the place of cats and vice versa. Another way of coming back the same therefore, but this time also as a remedy for the first sameness which was instead entirely indifferent.

Do you remember, Sergeant that evening a month ago when you stopped to have a meal with us? We were all slightly tipsy that evening and I started to sing one of our local songs. I sang the words softly to do not disturb the people nearby so that they might almost hear a distant voice, and you sang the chorus in a deeper and much more distant voice.

Then I felt I was back in my own place, when the snow dimmed the voices without entirely extinguishing them. Everything is as before: the road grey with crushed ice, the houses darkened by the great whiteness of dim light and that evening red below the clouds on the tips of the distant mountains: a red that gives no light but merely promises more snow.

Once again there is nothing to do about it; nothing can be changed. And yet, passing close to that place where we had the meal, and hearing those songs, enclosed within, there is a sense that something has also been done and concluded. Now the sense of inertia comes from the conclusion, from the ending to which nothing may be added: that is indeed truly the sameness of all things, men, cows, mountains, but this time a peace-giving sameness in the great quiet of the ending. Nothing to change, nothing to take away or to add. And then a woman like me asks herself: What is the difference between the uselessness from before and this consoling peace, between despair and happiness, if everything remains the same in the worst of before and the best of later?

The difference, in this sea of things always and everywhere various, but fundamentally always and anywhere with the same destiny is, I am convinced, in the arrival. When one arrives, let's say, at the farmhouse in the woods in front of the farmhouse from which one has set out one says with a sigh of relief: 'At least this is done!' Certainly the leaves rustle and fall as before: the red ones are tossed by the wind and fall to the ground with the first drops of rain, but now the immense rustling in every place in the world and clouds massing in the sky is no longer so distant and extraneous to us. It feels nearby and friendly, like a silent presence watching us.

We set out and we arrived! And because this seems to be not a single thing concluded but everything, arriving is also a return. We recognize what has always been in every single thing, this time without stopping at the apparent details. Looking around we respond to everything looking at us. With good will and calm we respond to good will and calm, with silence to silence: or better still, with our face we respond and recognise the face of serenity of any figure in the garments of everyone which could somehow also be our mother, if nothing else for the green of her eyes.

'But this is madness!' you will say, Sergeant. In any case this madness doesn't come upon us with a leap or by chance, but after a kind of journey, a long road. Once one has attained madness, one is aware of the length of the entire road one has taken. Whatever point may be the one arrived at, one thing is certain: it was a long difficult tiring journey. This journey now concluded cannot be divided or doubted, and one cannot go backwards.

Let's also admit that this arrival is terrible, however worse one may have feared it. What can be done about it? To have arrived is the truth now, not the journey one made before. Arrived! Therefore there is not a before and perhaps not an after. Even wanting to believe that there is an after, it is certainly not an after of the before, but an after in the sense of everything. What am I doing writing all this?

Oh yes! I forgot to tell you that I arrived just because I no longer know where to go and don't even distinctly remember any more where I came from. Family, my friend, you yourself, Sergeant, all around me you are all present: the world is present for me in a block. It is not true that the world is bigger or, as you believe, more open and more possible than this room; it is only more confused and more united.

I don't really know. Perhaps truth is different. Because of this conclusion, no one expects anything more of me, or no one expects me. And so it is as if I were expecting everyone.

'But,' you will say, 'these are the fantasies of a woman alone and abandoned. For a woman it could also be like this, but even like this makes no difference, because I cannot even say that I am the expectant one. Between me and the place in which I arrived there is almost no difference. Could one say a place instead of a spot, a hole instead of a whole, a thing that is open rather than closed? Open, patient, feminine, as you wish; but alone no, because even in this there is agreement and likeness as in the chorus I spoke about before. And choruses cannot be called a "solo", and if one does not say that, it makes no difference. And this, Sergeant, seems to me to be true also for him. If, as he wished, he arrived, he is like us and also for him "solo" or alone is not something one can say makes a difference.'

The attorney put the pages of the letter back in order, and gripped them tightly between his fingers. 'No,' he decided 'I hadn't read it well before. I cannot restore the letter to you, Sergeant' he said without looking up from the surface of the desk. And since no reply followed he continued: 'Perhaps the thing, as you say, is truly embarrassing, because they were true friends of yours. Meals, drinks, thick as thieves as you say in the South . . .' And he went on for some time, but in a certain sense, even knowing what he was saying, he did not listen to his own words. Instead he was thinking *'Napoletani*! They are all *napoletani*. In this universal neapolinity he had been right to not get married. Why bother to marry and have children if all of them, in one way or another, ended up being *napoletani*?

INTERMEZZO

To Giovanni Aquilecchia

Dear Giovanni,

At a certain point you may ask yourself: 'What sort of story is this?' In *Intermezzo* there is a quotation from Tasso, about Aristotle's definition of the unity of time. I can't give you chapter and verse, as usual I don't remember, but I do remember clearly Tasso's words: the unity of time is that fragment of time that is needed to listen to a comedy or a tragedy: a definition, as you see, as theoretically approximate as could be, unless one brings in this relative use of the concept itself, in which unity becomes 'that' unity of time, that is, the time needed for the content to reveal itself, whose unveiling at the end (at least in the case of this *intermezzo*) could change absolutely nothing, that it has no ethical or teleological meaning. What I am trying to say is that when the story is told, it appears to be nothing other than 'one' single consciousness of life in the sense of occupation of a lifetime; or rather, turning around the intentional genitive, the life of a consciousness, which is in the last analysis the unity of the story that is told.

At least these are my theoretical ambitions. Which, as you will see, imply in the form of contraband other ambitions of an ethical nature, largely mistaken, like all ambitions. But I am convinced that literature is the courage of an attempt (to understand) while being fully aware that failure is inevitable, to a greater or larger extent.

Thanks so much for the kind attention you give to my scribbles.

With great affection, your Michele

'I could have done without that!' he repeated in front of the empty lake. It was not the first time he found himself making judgements like this, with a precise literal meaning, but without any reference and then to continue to repeat them mechanically. But what could he have done without?

'Everything and nothing!' he thought he could say. This reply, even if it meant nothing, at least got him beyond pure and simple abstaining from doing something towards more vague moral regions, so that, whatever thing he may have omitted to say or do, he felt, thinking of it, could be epitomised as a long and indefinite regret.

'Oh, damn!' he said, kicking a branch of a laurel torn away from the nearby bushes that had made its own way up to the edge of the quay.

For a few seconds he looked at the water soaking the few leaves attached to the surface branches, almost dozing in the light, filtered from the morning mist. So early, with the sun still invisible, the colours of the place gave structure to the objects, and made him aware of their weight and distinguishing characteristics and, by implication, that night and sleep were still nearby.

He was looking at the water, leaves, mountains: distinct and diverse, as he had done before in other places, without making any sense of what he saw. Turning his gaze from the paleness of the sky to the more intense colour of the water or just looking from one thing to another, he measured the emptiness of difference: a dimension of nothing or of absence that seemed to him always greater than the things it separated, although these things were near and immense like an entire lake or the entire sky. He felt that this difference or separation was the recurring pattern of his life: the interval between one landscape and another of the various places he'd been; the journey from one city to another, often by train, through inscrutable nights or shapeless and fleeting distances.

This emptiness between different things was the dimension in which he often recognised himself with greater approximation: in a word, he travelled from one city to another, from one landscape to another and perhaps also from one thought to another, often, however, remaining in the middle himself and poised between these thoughts, because it would have been very hard for him to say he had arrived at something, except for the point of the next departure. In practice, he was always departing, so that departure could be said to be the formal and final cause of his life, as the ancients would have maintained. But departure was a theme not only for fantasy, but also the pretext for his most occasional and disordered memories: the commonplace of every mental event, from which sometimes images could emerge that were even clear, with high definition and propriety of design. In other words, while he was fantasizing or perhaps remembering, if he thought of a cow, or a whore, or a woman, his thought was cow whore woman scrupulously detailed to the most hidden downy hair, provided that with respect to these things he had in mind a 'himself' about to depart towards 'elsewhere' so that in the end he would not have been able to say where or when about these 'beasts', or why they kept meandering around in his mind.

'Phantoms,' a moralist would have objected. 'Fairies gnomes elves mermaids: figures from an intermediate world, neither of God nor the devil!' He needed to recognise that these images were not calling for judgement, but enjoying the neutrality of a manner of fluid thinking, without order or consequence. The imprecision was not in the word choice, but in syntax; and at this point it seemed irrelevant to insist that he could have done without it or, on the contrary, that these figures played an indispensable part in life and the world. So what did he mean by repeating almost obsessively that he could do without it?

'It's almost cold!' he said, huddling within his shoulders. He realised this October had been mild, almost like summer, and although the leaves were turning yellow and starting to fall, he didn't intend to unpack his winter clothes yet. Perhaps he should buy a new coat to replace the one he'd worn for seven years which was now threadbare. 'I have worn out seven pairs of shoes . . .' he murmured, thinking that perhaps the number of pairs of shoes worn out in the course of the life of his coat was exact; but shoes and coat aside, his wardrobe was perfectly good; he had an excessive number of shirts; he promised himself often to leave some behind in a hotel, but then abstained, afraid that he would be scrupulously offered the same shirts many years later should he happen to return. Perhaps he should have written in his ledger next to the name of the hotel, 'abandoned shirts', just as he marked other useful information, for example that there was mildew in the chest of drawers or that the sheets were damp.

What's more, his archive, as he called his collection of these notes, was improving every year and making itself easier to consult. There were many columns with cross references: finding himself on a train or in the corner of a café or at a station. He could manage in a few minutes to inform himself on the situation in which he might be about to find himself: a city to which it was not prudent to return frequently and others more tolerant: pleasant hotels and others that were gloomy, people of various characters and varied means. For the shopkeepers of various cities he had a double column: types of merchandise and names listed according to presumed economic situation. There were also notes on the physical characteristics of each person: weight, height, colouring; others about sexual habits, religious practices, ways of speaking, most frequent swear words, nicknames, degrees or professions of wife, children, brothers and even grandchildren. From a couple of pages of these notes he was able to draw out material that permitted him to talk about a place as if he had been born there or of a man as if he had known him all his life; but in reality, in spite of all his display of familiarity, no place or person truly existed for him outside of his notebook. Even he himself was a character from a notebook whose image faithfully followed a conventional type. In general and especially at the beginning, he was identified as 'the Boaster': the show-off poker player.

In towns he had not visited too often or recently he would recount on any pretext some most amazing wins and if any doubts were expressed about these boasts he showed every sign of sadness or even hurt, adding detail to detail in an obvious attempt to be believed, and rendering the whole story ludicrously confused. However when he was challenged, or even dragged to the gambling table, he managed with a few good hands to win a small fortune, which he pocketed laughing like a happy and surprised child, in jesting and yet haughty triumph over his adversaries. What's more, his tactics varied within this line of general strategy, and his facial expressions went through a whole range of emotions from arrogance to fear and showed such complexity of *arrière pensée* with frowns, sneezes, and scratchings, etc. that his adversaries' compelling need to understand what happened led to other games and subsequent losses. To distract them from these losses, he shifted to behaviour that was less guarded and more ostensibly revealing. In fact, having nothing to reveal, he confined himself to allusive phrases. For example: he cited vague contracts with unnamed banks, stopping abruptly before long as if he regretted these vague confidences. In any case, since he went around trying to sell small or large lots of different sorts of containers in paper, wood or plastic, there were those who eventually believed he was a shareholder or director of some packaging company. This would explain his choice of rather expensive hotels and restaurants. To distract attention he would also allow distinctly disagreeable stories to spread about himself and to circulate. He pretended not to listen, not to understand, while the laughs and allusions became ever more explicit, and then, suddenly and unexpectedly, he began to deny these things, but in such a heartbroken and awkward way that people felt sorry for him.

'No!' he insisted in a voice wavering between rage and sorrow: he didn't much like the local whores! And he certainly was not a man who needed to pay a woman for sex.

'Of course!' the others chortled. Women (it was said) made reservations to enjoy his favours!

The laughter deafened the café and the most serious customers shook their heads in sympathy. But by then many were convinced that he was impotent. Some inferred from this impotence that he had been cuckolded. Others, apparently more informed, spoke of a wife who openly lived with her lover at his expense.

When these last stories got back to him, he replied with rude gestures, obscene, violent and silent, but without bitterness; actually with a weariness so heartbreaking it might have been resignation. 'Perhaps', he thought, 'resignation was not entirely simulated.' Sometimes, spotting in the mirror, from obvious signs, the passing of years and accumulated weariness from his innumerable departures, he thought that the time would soon come for him to live off his earnings in some little town he had already visited. There was no town in his memory that didn't repulse him; but finally one place was as suitable as any other for the quiet and simple life he intended to lead, and in this sense any place could tempt him to resignation, like any other. Therefore he would no longer have lived in the sign of departure but in that of arrival and this changing of signs that he called resignation would have also changed the sense of the emptiness that he felt: an emptiness – he thought – which he saw perhaps without too much anxiety, after reversing his perspective, or looking backward beginning from the end. In fact why not simply let himself go to a banal, current perception of his solitude or of the emptiness that he saw around him; for example the perception of the life of a cuckold; perhaps a putative but tranquil cuckold?

'The cuckold! The old wanker!' children would have called out in unison when they saw him walk by, while he held his hands behind his back, keeping pace with their sing-song. He would have gone to his customary morning café announced, and so to speak, hymned by the children and sit at his usual table by the usual window, watching the people smile as they passed by on the pavement at the signs the waiters were making behind his back, referring to him.

'And where is your wife?' one of the more facetious would have asked, winking. 'Travelling!' he would have invariably replied, affording an opportunity for sassy tales of entire tribes, as far east as west, deep in the south as well as the extreme North down to the last old man and baby boy fucked by this travelling wife of his. He would have also had a chance to bask in the warmth of reflected glory, no longer an outsider in any sort of place, but a distinguished stranger in the right place, even if it was not his, now that he could be recognised by everyone through these stories of cuckolding.

He smiled with compassion: 'Fantasies!' he said. In reality he knew very well that children no longer paid much attention to cuckolds and for the dozen people with whom he spent most of his evenings, his existence and even the memory of him would be suddenly erased in the instant in which they were convinced that a game of cards played with him was an undertaking that was more hazardous than exciting. There would have been no further point in alluding to banks or cuckolds: his own character, constructed with such a profusion of vague details, would have vanished from the memory of all the inhabitants of the town as if he had already gone, leaving a phantom perhaps to go around the streets, the restaurants, the hotels, always more blanched by the wear and tear of empty days. Therefore where did this instant and unexpected nostalgia come from? Or, as the ancients said, this grief and anxiety return?

He looked around. The light of day had already brightened the entire sky but beyond the lake the slopes facing west (a mixture of steep woods and slow fog) still held on to the night: the mysteries and the cold ambiguities of night. In the houses beyond the road, behind the calm façades and the windows scarcely whitened with blind sheen, the inhabitants' lives and belongings were still silent: still as fearful of God as of the devil.

'I could like this place!' he admitted. The town and its surroundings suited his tastes and willingly he would have spent the rest of his days there. But could this really be the place of his nostalgia? Why not any other among the many that had *en passant*, as they say, touched his fugitive heart?

Then what place? In confusion, without any geographical or chronological order, he thought of mountains, sea, springtime, winter or summer or autumn: all seasons of transition and of exile, which appeared outside any chronological sequence. No matter how he looked, their diversity and singularity, though apparently strong, or even sensational, vanished or evaporated into an indiscernible neutrality, in a grey indifference amongst places, times and seasons. For example, there were so many narrow abandoned roads, in old towns, or in the old part of other towns: roads that at first did not appear to be made for the passage of people or carriages, but as paths for memory in their solitary immobile presence within narrow walls, narrow entrances, few windows beneath a band of sky so narrow and distant that it seemed to be, rather than an image of air and clouds, the image of a span of time in which the same light always lacking sun moved from morning to evening.

He shrugged his shoulders, annoyed. 'When all is said and done,' he asked himself, 'why all this sentimental eloquence, almost like whining?' His journeys had never been sentimental ones and if he could be called a vagabond he was an opportunistic vagabond, preoccupied only with his own survival in the world. Nothing but a gambler like many others (many even more able than he) he was constrained by nature to travel in search of local gamblers: the race to whom he owed his board, lodging and pension. Actually, at first sight, with his weariness, his wan and decrepid appearance (even if he was not yet wrinkled) caught by the mirror or, as one says, objectively, he wouldn't be called anything but a mediocre gambler, with a possibility of success only in the depths of the country: not the country of his liking but dreary disagreeable and necessarily deprived of any emotive content. 'Puh!' he concluded, spitting noisily on the planks of a bench.

And yet there were things he had seen and that perhaps no one else would ever see: things that were finished, past; things he had seen a year before and also things he barely noticed yesterday or even today at the time: in other words what was immediately visible to him and him alone: journeys aside, he would have said that a part of the world, perhaps in the depths of an unknown place was offered to him to be preserved by his gaze. Saved for what reason? For immortality? For a duration that stepped over but encompassed places, days, seasons?

Some leaves, shifted by the dawn breeze, screeched against the stones; others skidded slowly along the surface of the lake, dry, with their corners high like tiny brown sails. Only whim or chance governed relationship between insignificant incidents and things large or vaguely boundless like the lake, the world, time, in comparison with which he himself, looked at objectively, was merely a negligible or overlooked speck on a journey: something one could definitely do without, even if something in this obscure and indefinite journey, according to where the good or ill wind of fortune might blow him, accidentally could stay firm and fixed *par coeur* for a mere whim: the notes of a violin, childishly played on a street, the smell of cabbage soup in the entrance of a billiard room, the silhouette of a woman enfolded in her lovely summer dress by a gust of wind that had already turned grey and autumnal.

Marginal and incongruous as they may be, he felt that these special images, sensations or emotions were things he couldn't do without. If a division could be traced in his travels between the indispensable and the superfluous, the picture, dim as it may be, in which this feminine silhouette appeared, the child's sounds on the violin, the interior, extraneous, of someone else's house, hung on the side of the indispensable. For that privilege of shadow or chiaroscuro that belongs to memory, these tiny details emerged in their outlines with scant precision. Things he had seen only once hurriedly and out of the corner of his eye seemed to have been turned exclusively to him that time or things he was seeing for the first time immediately returned his look the way one returns a greeting with the easy courtesy of small places in the country.

What's more, he told himself, adopting an expression of intimacy and trust, why shouldn't certain events, circumstances, or people be inclined to be courteous to him, although they didn't know him, since he himself was courteous with everyone first, either calculatedly or spontaneously? Ready to yield his place with a smile to ladies and old men, condescending and anxious to avoid even the slightest disagreement? Most of the time this courtesy was returned with the same spontaneity, identical almost in all respects to his first courtesy: almost a reflection of the cold brightness that all reflections add to the original images. Other times this courtesy of reply was charged with a question mark that was more or less explicit, more or less discourteous, but at least *prima facie* it always remained courtesy. Long live courtesy therefore! Why make too fine a point of it?

There were cases of transition, though: true and authentic signal changes, which let people and things pass quickly from the warmth that might be slightly mannered on first meeting to weariness and boredom. But perhaps it was his own weariness, his inadvertent indifference that things promptly echoed. Sometimes this passing was so abrupt that the same scene could be said to have two lives. So a single memory, the same picture with the same figures in the same position, with the same light and equal components of the landscape, which at first looked welcoming and even festive could suddenly shed its initial liveliness as if it had been discarded: that is taken down from the easel and stuck in a dark and dusty corner, to persist implacably in being perceived as a forlorn sketch left in a state of grisaille through a lack of confidence. And memories or fantasies like that were just the sort of things he could have done without.

He had reached the end of the pier and stopped to retrace his steps. The sky was now uniformly bright and clear; the sounds had even assumed their daytime tone, customary and therefore reassuring; but he still felt the watchful weariness of insomnia. The card game usually ended very late and after hasty farewells he found himself facing the dawn alone and weary, stupefied by the new and clean insignificance of the world, rain or shine. The clean rain, the clean light, the houses in their twilight colours, distant sounds, only he was there to see or hear them. A few trucks arrived, disappearing more speedily than they would at other times. To persuade the new day to get down to work, the apparel of the world, from mechanics to construction, followed a practice of well-known simplicity, or even poverty, starting with trucks going to unload bricks and trams going to unload workers. 'But, I ask myself, what can I make of all this banality?' Since he felt excluded from participating in the activities incumbent on that hour, the town seemed full of places that were uselessly vast. Even what seemed to be nature (parks, gardens, simple streets on the periphery that lost themselves in unknown countryside) gave him the nausea of a vagabond, the dizziness of distances without a destination, composed of emptiness behind and emptiness ahead. 'In this state of mind how can one sleep?' he asked himself. 'But,' he added, 'if there were a God, I'd really run to him!' Instantly, this uncalled-for burst of religious pathos bolting into the middle between the emptiness of the labouring city and his personal insomnia gave him nausea. 'But how silly, how silly!' he said automatically giving himself a resounding slap on the forehead. 'Very strange, after all!' he added more calmly, considering that he wasn't used to swearing, but actually at any mention of the divinity ran and so to speak darted out of his remote den or borehole towards the bright light of the public square. And then, what relationship could there ever be between the emptiness of his own solitary laziness and the resounding emptiness or, rather than emptiness, almost boundless availability for work and days of a city still certainly sleeping, but at least sneakily if not joyfully populous? 'It's better to think about whores!' he told himself. 'Long live whores!' he exclaimed in a whisper, but with emphasis in the grim silence that had suddenly taken over, predictably like one of the preparatory phases of the working day. 'At least everyone would agree that whores are a diversion,' he thought, forcing himself to imagine arses highlighted with pink and thighs round, like parian columns . . . 'Even I . . . Only for distraction,' he excused himself. 'Only to calm me down before going to sleep. . . . !? Then let's walk!' he concluded, shrugging his shoulders. 'By walking, sleep will come the way it does every morning.'

That morning however had something special, something gloomy and insistently nocturnal, despite the full daylight;

something like a prophecy or a bad omen hard to bring in line with reason. Leaving the apartment in the suburbs that one of the local policemen rented for the game every Saturday, he had turned a corner perhaps earlier or later than he should, and found himself facing an enormous empty road that apparently went on for miles along the banks of a river without a house in sight. The road was marked by huge plane trees that were lost in a vague curve, in the distance where the domain of green became glassy and grey.

'Damn them! But watch out for where they hid themselves for a game!' he said, walking along the bank in the direction the water seemed to rise towards the lake. He had been walking with long strides for about ten minutes when a couple of young people emerged from behind a thick plane tree: a man and woman about the same height, both dressed in grey clothes with blue stripes, with their eyes wide open and their hair damp and dirty.

'Do you want this whore?' the young man asked, quoting an enormous price.

He shook his head and the other man pulled out a knife.

'Wait' – he then heard someone shout behind his back. 'Wait, you son of a bitch!' Both young people fled and an old policeman immediately came up to him, mounted on a creaky bicycle. He ran past him chasing the young people but they were far away by now and called out from the shelter of the plane trees: 'We know you're a gambler! We want our share of the takings!'

The policeman put his foot on the ground with a gesture of weariness and he went up to him: 'I ought to thank you' – he said with his best smile. 'Were those two attempting a robbery?'

The other looked at him, sternly inspecting him from head to toe: 'You' – he said pointing his finger at him – 'don't come to my house again. You stand out too much. You don't know how to keep your place.'

He bowed slightly: 'As you wish' – he said – 'but thank you anyway for your hospitality and your protection.'

'Bla bla' the other said, pale with rage. 'Why don't you stuff it up your arse! Don't you know how to talk like other people?' And so saying, turned the bicycle in the direction from which he appeared and went away pedalling and farting with increasing speed into the mist.

Although he wasn't worried about it, this episode of the pseudo-burglary embittered him, because burglary and the discourteous behaviour of the policeman appeared to be signs of rejection: after barely a month, the city had begun to rebuff him. There were certainly other places where he could have gambled safely, even with very large stakes and there was still half a dozen players in town who hankered (as they said) to give him a lesson in cards, at least: nevertheless, the tone of the people had changed for the worse, that is, curiosity about him diminished, while a distant and extraneously arrogant attitude against him became ever more obvious.

'It's cold!' he said, pulling up the collar of his jacket. Obviously it was not true: one could even say the temperature was pleasantly cool. 'Pleasantly cool!' he repeated. 'Pleasantly cool . . .' And to get out of the block of the iterative phrase he mentally added other notations of a tourist and publicity nature about the mildness of the climate and the solemnity of the landscape. This old part of town, the hotel where he had spent the month, the gardens along the lake were familiar to him now. A lost familiarity, he thought, typical of departures and farewells, as often happens when one brings back memories, while packing, and one sees clearly how these memories now, customary still as they may be, are already inevitably also extraneous. He could already say of every shrub, every bench, every outline of a house, while he was looking or remembering that he had looked: 'How strange!' meaning an intermediary weariness with this comment, a separation between himself and what he was seeing that could not be filled. Speaking of cold, it was of this almost watery diaphragm of weariness between himself and the place he wanted to talk about. In other words, however pretty one might concede the town the lake and the countryside around it to be, dawn pounded these parts too coldly. And then there was too much still water: a place for carp and tench, rather than for men.

'No fish passing through here, I'd say,' he said, leaning over a little to look at the water of the lake. Images of fish or even outlines of discussions about fishing made him sleepy. Once, stretched out on his bed, the same light that inevitably filtered into the room even with the blinds drawn mottled a piece of furniture or a corner of the ceiling, and he felt that it streamed with the rhythm of water, which he could conjugate very well with figures of tench and carp. The world slowly but progressively emptied itself of objects, the sky of clouds and his mind of irritations, and he prepared himself for the silent arrival not of sleep, for which he had hoped in vain for so long, but of fish, each bigger and more resplendent than the ones before, always more incredible and imaginary, always more dreamed about.

A bench was almost hidden in the midst of laurels, four or five metres from the edge of the water: it was made of cast iron, painted with white enamel and looked inviting to him. He was weary and sat there with his legs stretched out. The cast iron was certainly cold and hard, but he found something reassuring about the shape of the bench and its location, protected by the shrubbery. It was old fashioned, if not antique, and expressed a hereditary permanence, so to speak. It was a modest inheritance however, not a monumental one: actually part of everyday and ordinary furnishings. For years, perhaps even a century or so, people had sat there with intimate indifference, faithfully nodding, even sometimes napping, sometimes meditative, without causing any changes through this momentary pause for anyone's destiny, fate or the way things went. Sitting there he asked himself if there might be a relationship between the volutes, the flowery grotesque charm of the wrought iron and the innocence of sitting. Perhaps someone could have even slept there. Sirens, tritons, sphinxes, tendrils, masks, which could be fingered more easily than seen because the bench had been painted and repainted so often, adorned the wrought iron the way inarticulated thoughts adorn sleep. What's more, once he had sat down on this bench, watching the vague waves of light on the surface of the lake, he felt that the ornamental and gratuitous character of sleepy thoughts accorded well with water and even with fish, their elusive nature, their way of coming and going indifferent to the direction and actually disoriented; that without this disorientation the great distances of water that were unexplored would have appeared foolishness to any sort of fish.

He admired the lacustrine and implicitly piscatorial quality of the place, but given a choice he would prefer a town by the sea for a long stay. The water is heavier and undoubtedly more gloomy by the sea, so that the well nourished, but somewhat futile grace of the laurels would not have done well. A place by the sea on the other hand (any one of the places he remembered) had gardens or simple flowerbeds along the walks with more desert-loving plants: pittosporum or palm trees, that could hold their own in the salty atmosphere, when the breakers swept over the seawall or breakwater barriers, and hurled themselves against the first row of houses. Almost dreaming, in the fresh breeze of a pleasant morning, he could now see the foam on the breakers. Even without a breath of wind or under a uniformly rainy sky, although a drop of rain had yet to fall, in a light that was steady and homogeneously pale, the sea continued in its inertia to beat against the shore with waves darkened by algae in chaos due to the storm a few days before: a rough and stormy sea, in other words, empty and sporting white curls all the way to the horizon. On land the road was bedecked by a long row of pale two or three story houses almost alike, without shops, and large curved doorways prudently semi-closed as defence against waves which still washed the pavement every so often.

Continuing as in a dream to walk along this space, framed by houses and the sea, he asked himself with every step: 'Is this the setting for my nostalgia? Is this the place for my return?' The place seemed almost right and cool: washed down every once in a while with buckets of seawater, but still far too vast.

He was walking quite slowly so as not to disturb the uncertain and suspended contentment of this approximate recognition of his: the almost-ness of his contentment in fact was such that it could become more precise just as easily as it could fade away. With bated breath he was considering just how precarious this equilibrium was when a little boy about ten burst out of one of the houses. The street had been silent and deserted until the child ran up to him at great speed making loud engine sounds. The child almost ran into him, then stopped abruptly with the noise of screeching brakes, and looked at him for a moment in silence, or, so to speak, with his motor off. Then he started again and ran off at great speed down a side street. But in that instant when he and the child looked at each other with reciprocal indignation, the place seemed to have become false and ruined.

'Then this can't be the place,' he had said, looking at the landscape which now appeared to be irremediably dreary in colour and awkward in plan. But aside from the landscape, the malevolence in the child's behaviour weighed on his chest with anxiety, because it was as if the child had asked a question with his stern glance: 'Where do you live?' And not knowing how to reply, the other, quoting the Psalms, would have added: 'He who has no house is like a wild beast in the forest.' But in this dialogue, which of the two was he truly himself? The questioned one who did not recognise any place, neither outside nor within himself and therefore didn't even know himself, or the silent voice? This was the question that a residual consciousness on the point of blurring into sleep could place in the silence of the other.

'Perhaps,' he thought, 'the self itself, the ego or so-called subject is merely a question, or more likely a sentence of the type: I could have done without that!' That is a sentence summarily correct in grammar, to which was added a long commentary both useless and prolix.

He opened one eye prudently and saw that daylight now slid brightly along the roofs of the houses and the tops of the trees. 'Bah!' – he said, stretching – 'At this point I might as well go to sleep in a bed.' As he said this he got up from the bench and went towards the hotel.

II

My dear, I keep writing to you and fear that this letter will be too long for your patience. It doesn't matter if you get tired; put it aside, you can continue reading it the following day. Read it in installments, which is, after all, the way I write it. Not that I like writing very much. I would have preferred to be with you, looking at you, respectful of your silence, as you usually ask me to be, but since I can't be with you, I am writing to you, and thinking about you, or rather thinking about us, because I really don't know when and where thoughts and reminiscence of you end in my head, and where and when memory or preoccupation about myself begins. But writing as I do now, I feel that, if we really wanted to, we could distinguish these two dominions, yours and mine, as background and figure and there where the figure is mine, I feel that the background is yours, the painstaking and patient questioning of your eyes as you listen, and your radiant, calm expression without which my figure (or my portrait) could not exist. There is something about our reciprocal curiosity that is indivisible and yet in two parts which men fail to understand because their manner of being curious about us, that is their curiosity about the feminine, is always a mixture of sacred and profane, so that the mud of the profane spatters the transparency of the sacred or vice versa. They see the two sides of the feminine as an ambiguity between obscenity and modesty and end up adopting both at the same time without conceding even a provisional priority to either one. They don't manage to rescue the feminine because they never know when to avert their gaze, to avoid looking at something it is not right to see. I recall a story that you told me about one of your lovers (one of our fellow students, as I recall) who positioned himself beside you as you were lying naked on your bed and got carried away contemplating and describing your physical attributes: your forehead, eyes, mouth, breasts, etc. He elaborated these details with good examples from literary tradition, but when he arrived at your sex, in the silence of the poetic fountains, instead of being silent, he tried a new comparison: 'It is a rose,' he said, 'very simple with two small internal petals: it is an eglantine rose,' and since you mocked him, he said, spitefully: 'Rose, I said. Stinking, but a rose.'

How sad that stinking can find its way into the floral, and decline mingle with health, and death leave its mark on life. How is such contamination possible? I would like to ask you so many questions about this, and actually about everything. And not only questions, but also, respecting your sacred silence, if it is all right with you, nod, wink, and make all sorts of signs, affirmations, negations. But isn't silence the double of the word? I mean, aren't darkness and shadows the way we discern light and colours? How many things do we know that we don't mention, while the unknown is right in front of us! If I think about knowing you, you are 'black wisdom' around my 'figure of an unknown woman,' and so the game becomes obsessive vice versa, the being of one continually pursuing the appearance of the other, or, on the contrary, pursuing the being of the other with one's own appearance. And so we end up always agreeing, the two of us, on an unambiguous meaning for the ubiquitous duplicity of existence, even at the cost of lies and pretence. If it weren't for these stupid fights about money that you tend to keep going at all costs, we two would end up thinking the same thoughts at the same time, in the same room, this one or another. Actually we wouldn't even need questions and answers because even the proudest of silences, the silence you prefer, would be transparent between us.

Getting back to what I was saying. I was down in the hotel restaurant: the usual people, usual melancholy, actually malaise which I'd call moderate, even comfortable. Why I am telling you this now? I could tell you all about it some other time. Now the thread of my chatter, or our chatter, our ideas, imposes itself with saving force on the ambiguous mediocrity of circumstances that sometimes oppresses me with unexpected violence in this hotel. Between the two of us, I then start thinking, sometimes, many times, most of the time all was clear and luminous dawn if not actually sunny. Our laughs and winks and the stories we told each other were always able to contain an unambiguous meaning. Not important meanings, but meanings firmly settled within their expression. What were they all about? If I were to hazard a guess, I would say futility. How we loved futility, the glory of our youth without shadows! Hours of contemplation of ourselves froze us in happy admiration at the mirror. In front of two mirrors in the same room at the same time or our faces next to each other within the same frame until the light fell, and darkness touched our features, threatening for a moment to penetrate our beautiful image. But we didn't fear the darkness because of our beauty. We weren't looking at beauty when we looked at ourselves; we knew very well that we were only appealingly young, and that what we were both contemplating was rather our seeing ourselves beautiful; it was the joy of our unambiguous gaze turned on ourselves; the joy of the reflection in which our intentions in looking coincided with our being, our substance in the same meaning without margins of misunderstanding. Futility? Certainly, but triumphant futility. What is more futile than wanting to see yourself beautiful and succeeding?

Believe me, your lawyer is a scoundrel. From the standpoint of law your action is merely rash. From the economic point of view the question is as marginal for me as it is for you and I would concede, but I don't like to encourage your tendency to be arrogant, which has always been a big source of trouble between the two of us. But as you wish. I am not writing to you because I want to talk about this. I wanted to tell you about a strange, actually extraordinary adventure I had this morning. Just think, I saw him naked!

But let's start at the beginning. His room is directly opposite mine and as I was about to shut the door behind me his door silently fell open and there he was right in the middle of the carpet, naked except for a towel around his head. Probably his door hadn't been tightly shut so the air current when he came out of the bathroom was strong enough to push it open.

I stood there immobile, stunned, thinking how it would have been easy and opportune to make myself silently invisible because of the carpeting in the corridor. I saw his shoulders, the fragile thinness of his ribcage, the narrowing at his waist, but he also had two dangling empty pouches on each side of his waist, dirty with a bit of hair about six inches long that looked very black against the almost mortuary whiteness of his skin, which was smooth and hairless on the other parts of his body. It wrung my heart to see he was just skin and bone: his smooth buttocks dangled down like two empty bags as well.

'Well, well' I thought. 'Does he also have a dangling arse?'

At this point the door creaked; or perhaps he shifted his eyes from the towel he was using to dry his hair and saw something that wasn't right reflected in the window pane; in any case, he made a leap, grabbed the door handle to shut it, but when he saw me standing there stupidly in front of him, he took time to bow soberly before banging the door in my face.

How strange! Why can't I get this ridiculous scene out of my mind this morning? I have seen many naked men before: handsome, very handsome, ugly, very ugly, while he didn't belong to any of these classifications ... he is merely pitiable. One feels sorry for him. How strange is a man that makes you feel sorry for him.

I don't know! Even this seems to be a tale of contamination

and interference. A naked man of a certain sort, come to think of it, could possibly be put into a landscape, change the tone and relationship with the light. The colours and the lines change their meaning and reciprocally also the nakedness of the man changes its meaning. I'd say that a naked man that one feels sorry for could be transformed into an exquisite nude, with a bit of landscape and perhaps a bit of background music.

But in this case, my dear, I admit we are still in the realm of ambiguity far from our shining youth, from the happy certainty of the futility we share.

My room is pleasant, otherwise I wouldn't spend hours here lying in bed, or sitting at my desk to write to you. On the ceiling I see reflections move like gleaming waves; but the water is far away, barely visible in fact beyond the poplars at the edge of the hotel garden. The poplars are pure and severe trees; also, seen from the window, that is, looking north towards the lake, they have their tops constantly illuminated because their height is higher than the shade of the houses and this high light gives them an indulgent appearance. Everything looks indulgent to me: the empty garden, because it is already somewhat cold with the hotel's white tables neatly arranged to receive improbable guests, the wicker armchairs empty day after day and the little paths of boxwood and gravel darkened by the shadow. Will you also indulge me in this installment of long-winded talk? Just think: otherwise what could I do in the afternoon after spending all morning drinking the waters in installments, one gulp every half hour?

I keep the same rhythm, although not quite so punctually, let's say, every half hour or three-quarters of an hour, I raise my pen to write you a line or two; at times though I make alterations to what I already wrote you; actually some pages were so messy with alterations that I had to write them out again so you could read them, and I could as well. Don't tell me this procedure of mine takes away spontaneity. Between a letter like mine and a normal letter written and posted in half an hour is the same difference between a painted portrait and a snapshot: a difference in the amount of time. In a painted portrait there are layers and layers of time, poses and behaviour in storage, and this stratification, this thickness can't be left to sediment by chance: it needs to be studied, thought about, interpreted; let's say that in this case the one who writes, reads, re-reads and also makes a few corrections, as the work of interpretation and amendment is more on the part of the reader than the writer. And the same observation would also be true for the meanings that are inserted more in the reading and interpretation than in the writing. The latter, the immediate recognisable *prima facie* meaning in a snapshot can be only a familiar and habitual reference: the way I say the witch when I mean my dreadful aunt. (Damn her). *Littera occidit*, the letter kills, one should say. *Littera necat*, the letter slays. Is this the spontaneity you are so proud of? Then I can do without it. And yet it's not so important that I write you as spend time thinking about you in the pleasant silence, calm light and graceful leisure of this room; naturally the time I spent thinking includes the duration of just as many repetitions and variations.

But now I must stop talking always about you, or I shall end up getting bored. Let's talk about the naked man. I was telling you, it upset me. What does it mean?

It is strange that I ask you the meaning of what I tell you. Or at least it would seem strange to anyone who didn't pay attention to this duplicity of reading and writing of which I think I have already spoken to you. As far as we are concerned, I am the writer and you are the reader, and I think we are part of the same mind: we are closer to each other than most people and yet in our case there are several hundred kilometres between us, at least now, and therefore optically we can't see each other. But haven't I already written you something like this? I'll check on it! Now I want to say something not about the two of us, but about him, my naked man: that I find him always visible, even when he is closed behind the doubly-locked door of his room. In his absence I turn him again and again, I make him walk and sit and bow. And how he obeys me!

I saw him dressed about three days ago. He was sitting in one of the armchairs in the hotel lobby with a book open on his lap. I was just passing by, there was no one else around at the time and since he had already smiled at me when I was at the foot of the stairs and continued to smile when I stepped onto the marble floor, I passed by him as I went to the door (his chair was in my path), I couldn't think of anything better than to ask 'What are you reading?'

'Ah' – he said – 'this is a book about chess.' And then started to tell me something about this sort of literature. I felt I should stop and listen while he spoke, and I swayed towards him, or more precisely towards the open book on his lap.

'A book about chess,' I thought in the meantime; 'what could be more boring?' When I'd finished this thought and he his elucidation we waved goodbye with more courtesy than friendliness. 'Let's see,' I asked myself as soon as I was outside, 'what sort of eyes does he have? And his hands? What are his hands like? Is he wearing a grey suit? Or beige?' I didn't know how to say anything of any sort about him, except that maybe his hair was grey, possibly not very thick but sufficient: in other words, he wasn't bald. Just think, that after the chance discovery (or should I say 'invention'?) of the 'nude', if I now close my eyes, I might tell you, at least for an instant, how many hairs grew out of his left nostril; but only for an instant, as these details dissolve into bright radiance, indistinct, in the totality I immediately recognise as his face: a face unlike any other, unique, unforgettable even in the indistinct flash of a vague and uncertain memory. What else can I see of him with my eyes closed? Everything! that is also those things that I have never seen.

'All right,' you will say, 'you are seeing him in your imagination. Isn't that true of us? Don't I succeed in imagining you wherever you may be? Didn't you even say that it is impossible to escape my gaze?'

That's actually how it is; and perhaps the difference doesn't come into this seeing in imagination or in reality; but there is still a difference. I search for it in this special seeing or fantasizing and probably make a mistake, but the difference remains: it is the way I think of him that is not the same as the way I think of you or think in general; actually it is not thinking or imagining or seeing as one usually sees with the eyes or the imagination, but seeing and thinking through another filter. Hope? Desire? I can actually see you or imagine I see you *ad libitum*, whenever I please and this also gives me pleasure and yet I hope also to actually see you face to face. You might think that's just the same. But it's not! As for him I only try to see him. Perhaps I desire him, but without any success, since I am tormented between doubt, uncertainty, even fear. I really don't know whether I even want to see him again.

Chance certainly plays a large part in our relationship. For example, if chance had not brought us both to the same orphanage when we were three; if we hadn't been kept for another eight years by the same nuns; if your aunt and uncle hadn't decided to take me into their house as well after we took our school-leaving certificate, if we hadn't gone to the same university, studying the same things . . . if, if, if . . . This nearness we share which I invented, and of which I continue to speak, to the point of obsession for me and nausea for you, would never have existed; I would even say that the very idea of nearness would not have become for me, more than a thought, an instrument of thinking or in general it would never have assumed the central position it now has in my thoughts: nearness and near would be expressions in common use as in the phrase 'my near neighbour' or 'this part of town is convenient because it is near the shops'. There, as you say, our nearness is mere chance, with no dramatic dignity and is no basis for the great scenes for which you say I have a tendency. Never mind. This idea, even if born arbitarily in my mind, is born completely formed, like Minerva in her armour: it was a revelation, an illumination, a parousia. At a certain point, in an instant, all life became a game of 'nearness': impermanence, the past, the future: changes in the body and in consciousness have no effect on it: no misadventure, no recognition, no resolution and catharsis: 'we', that is the duplicity and very sameness of this dual number are the nearness and this nearness is a constant invariable like destiny. Even if what I tell you will only inspire you to depart again towards the distance (or some other form of disrespect) the calm, the constancy, the banal inertia of this idea remain unchanged. So its unambiguous meaning too, perhaps, for despite all your shouting and raging, you will always return to the calm and unambiguous futility of our relationship. A relationship, I hope you realise, that requires neither reciprocity, nor a complement of our two subjects which after all in the expression 'we' come later, when all is said and done. So this 'we' is more like solitude than companionship; in our case it actually emphasises the meaning of solitude, as if I buried myself in an empty church, angrily telling myself: 'One who is alone almost stands on the brink of nothing.' To ease your conscience, let me add that it isn't even important that there is love between us. So it is stupid of you to confute this hypothetical love of mine with spite. Even the hate which I have shown you at times serves no purpose.

Do you remember? I hadn't seen you for a year. Only when certain silly people mentioned a coma to you, did you rush to see me and weep on my hand: you even left mucous on my hand. And with your mucous between my fingers, in that sort of horizon that comes between one breath and another, confusedly I saw myself hemmed in on one side by a big wall of hate for you and on the other by the great desolate expanse of death. I was desperate. How could I die like that? I asked myself. Suddenly the hatred disappeared, death disappeared, and I disappeared. There was only the futile simplicity of your tears, the indivisible unambiguousness of our nearness.

But I have said and written this and other things like it to you so many times, and even without writing or telling you about them I would continue to ponder. You could do nothing about them, no matter how much trouble you might manage to bring me. Why don't you tell your lawyer to stop bothering me? I will not come to the hearing; it is not necessary and I have already given instructions about it. After all, what do you want? The house in the windmill which we acquired together is *pro indiviso* and stays that way: I don't want to sell it to you, nor buy your half. It is ours in its entirety. Use it as you think best. Burn it down if you wish.

But that's enough silliness; I want to tell you about this man: my naked man. I now see him dressed every evening from seven to nine. We dine at the same table and he talks, while I more or less only watch him move his mouth, speaking or chewing. At nine punctually he stands up, bows and goes to get dressed before going somewhere for 'a little game', as he says. Note: it's not that he wears evening clothes, but actually takes off the rather elegant suit which he wore for dinner and dresses, I'd say, like a hunter with boots and loden jacket. 'And your shotgun?' I invariably ask.

Joking aside, there is certainly something clandestine about these games. Because of the boredom endemic in this town, a great deal of gambling takes place, but since gambling is not permitted here, for all I know, or is actually considered a crime, gamblers are blackmailed by the police and have to pay protection to the local racketeers. It's not clear why official gambling places are not permitted, at least in the most boring towns, with licenses that would bring some revenue to the local coffers. As a matter of fact, we tend to favour crime, our most flourishing national industry, which everyone says is of great interest to our politicians. So be it. This is a mere digression: one of the many paths a thought can use to go off on its own, leaving the main one, the true and authentic thought, to take the principal road.

So many digressions, seated next to him! The evening shadows, the desolation of the garden, the plates with gold rims on the white tablecloth, the sounding of the hours, that slightly raucous sound of old grandfather clocks in good hotels which recite the hours of semi-public, severe luxury, from a corner of the stairs whether their authenticity is true or false, quite different from the poor empty private hours that are harshly announced by an alarm clock in the kitchen. What peace in day dreaming, and lazy thoughts. But what was the principal road, that on which the main thought was advancing? Here it is! If I were to express myself with a phrase, I would say the phrase was 'Next to him'. 'Next to him!' I continued to think in the first place of this other nearness, that is of the nearness I had this time to my naked man, now correctly dressed in a handsome beige suit perfectly in keeping with the decisiveness of his features: his nose slender, but strong, his eyes perhaps too hidden beneath thick eyebrows, well defined cheekbones, a wide forehead with a lump or two, crossed by two horizontal wrinkles and his chin with almost too graceful an oval. A handsome face, one would say, but too pale for my taste. Did I really like this man? Outside the digression, however, within the principal migration of thought, there were many other states of nearness, so many memories of failures at getting close. People who came up to me, almost brushing against me and then vanished: he was only one of a procession. It wasn't so much thinking of him as finding he figured in my thoughts. In case the refrain 'next to him' in its repetition could have meant: 'What's this? Still here? When is he going to leave and get on with it?'

I feel I can hear you say: 'How complicated and ambiguous you are for one who exalts simplicity, actually the 'futile simplicity of unambiguous meaning'. I remember well how my bad habit of giving adjectives to abstractions was one of the obligatory moments of our arguments: the strength, or even the support of our hatred.

'Then what is simple?' you may ask.

And I: 'Something you can almost no longer think about. An example would be death or something on the verge of death, destiny or something on the verge of destiny: the two of us, I'd say.'

Invariably your reply was partly philosophical chatter about the illegitimate use of giving adjectives to abstractions and partly foul language and since you have a particularly charming way of using obscenity I enjoyed it.

We certainly never talked about philosophy at first, in the truly simple stage of our relationship: we didn't speak, I'd say, or we spoke without paying much attention. We talked about fantasies or sensible things or gossip. Especially gossip: about someone's nose, or the way someone else wore their spectacles. And that person with six fingers on his right hand, do you remember? One day I said to you: 'Do you realise your aunt has started to calculate what I owe for living with you all these years?'

And you: 'What do you care? You're three times richer than all of us put together.'

I was disgusted. 'If your uncle were still alive' – I said – 'this never would happen.'

And you: 'Do you feel that everything is owed you? Who do you think you are? My sister?'

'How can you say "owed"', I asked, 'when she's given a cheque equivalent to a high-school teacher's salary and on top of that she also includes my groceries, cigarettes and some dreary clothes?'

The next day I moved to the Hotel Inghilterra: a much more comfortable place than your aunt's house, if not more economical.

That was our first argument.

Your uncle! What a character he was. But I'll write you about him in the next instalment. Now I'm tired.

No, my dear. Your house would not be called a princely home. It was a very large apartment on the first floor with an L-shaped corridor, that is a corridor that bent into a right angle at a certain point, with many doors that inspired suspicion when they were closed and led to hurried and watchful behaviour. No one stayed in this corridor except to go from one room to another and then close the door behind himself.

The rooms were a bit better and at least some were less dusty and dark than others and there were also rooms I never entered. Our room was one of the brightest I saw. Two windows, longer than wide and with glass set in tiny panes, looked out on a square full of lime trees. In the winter these trees were pruned down to the trunk, leaving stumps that sprouted leaves in the spring and flowers that bathed the square with stagnant fragrance.

My memories of the square and the house are concise: memories that begin with a teapot in the kitchen and end in the map of the area and so for the time the years, the months, the days. I begin with May for example, but then I wander towards October, going through December incongruously, a winter, many winters: seven in all. Certain winter days there was snow on the window ledge: the sounds of the square and sometimes from the surrounding streets came through snow and fog as if through time, presenting themselves almost as reports of sounds, which had taken place somewhere else perhaps, rather than direct sounds. For example, once there was a quarrel in the square: the restaurant owner argued with the butcher about the quality of meat; his argument could be distinctly heard, but so isolated by the snow I asked myself: 'could it be that these are the same points the restaurant owner made many years ago or that they are the complaints of another restaurant owner a hundred kilometres away?' How obvious the ubiquity and fundamental equivalence of life seems on snowy days! Snow aside, through the years, my memory tends to compress all events into a single year: that year I wrote my thesis all alone in our room, as you had decided to find a university that would be congenial to you, or which better knew how to value your talents.

It was the start of your wanderings, but that is another story and now I want to tell you about your uncle and how I managed to wash his feet that year.

It was summertime. July or rather everything that I call July in the summer: the green of the plane trees so intense it looks almost black, the shrubbery too thick and that nonchalance some animals take as they go about their business. The month of happy dogs, I call it. There are many dogs in our part of town probably because of the restaurants and the market: young dogs usually chained or muzzled to keep them from jumping up on each other to couple in public but they can still whine and tug towards each other. And when they are taken by the dignified matrons to walk the market during their shopping, they obviously watch out for each other and look at each other admiringly and in their hearts become happy.

A digression, as you see, this about dogs. But how many digressions are in my mind: not only about dogs and cats, but trees, birds, mountains, calm air and tempest. My mind would lose its way and get lost in all these digressions if it weren't for you to give them a firm foundation.

So, as I was saying, I managed to wash his feet.

Let's say it was July. You weren't there, she was out, looking over her shops and the old man and I were alone: he was in his wheel chair, shut up in his room, with the shades drawn and a long spiral of light seeping through. Every hour or so I went in: 'What are you doing?' I asked. And he shook his head with a smile but said nothing. He didn't read, he didn't smoke: he was silent, but one day, after his usual smile, he asked me: 'Do you see this vase of blue glass? On the oval table, with the silver feet?'

'Yes!' I said. He explained that it was a wedding present. It had been in that precise place on the table for as long as I could remember: 'Things' – he said – 'last . . . they don't have their own reasons for being, therefore one would say they don't exist, but they last. On the contrary, we are destined to perish, but we exist or think we do.'

'That's right!' I agreed, more confused than persuaded.

'I told you this' – he explained – 'in response to your question. Why not read, or play a game of solitaire? Do you see, if one asks oneself that a pair of fundamental questions consigned to us by the philosophic tradition regarding the most negligible thing, that is all one needs to lose time. These questions always bring circular thoughts that are practically infinite.'

I nodded again demurely and then made a suggestion: 'Shall I wash your feet?'

At first he refused, but after a few days of insisting, he let me do it. His feet were white as wax, very thin with long tendons and joints showing and perfect toes and toe-nails. I complimented him many times on his feet. The nurse came every day at five and every week brought another nurse with her to give him a bath. They dumped him into the soap and water and a few minutes later pulled him out again swearing.

'I'll give you a real bath . . . a bubble bath,' I suggested; but I didn't manage to persuade him: 'Go away' – he replied smiling – 'go away and read another book!'

He died one morning before noon. I opened his door then and saw him on his chair with his head leaning forward as if hunting for something he'd dropped. Later I was told his denture had fallen out.

Why did I tell you this story about washing his feet? I no longer know. The mind is an intricate maze of words: an anxious maze, which, like all mazes, hides many things one comes across more or less unexpectedly. Death is hidden there and, as you see, is encountered there. Is love hidden there?

Perhaps in the thickest leaves and shadows: I wouldn't be surprised. Your uncle's death was hidden instead in the transparent heat of a July morning, in the month of the happy dogs, that in fact paid no attention to the coming of that death, nor the subsequent fall of the denture. So be it. I wanted to talk about love with you, too (obviously of my love for the naked man), a love still uncertain, still hidden in the thickness of myrtles in the maze of my thoughts.

Suddenly in the hotel foyer both sides of the door opened and two men, one shorter, fatter and more bald than the other, came in shouting.

'If it's about money' – shouted the fatter one – 'I don't hear anything and I don't want to hear anything!'

'But let's talk about it!' the taller and less bald one said, following him.

'No discussions' – the first one replied. 'Money is arithmetic, not friendship and certainly not relationship. There is nothing to discuss.'

The second joined the others in the middle of the room a few metres from the chairs where they were seated, grabbing his shoulders: 'Calm down!' he suggested in a more quiet voice, while he offered them a smile of complicity or excuse.

'All right. No friendship. But isn't there a certain trust?'

'What trust?' – the other replied getting more angry. 'There are documents, right? Pacts and agreements, the notary public. What does trust have to do with it? And after all what are we? Relatives? Friends? Just two guys who must keep their pacts. Now tell me: Why talk about it?'

'All right!' – the other man conceded, 'but sometimes unexpected things happen: necessities that couldn't have been foreseen . . .'

They stood silently facing each other. Then the taller one stretched out his arm and smiled several times: 'No friendship! Well then let's speak frankly. Let's speak like one shit to another!'

'But where do you think you are?' the old lawyer shouted, banging his fist on the little table and making cups and teapots rattle and shake.

The gambler got up from his chair, and took a few steps towards the new arrivals: 'Let's see!' – he said, conciliating – 'there are ladies here. Wouldn't it be more appropriate to find a public toilet elsewhere?'

'Oh, yes!' – the smaller, balder one shouted, incongruously raising a hand as if to point to the ceiling or the sky – 'he is the shit. I'm glad to leave him in good company.' He moved to leave, with a sort of bow, and the other followed closely behind him, turning several times to smile and stretch out his arms towards them.

'Close the door behind you,' the lawyer shouted after them; but the two men paid no attention; so the gambler, who was the only one standing, went to close the door.

'They didn't look wet to me!' observed the old lady with a smile. 'So it must not be raining very hard.'

In reply the younger woman took one of the old lady's hands in her own, nodding. He saw they continued to exchange smiles. Between the two of them, it might be said, a flow of sympathy had been established: a traffic of benevolence that was mannered and a bit dull, which irritated her but also she found reassuring and almost protective, wrapping her with motherly touches in a blanket of mental vagueness: a sort of bland idiocy, calm even in the midst of turmoil. In exchange every so often she felt obliged to say something in the old lady's ear, who heard these words blended with the buzzing of her deafness, and managed to construct a sentence that was syntactically correct every once in a while, even if eccentric in the course of normal conversation. What's more these sentences the old lady invented – she had observed – were either on a most general subject or vice versa on some fragment of detail. And since there was a freedom from logic in these women, the sentences offered marginal ornament and sentimental effects to the conversation and sometimes were very pleasant.

The deaf old lady continued to smile at her tirelessly, holding on to her with two fingers or her whole hand, while the old lady's husband, the man everyone called the lawyer, was involved in a thorough discussion of the value of colloquial speech. The old man maintained that the value of spoken language and the value of the nation that spoke it were one and the same: a word like shit or arse should be understood in reference to the entire country, which, in fact, was universally considered shitty and sansculotte. 'What a filthy country!' he said with sadness, shaking his head of thick white hair, while his slanting eyes, sliding towards the outside of his face, stayed fixed in stubborn contemplation of a piece of porcelain on an *étagère*.

'Don't give it another thought, sir!' the gambler suggested timidly.

The old lawyer took his azure blue gaze from the azure blue vase and examined the man who had spoken to him with almost military severity: 'It's a disgusting country!' he said, breaking his words into syllables and staring at the gambler.

He quickly replied: 'Of course, most certainly! It is just as you say!'

She also nodded her head, as soon as the lawyer surveyed her face thoroughly.

After a few moments of silence the lawyer's voice continued the exposition in tones that were sometimes indignant, but more often solemn and didactic, and no longer with any hint of blame. Actually – she said to herself – once the group had accepted the superiority of a leader, in their case the lawyer, the group was calm; they were among friends. Even the gambler seemed to agree: his unwavering smile was an expression of invariable courtesy for the lawyer's oratorial artifices. The old lady closed her eyes and rested her head leaning on the arm of her chair, and without releasing her hand, appeared to be sleeping. Her calm and weary breath lifted her parched bony chest rhythmically, emphasising the fragility of her body. Nevertheless – she thought – there was nothing physically fragile about her frame, which was taller than normal, even if angular; actually the old lady still walked, at least on hotel carpets, with the proud carriage of a great lady who was once beautiful. Only when, sunk in the chair, apparently succumbing to a broken sleep, she held on to her hand, or woke up for a moment and gazed up at her, as if from the depths of a dog basket, with almost canine hazel eyes did the old lady look undefended and fragile.

'Is it raining?' the old lady asked at a certain point, trying to shake off her sleepiness. She reassured the old lady by saying no, and going into detailed information about the blue sky and how one could even see the stars: it was an extraordinary night for October, and even warm. There hadn't been one like it for years.

Everyone agreed; and it seemed to her that by means of this agreement the gentleness of the night and serenity of the stars had entered to participate in the domesticity of the gathering: a domesticity perhaps a bit feigned or even forced but which emphasised the old lady's smile with a certain tone of authenticity. 'But look!' she said, astonished. Behind their apparent inertia these people went about loving each other blandly and this activity had even managed to bring something cosmic within: the evening breeze, the air of the dark lake, the trembling leaves high on the poplars.

She smiled gratefully at everyone, beginning with the old man, who silently acknowledged her smile with a half bow.

She turned to the gambler, 'Do you have your usual game this evening?'

'Not tonight' he said, 'someone new was supposed to come, but now there is a change and everything is postponed to tomorrow.'

'Why?' she asked.

He laughed: 'The man is new in town and today is Friday.' He paused, 'Don't you understand? Superstitions and gambling go together and as the saying goes, "Never marry, never part, never try to start on the days of Venus and Mars."'

They all laughed quietly: and then fell silent. The only sound was the old lady scratching her knee, because she wore thick elastic stockings which squeaked when she scratched them.

In the music room, as the place was called where the four of them spent an hour before dinner, the air was so still that the smoke of the cigarette, which the gambler had held immobile for some time between his fingers, rose in a vertical thread up to the height of the cornice of the *boiserie*. Silence arrived at unequal intervals, interspersed with sounds which seemed to have an implicit destiny of silence. At a certain point she thought that this sort of interval was no longer a parenthesis in reality, but all reality, and that just everything else in the world was parenthetical without its own plan, but tentatively through testing sounds: in other words a chance accumulation of differences which, on the one hand created the impression of being both dull and vast like the night or the lake, and on the other provided dignified isolation for transitory themes that were not necessarily present, but could also be memories.

The two old people were a mine of discreet memories. They cited them every once in a while almost whispering as if they were in private, but then, because the old lady's deafness required clear and distinct sounds, everyone ended up joining in. 'Leonardo' – the old man said, and the woman retorted: 'What ever became of him?' 'Michelangelo!' the old man said somewhat later. And the old lady: 'What ever became of him?' And so they continued their rehearsal. This one vanished, another disappeared. It saddened them, but they were also resigned, as if these disappearances were prescribed by destiny for people, created, you would say, only to vanish from their (private) horizon. But if, leaving these people aside, one speaks of objects as in the phrase: 'The hotel piano is out of tune' or: 'These bronze candlesticks look to me as if they were forged yesterday', other pianos and candlesticks and chairs and tables emerged from the past. 'What ever became of the Venetian mirror?' 'Where is the maiolica lamp?' My God, they seem to ask themselves, why were there so many things in the world and why did they all have to end?

She closed her eyes. 'What ever became of him?' she asked herself, referring incongruously to the gambler. To herself she now referred to him familiarly as 'her naked man'. She thought she saw him in his room, not naked, but properly dressed, sitting in a comfortable chair with a book in his hands. Now he was leaning slightly forward to read the book, then shifted his head back to meditate on what he had read, using his index finger to keep his place. The title of the book was: 'The game of chess: Famous matches and their variations'. My God, she commented, covering her face with her hands, couldn't he read something more amusing? *De sensu rerum et de magia*, for example. Time seemed to have stopped flowing in this imaginary room: the man, his book, the silent afternoon had come together by chance in a greenish and lacustrine way with fleeting bright streaks of colder and faster water. There was no trace of intention in this picture that she made of him, no title she could give it except for 'regret'. But, she felt, it was not a central moment of deep regret, but the onset of a sense of sadness which would be present for an incalculable length of time.

She leaned towards him, almost brushing her lips along his ear: 'Do you know I've seen you naked?' she whispered.

He turned his head towards her, at the same time drawing back: 'I am so sorry,' he said, 'I apologise.' He went on to say that the chambermaid, who was changing the sheets had left the door ajar so she didn't have to bother to open it again when she returned with clean sheets.

'Oh!' she said. 'It's not important'.

In the meantime the voice of the lawyer had become menacing, obviously impatient of their 'aside'.

'You young people' – he roared – 'with your carefree optimism . . .'

The gambler shook his head in agreement: 'That's not the case. That's not the case at all.'

'What's not the case?' the lawyer lashed out at him.

'That we are optimists!' the gambler quickly made himself more precise.

'After all,' the lawyer replied with residual severity in his voice, 'if it is really true that the world is changing, this change, at least here, is always for the worse.'

She thought about the empty docility in the gambler's smile: similar docility, in the case of the lawyer, was so obviously disinterested as to appear actually suspicious. 'Perhaps it's only mocking!' she thought and yet she found this mocking of the old man's arrogance distressing.

'Isn't it getting a bit cold?' the old lady asked, tugging at her sleeve.

She reassured her with a gesture and a smile. The *boiserie* on the walls, the carpets on the side by the windows which faced the river, the daily waxing of the furniture, the small grand piano in the corner, once again gave her that same sensation of stagnation, of enclosed time, but just at the outset, and the same sentiment of regret she had had when she imagined the gambler's room, while he was reading about chess. 'But after all,' she asked herself, 'what does a stage in an empty theatre stand for?' Certainly not for a comedy or farce that we spectators don't yet know, but, for that span of time needed to listen to a comedy or a tragedy: the stage represents time as a discrete unity, not its hypothetical content. And now this room in the hotel was staging the same type of representation which may take place in a theatre, but in a coarser and more peremptory way and also in a way more commercially evident. The music room haughtily represented what the hotel was selling: the time for the stay. 'But why are there regrets?' She shook her head undecided.

'What beautiful hair!' the old lady said to her, almost caressing her head with long and admiring looks.

She smiled at her: 'Such regret!' she was thinking. And then long afternoons came to mind from many years before which she had spent in front of the mirror lost in protracted contemplation of her own face and expression, trying, unsuccessfully, to find in her features, her eyes, the line of her nose some sign of drama, comedy, even farce or at least the title of the play to which she had dedicated her long empty time. 'Beauty?' she asked. 'Love?'

'That's how it is!' the contrite gambler was saying to the lawyer. 'It's just as you say!'

The lawyer seemed satisfied: 'Certainly' – he admitted – 'this is only chatter about the way things appear today. It would be best to look closely also at the national history in the various episodes of the country, in order to be able to say with conviction that each century is "the century of shit!" and every national hero is "a real turd". In other words it's important to conduct patriotic discussions with care and detail, not just get rid of them in a hurry, because the material is so disgusting. This will be the task of future generations . . .'

Beyond the closed door the grandfather clock in the corner of the entrance hall could be heard striking eight and was immediately followed by a bell rung by hand to signal that the restaurant was now offering residents of the hotel its fixed menu.

'Dinner?' the old lady asked, straightening up from the depths of her chair.

'That's how it is!' the lawyer said, looking at her severely. 'Time to eat!' he added accentuating each syllable and poking his hand in front of his open mouth as if he were eating.

They all stood up. The old lady was first, showing almost athletic agility.

The bell was rung again.

'*Ad conventum conventuales!*' the lawyer commented. And then he turned to the gambler as he did every evening: 'I hope that you at least know how to find your beautiful guest a better restaurant than this dreary den of ours!'

As he did every evening, without replying, the gambler bowed to the old lady and she took a step forward to let herself be kissed by that woman on her forehead. After that, the lawyer, took the old lady's arm, clamped under his own, and then strode towards the doors of the restaurant, sometimes dragging her, and sometimes letting himself be dragged by her. As they did every evening, they stood and watched them go.

III

'What do you think of this place?' she asked.

He was undecided for a moment: 'I might be able to like it,' he finally said.

She laughed: 'Why use the conditional?'

'I have seen so many places,' he replied. 'This is yet another place. There is the lake, the trees in this public garden: the houses are attractive: and the paintwork is beautiful, I'd say. At certain hours of the day with the light at a certain angle I have moments of enthusiasm. The place and its setting are elevating, approaching the self-sufficiency of a castle in the sky. It could be, as they say, the place of my dreams: it floats between deja vu, the conventional and the unreal in the sense that it is detached and situated some metres above the level of common reality (whatever that might be).'

'Umh!' – she conceded. 'Is this the only place where you have perceived this vertical transcendence of a few metres?'

'Oh, no!' – he laughed. 'That's the problem. I have felt this dislocation in many places. As soon as I leave the station in any humdrum place with the idea of spending some time there, a month or two, let's say, the humdrum place detaches itself immediately from its position on the rail map or tourist circuit to become the place where I'm staying. One might say it is natural: my egotism changes the facts. But this doesn't seem to be the case, because on the contrary what strikes me is the way this place does not suit my plans: the place is actually transfigured once I have some relationship with it. The face of the city begins to express anxiety, anguish or, on the contrary, queasy joy, a tendency to mock things, as if these passions were not mine but belonged to it: the city in flesh and blood or the city as protagonist, with a role that is important, if not superior to my own, in the events that are still unknown but are about to happen. In other words, it is the protagonism of the places that sometimes irritates me, sometimes oppresses me, sometimes moves me and more rarely makes me happy. Haven't you ever felt you've fallen under local influences?'

She shook her head. They walked along the pier silently for some time: 'Shall we sit down?' she asked, as they passed a bench.

'You don't like this place,' she said, 'but you are trying to like it?'

He laughed: 'It's not quite like that. The town flirts with me; it arouses me and then rebuffs me. If there is anything I am trying to do, it is to make myself accepted once and for all. If this should happen it would only be a mediocre success: a minor joy, actually a faded and almost boring pleasure. In other words, as a temptress it does not offer great and irresistible temptations.'

They both laughed: 'Yes, that's true!' she admitted. 'Even the tourist brochures show the boring pleasure of the place between the lines.'

'Do you come here every year?' he asked.

'Yes, I do!' she admitted. 'I am a creature of habit. I don't need the cures that are on offer here, but boredom, as a gentle massage for the soul.'

'There are no longer any souls' – he interrupted her roughly.

'No one talks about them anymore and what is worse, no one talks with their own soul anymore. When one is alone, one just talks.'

'What a strange idea,' she commented, vaguely annoyed.

'Perhaps it is out of fashion,' he corrected himself, conciliating. 'A word that is out of fashion: that's all.'

They were silent for a while. She ran her fingers through the fringe of her turquoise shawl.

'And your mother,' she asked. 'How is she?'

He was looking at her shawl and the way she was fingering the fringe.

'Very beautiful!' – he said. 'Is it silk?'

'Out of fashion!' – she laughed. 'But you're right: it is truly beautiful. My grandmother wore it, they told me. So your mother is well?'

He shook his head, to say no in silence: 'She's dead,' he said after a while without stopping to look at the shawl.

'My God!' she exclaimed. 'When?'

'Fifteen years ago or so,' he replied in the same vague tone.

She turned to look at the lake, with her back to him, to hide her astonishment from him: 'But didn't you tell me yesterday that you were going to see her before the end of the month?' she finally said after a full minute of silence.

'I was lying,' he replied. 'I always lie when I speak of my mother. And then' – he continued, pausing with a tone of excuse – 'even when she was alive I only managed to see her for a few hours a month. In her last year she didn't recognise me: they brought me to her and she leaned forward with her head and drooled; she was curled up in her chair in a way that made it impossible for her to see anything of me but my shoes, until someone passing by managed to straighten her somehow. I was young then' – he continued with the tone of one trying to explain. 'The room was almost as long as a corridor, with big windows overlooking the garden. In the winter reflections of the snow between the trees, the earth and the branches filled the lacquered yellow walls with strong gleaming streaks that were completely senseless. "What does it mean?" I used to ask myself. It was a common old people's home, that's all. Like all of the most common things, from a certain point forward, it was only appearance: an insistent habit of appearing one way rather than another: pure appearance therefore, lacking immediate sense. As a young man though, I always used to ask myself about the meaning of everything, especially when this supposed meaning seemed infinitely far from its appearance.'

'I am sorry,' she said.

He shrugged his shoulders: 'Perhaps that which we see would mean something if we were different people.'

'Why?' she asked, disconcerted.

'I don't know,' he replied. 'Perhaps there are meanings on one side and men on the other and then subjects and meanings draw near each other, and it might even be predestination. Not everyone actually understands everything, but only what they have been given to understand. I understand little or nothing, but I think that if I were a different person with a different predestination I would understand somewhat more: certainly something else, and possibly something more amusing or pleasant. And you, *signora*, do you understand everything?'

The evening air was clear, but not cold: actually rather soft, she would have said, while in this soft air what he was saying seemed harsh to her somehow: an adversity made of words like the flight of obstinate birds.

'Explain yourself!' she encouraged him.

'I was thinking about my mother again' – he said – 'at her insistent looking at my shoes which I had carefully polished for this reason before going to see her. Well, sometimes I thought I saw her attempt to climb up: her glance attempted to rise along my legs up to the knee. She couldn't do it, but my God how hard she tried, what desperate determination. And what weariness in this attempt, just think, if she had succeeded!'

'What?' she asked, confused 'Succeeded in what?'

'That's right! What?' – he laughed. 'That's how I am: I see something flat on the ground and I climb up, pulling myself up gasping along the vertical: from the city (this same city, I say) to more elevated utopia: a transcendence of thirty metres, let's say. But, as far as my mother is concerned, I felt, since she was not predestined to meanings any more than I was, that instead of actually exhausting herself to capture one or another, she tried to climb up to the place of all the meanings. Amusing, isn't it?'

'No' – she said. 'It's not amusing.' She thought there was something grimly blasphemous in what he was saying, but perceived behind this cursing grimness a troubled and troubling sentimental luminosity.

'Did you love your mother very much?' she asked.

He didn't answer: he kept looking at the ground and kicked leaves out of his way every once in a while.

'I don't know,' he said finally. 'I often speak with her about this "love" (a fantasy, of course), but we don't manage to understand each other. There is a certain reticence and then (always in fantasy) we can't find the right words. Don't worry. I am talking about "fantasy", not phantoms. But what harm would there be in talking with a phantom every once in a while? Once, at least, one used to speak with one's soul or guardian angel. A few madmen risked even speaking with God: in other words with another different from oneself, because it is indeed the difference between the speaker and his imaginary interlocutor which saves the reason in every fantastic discussion. Today however, everyone talks to themselves in complete solitude, which is like talking to the mirror. A boring practice, I'd say. Don't you agree?'

'I agree,' she said, forcing herself to smile. 'It is very boring talking to a mirror. But all women do it. I do.'

'Don't worry about it,' he said. 'You don't talk to your mirror: you simply look at your beauty: you check on your clothes, your elegance and this is a normal use of the mirror and could even be pleasant, just as it is pleasant for me now to look at you: anything may be pleasant to look at, anything which comes into sight, provided you don't search for the meaning. Saying "talking to the mirror", I meant instead asking oneself the meaning: of its own meaning, what's more! Is there anything more silly and ridiculous?'

'You're not going to tell me the usual stupid things, that nothing has meaning and that life is a tale told by a drunkard?' she protested.

'Very well' – he admitted – 'this has been said too often and I might have been going to repeat it to you. Sayings have their way of making themselves repeated. But my intention was different: I was speaking only and uniquely of my face: my nose, for example. What is the meaning of my nose? I am not talking about noses in general, but about mine as if it were a potential justification or at least explanation for my presence in the world.

This certainly is stupid; instead, asking: "What is the meaning of the nose of the first person who passes by?" could be amusing.'

She shrugged her shoulders: 'And the house?' she asked. 'Don't you have a house in the country?'

'In the mountains,' he corrected her, 'in the mountains I saw a house I liked very much. Imagine a field in the mountains, at about a thousand metres, four big-bellied horses moving in front of a house. It is already dusk and there's no sight of the sun: grey air, trees with red and yellow leaves, outlined with other mountains in the distance beyond the valley, beyond an abyss. The house was small and the plaster looked old, in some places crumbled, and was originally pink, I believe: three windows on the first floor, the middle one under a triangular top floor; and, on the ground floor, doors bolted with planks. Obviously the house was deserted.'

'So you bought it?' she asked.

He made a face: 'I certainly can't buy everything I like or find interesting!' he said. 'Can you?'

'Sometimes' – she replied – 'sometimes I could . . .'

'In any case' he continued. 'Whatever I might have led you to believe, I don't have a house anywhere. The idea of owning a house is a diversion for me.' He started to laugh. 'It is not that people interrogate me directly about my existence, but in certain cases I detect a sort of uncertainty in others. Their uncertainty communicates itself to me in an unpleasant way, because I am always uncertain myself: "But after all, who am I?" I ask myself. And I wouldn't feel at ease or at least I wouldn't think I felt at ease if I didn't have a house. The one with the house is a fictitious self, and if I must confess it is something I made up without much forethought, put up very quickly, when I saw an opportunity; so it is possible that I did speak to you of a house in the country.'

'You're a strange character,' she commented with irritation. But since she wanted to encourage him she continued, 'but very, very interesting.'

'Really?' – he cheered up. 'Then to continue with the confession, I'll tell you there is also an aesthetic motive for my house in the mountains. After my mother's death, since I imagined speaking with her for many years, I didn't feel it was decorous to hold our conversations in an old people's home. A house that was slightly isolated, exposed to bad weather, would be much more appropriate for an intimate conversation, like ours, that in fact turned on the fundamental polarities of existence: consciousness and being.'

'Consciousness and being?' she asked, clearly astonished. 'You were saying your mother could no longer recognise you: you described her as demented. Forgive me, but were you thinking of her as she once was? An intelligent woman who knew something about philosophy?'

He shook his head, smiling. They were silent for a good minute.

'Shall we get up?' he asked.

She didn't answer and they remained seated, although he turned around, clearly not at ease.

'All right,' he finally admitted. 'My mother couldn't even manage to read a newspaper. Before she was demented you might have called her silly.'

They both leaned forward towards the fallen leaves with a movement strangely simultaneous.

'I am the silly one!' she said. And after a moment of silence added, in almost a whisper: 'Forgive me.'

He sat up straight. 'Meanings!' – he started to speak again in a tone that sounded almost happy to her. 'I spoke to her among other things of the predestination of meanings, as I already have talked idly with you. For example, in my wanderings around unknown medium size, or small, or even very small towns, I sometimes happened to get hold of the meaning of something: a doorway, a bush, anything at all. I don't mean meaning in the strong sense, for there is no meaning to speak of in a wall, a tree or a town square. It was more like a recognition. I suddenly recognised the square, the trees around it, the small cast-iron fences around the flower beds not as things already seen (for I had never seen them before), but unexpectedly I found that we, the things and I, were almost face to face, on the same level. I recognised, so to speak, the gate and I shared the same intellect, despite the enormous difference that at first sight my figure presented with respect to the gate. The gate and I were predestined, one for the other and it was this reciprocity of destiny that lent meaning as much to the gate as to me. Amusing, isn't it? My mother seemed to understand this. In fact she spoke to me often about a stone staircase she had seen in the house of a cousin. She immediately wanted one just like it in her own house, but it was impossible, and after many years she grew bitter about it. "But nevertheless this is always your stairway," I tried to console her. Certainly there is also a sentimental side to this recognition with respect to destiny, but it is not the effect of habit or possession. There are actually places which remain almost secret to everyone, although many people go past them. Of course I am not talking about main streets or municipal squares, but of places that are out of the way but not private: a courtyard with a horse chestnut tree in the centre, for example. Children run around it shouting, pigeons coo and shit on its leaves, plaster fades and fails; yet in all this bedlam, the secret stays closed, sealed to all, until I arrive by chance. I pass and probably will not pass by again; and yet immediately the secret is offered to me at first glance. The place, it appears, was waiting for me, on the opposite side of a destiny we both shared. It almost brings tears of gratitude to even think about it.'

He suddenly stopped talking and started rocking his head up and down. She started to repeat the same movement after a while. She felt uneasy.

'That's lovely!' finally she made an effort to say, 'confused, but lovely!'

He raised his head and laughed. 'I am the one who's confused,' he declared. 'I am, above all, a confused man. Shall we get up?'

'Yes' she said, getting up. 'Let's go and have coffee.'

They crossed the garden through rustling leaves, mostly red on the branches and brown on the ground. The breeze from the lake made the rustling leaves screech against the pebbles. Evidently the dustmen gathered only part of the fallen leaves, leaving at least half under the benches, next to the flower beds and wherever it was hard to collect them; this let the wind which usually started blowing in the evening toss them around, making them more dry and liable to fly with each passing day. Apart from the leaves there was an atmosphere of neglect, a careless nonchalance that was typically autumnal.

'Don't you like to gamble?' he asked, apparently just to say something, walking too close to her and yet with the hampered look of one who is afraid of banging into her with every step.

'You have already asked me twenty times,' she replied with a
show of patience, 'and every time I have told you that gambling
bores me . . . the mere sight of cards wearies me.'

'It also wearies me,' he interrupted her. 'What's more,' he
added, 'this is the best disposition for a gambler. It is tiring.
Everything else in comparison is a diversion if gambling is one's
work, as it is in my case.'

'I understand,' she said, 'you're a professional gambler.'

'More or less,' he admitted. 'What monotony, what boredom,
as you say. Nothing ever changes, except places and people, but
seen through the eyes of a gambler they are all more or less the
same. The seasons change,' he admitted, 'but there are only four
and in any case they change everywhere.'

'And yet you have liked certain places.' 'Well!' he said, 'yes,
but only a few, tiny places: a street, a widening, sometimes only
a courtyard, while the rest of the town remains inhospitable,
cold, uncomfortable. Certainly modern towns are worse than old
ones. But even old ones or somewhat old ones express
desperation. Just to see certain porticos, rustic, simple, yet
solemn with seasoned nineteenth century boredom. Sometimes
even the clouds above the houses look nineteenth century,
especially those around town squares.'

'Nineteenth century clouds?' she asked, laughing.

He shrugged his shoulders: 'The sky' – he said – 'doesn't
escape dating: a nineteenth century house has clouds of the same
period around it: trees, too. When they spend time together,
things end up looking like each other.'

They reached the square in front of the hotel, but didn't cross
it; instead they turned right, towards one of the cafés that still
had tables outside, under the trees. The tables had dry leaves on
their red tablecloths and were empty. The two waiters for the
group of tables where they were sitting looked at them
hesitantly. The wind was growing stronger. Leaves swarmed
around their heads and the movement of air made the space
transparent and places in the distance appear even further away
and more difficult to reach.

They continued to talk somewhat at random and distractedly
until their talk became fragmentary and – he noted – even
grammatically incorrect. She said there was something strange in
the air. Lights and shadows followed the caprices of the wind

and people looked restless. A child ran past and then stopped near a tree about ten metres away and started looking at her sternly. In the meantime he spoke of this house of his imagination and desire, and the need sometimes for 'putting down roots.' 'Houses and women,' he said, 'represented stability, the security of the following day.'

'Even the women?' she asked.

According to him, women were the equivalent of houses, but it was very hard to talk about women without being obscene or foolish. That is why he had spoken only of his mother, as if she were now one woman and now another available for all variations of experience, though he was terrified of seeing her vanish into the generic at one time or another, right in the middle of one of these little evolutions. 'And yet' – he added – 'what I find especially moving is that my mother once existed completely independently of my imagination or my own memories.'

He was silent for some time; then he took a brioche from the little basket the waiter had brought with the coffee, tore off a piece to toss to a big pigeon that was coming up to them, dull grey, and ruffled by the wind. 'Do you see it?' he asked her, laughing.

She nodded: 'Once again I need to ask your forgiveness. I didn't mean to be arrogant or indiscreet!'

'Oh, no, no' – he interrupted her with a reassuring gesture – 'I am actually grateful, because, you see, when I was speaking to you about my mother, an idea came to me: a sort of meaning, or rather a sort of parallel image. I felt I could see her, this poor woman, with her shiny shawl as if she were about to cross one of those immense fields after the harvest: a long stretch of stubble under implacable midday sun. "But where is she going?" I asked myself. In a certain sense it wasn't really her: the features were not recognisable: actually there were no features. It was more like the shadow of a cloud: an opaqueness moving across the sunny field. She went on and on, dissolving herself in a flash during her journey before completely vanishing. That's how she was in the final days: demented and almost on the point of vanishing and yet she was still alive, still going.'

The child whom he'd beckoned to take a croissant went away again silent and discontent.

'Are you leaving tomorrow?' she asked.

Without replying, he began to look around almost suspiciously and to turn around on his chair so that he ended up almost with his back to her. 'I want to make you laugh,' he said suddenly, without looking at her. 'You know that I was about to fall in love with you?'

She was silent for a moment: 'How incredible! Is that what makes you laugh?'

'No,' he replied, 'what is ridiculous is that I thought you were rich or, at least, it is ridiculous that I fell in love with you to the extent I presumed you were rich, knowing nothing precisely about this presumed richness of yours.'

'Are you telling me this to make me laugh?' she asked.

'More or less' he responded, continuing to talk into the wind.

'How incredible!' she repeated, standing up.

He stayed leaning over, offering morsels from a brioche to another pigeon and apparently speaking with it. 'There, my dear,' he was saying, 'peck at this!'

She sat down again, shaking her head: 'Let's be reasonable!' she said, brushing her hand along his shoulder. 'I don't think it's a good idea to go on laughing in each other's face.'

He shrugged his shoulders without turning: 'Well,' he said, 'I am leaving tomorrow.'

There were now three pigeons approaching or withdrawing, alternating sudden impulses of prudence with brazen audacity. At a certain point, a ginger cat approached, ignoring the pigeons, also ruffled by the wind, and also wavering between audacity and suspicion.

'Would money be useful to you for gambling?' she asked.

He tossed the remains of the brioche out in a single piece, which the cat bit into, delicately stretching out his neck and chasing away the pigeons, and then he calmly turned the chair around.

'To stop, actually,' he said. 'I actually think about stopping every time I feel physically tired and the mere thought of a green baize or a deck of cards makes me nauseous. "Better take a train!" I tell myself. And also I can no longer bear this place. After all, where would I live if I weren't travelling?'

'I am not very rich after all,' she said. 'I have what I need and a little bit more, perhaps, but not much more.'

He nodded: 'Would you like another coffee, or something else?' he asked.

In reply, she started to praise his hair, which was grey, but thick, and the right colour grey, she said and was very becoming now, ruffled by the wind. 'Very!' she repeated finally, almost automatically, without daring to believe her own voice. 'When I first saw you,' she concluded making an effort to free herself of that rash repetition, 'I told myself that you had very beautiful hair.'

He started to laugh: 'I think you're teasing me,' he said. And then, without listening to her, he went on to talk about gambling, and the characters he met who were all alike.

'Of course, no one expects to talk about music, or literature in a gambling place, but there is only talk about arse, real or metaphorical. Eventually, I get tired of all these arses, and I leave almost to escape the avalanche of bums that follow me. For a while the train gives me the sense of distance, of being almost unreachable. I also sense the possibility of another me, starting a new life, *Incipit vita nova*, as they say. And what a new life! First class! So I always travel first class. I know perfectly well that this is merely the old me running away without reason and without destination. As they say, *quo ibi iste fugiens*, whither shall I flee . . . with whatever follows.'

The wind suddenly stopped and the last sun of the day shone on the tablecloth at an angle, highlighting the tiny oval yellow leaves, thin as paper, which, even without wind, continued to fall from the nearby trees. The setting, still the same with trees nearly bare of leaves, the cat and the pigeons, when the wind stopped became, if not pleasant, at least peaceful. But, she thought, it was as if this change hadn't begun at the beginning, as happens with every phenomenon that is new or different from what precedes it, but from right in the middle of the new appearances: actually right from the centre of the new phenomenon, so that this new serenity appeared still busy putting itself into being and although at first sight it appeared perfect, it lacked foundation. When she was travelling one time, she had had a similar sensation of changes that were continuous and as unexpected as lacking foundation. The name of the famous city which she had yet to visit and was due to arrive at late that evening did not suggest more than a limited sense of night and rain, since it was already raining. That rain, like the wind of today, was intermittent, with sudden showers. When the rain stopped, the train went into a long pause of calm, through large stretches of bare woods. Then the rain started pouring down again thick and grey, and later, at sunset, she no longer felt she was carried by the train but by the caprices of the rain. She felt she was passing from one squall to another, and that the squalls attended her, like train conductors, sometimes rudely, with heavy drops, at other times with speedy and crystalline efficiency, and occasionally with good humour, almost joyfully with a shower of drops reddened by sun.

He had gone on talking about gambling and cards in general, but she barely heard him, as she was beguiled by the lustre of the sun on the surface of the tablecloth and by the leaves around the white cups and saucers. The cat, reassured by the absence of wind, sat on the paving stones a short distance away and watched her.

'You won't believe it,' he was saying meanwhile, 'but handling cards, hand after hand brings prophetic accumulation and addition: an increase in the power of significance of the game. Figures that have no direct bearing on the game suddenly come out from their neutrality like a summons: naturally an indecipherable summons, but no less threatening for that. Take the ace of spades, for example. Why did it come in my hand four times in a row the other night? It was also late and anxiety was struggling with sleepiness also on the faces of those around. Moments thick with silence, smoke and repugnant odours filling the air. Outside the window, beyond the clouds, were stars. Everything in the world is uncertain, everything could take a turn for the worse from one moment to the next and the same immobility of the stars or at least the regularity of their coming closer and going their separate ways, the sequence of their conjunctions are signs.

'For example, listen to this: according to Cardano in the individual born when Venus unites with Saturn there will be a tendency to sodomy, or to be attracted by old women. Well, I am certainly not a sodomite, but I was born with this conjunction. "What does that mean?" I ask myself. It means that even a defeated sign, just because it is defeated, preserves its prophetic potential: a durability that it would not otherwise have. In fact, if I should recognise myself as one who fancies arse or old ladies, the prophecy would forfeit its mystery: it would lose its quality of uncertain and incomplete revelation of the transcendent and place itself in the full light of immanence. There is always something unfinished about the threats of the stars and other prophetic signs: a virtuality continually threatening which provokes us to flee. That's why I am leaving. In other words I could say that I am leaving because I am superstitious.'

'So you believe Cardano?' she asked.

'No,' he replied, 'I am not convinced. But as I was saying, I try to leave before some misfortune befalls me.'

'For me,' she said, 'it would be the greatest misfortune if someone were close to me not for myself, but for my money. I have always been obsessed with this suspicion, and not out of avarice, believe me: I think it may be out of pride. But there are times when I think that in certain circumstances, I could accept this supposed misfortune, not only with resignation but even with joy.'

The sun was gone: the cat was lying with his head on his crossed paws. A pigeon stopped a metre away and started to nod haughtily at the cat.

'These beasts!' she said. 'In the country I have dogs and cats who live together in love and harmony. It's an old house,' she continued, 'at the top of a hill with an apple orchard: nothing but apples seem to be grown around there. In this season it's not much, but you should see it in springtime: the red of the blossoms is a triumph.' She paused a moment. 'I was about to tell you that it is very lovely, but I don't want to lie: even when in full flower, if the sky is cloudy or rainy, all those flowers in the orchards are prisoners of the clouds and trapped by the trickle of rain. So it's sad.'

'Is it a nice house?' he inquired.

'It's large, nineteenth century,' she said. 'Come to think about it, even the clouds there look nineteenth century.'

He nodded without speaking.

'The wind has gone,' she continued. 'This is a splendid, dry autumn: excellent for wine.'

'It's a bit cold,' he said, looking around. 'Here the sun sets early because of the mountains: we are already in shadow. Don't you feel cold?'

She shook her head. 'Perhaps I'll go to the old house tomorrow.'

They were silent for some time; he was leaning forward with his hands clasped between his knees.

'You even have a good profile,' she observed.

This time he turned to look at her questioningly, and then shrugged his shoulders: 'It's getting late,' he said finally, indicating the hotel sign which had just been lit. 'Tomorrow I have to leave.'

'So do I,' she said.

He stood up and began swaying from one leg to the other, with his arm raised to summon the waiter.

She inexplicably started to cough: 'Would you like to come see my house in the country?' she asked.

'Oh, you,' he said, turning to the waiter. Then in a more quiet voice: 'To do what?' he asked, without looking at her. He put money on the tray next to the cups and the basket with the rest of the brioches which the waiter had already placed there. She stayed seated while he bowed vaguely in her direction and gave her a last faint smile. Then he turned and went towards the hotel without saying a word.

Suddenly she felt almost cold, just as the shadows suddenly seemed to have become more dense in the interstices and around the edges of things, reinforcing the corner of a house here, the profile of a portico there, or, up higher, the line of a roof, while the sound of traffic, without diminishing in intensity, had turned into an evening sound as well, more shadowy and soft. It was still light, but the signs and neon words already glowed with nocturnal force and in general all things, from the table to the chairs, the trees to the lake, seemed to be preparing themselves for the solitude of night, starting to appear more authentic, almost without heeding men, but comporting themselves, so to speak as they were: the tablecloths behaved like tablecloths, the cups like cups, the trees like trees: the lake behaved implacably like a lake, settled in its watery inertia. Later, perhaps, during the night, the wind would have tempestuously shifted masses of clouds from one side to the other, but this movement would not have changed things substantially, nor would the following day change them, nor the years. Much time would have elapsed, but the lake would have kept its lacustrine customs with obstinate simplicity.

NIGHT (1948–1987)

To Armando Vitelli

They say I'm crazy, so don't pay any attention to what I say. What I do and have done can't be understood in the normal sense, of good common sense or any other sense, because it doesn't make sense. Now I think this is too broad a view of madness because even the most crazy people make some sort of sense. I think a lack of sense applies more to the collective than to the individual. A group can be called unreasonable or senseless when it behaves in a strange or absurd way, but even the most unseemly behaviour doesn't necessarily imply that an individual is senseless.

So be it! I don't want to set forth rules or make any firm declaration at this time, but only refute that damaging prejudice that I don't make sense. It's not true. I am preoccupied with meaning almost obsessively: my very gesture is preceded by doubts that it's sufficiently significant. I ask myself, for example: would it be significant to raise my arm? And because I am uncertain, I raise my arm, and wave my hand about to allow the significant to triumph. I make a great number of emphatic signs, so there will be no doubt at all that my gesture intends to be significant. I am sure that the most terrible thing about life is its tendency to dim meaning. And since I am a reasonable man I try to remedy this tendency, which is also a tendency to thoughtlessness, and to nothingness and I tend to exaggerate, with too many signs and possible meanings for each and every gesture I make, from washing my face to combing my hair. It is horrible that Plato says there are no ideas for dirt, hair and shit. If that were true, a man would find himself face to face with non-thought and nothingness every morning on the pot.

Certainly something with meaning doesn't necessarily mean only one thing to the exclusion of everything else: I believe that an unambiguous meaning is more the object of hope than the result of the process by which meaning is produced which is

117

always a laborious and misleading process. When I say that I want every gesture of mine to have meaning, I am trying to say I would like it simply to show in a general way, that it is a human gesture and not like the movement of a buffalo. In fact even if some people keep calling me 'buffellow' I don't think that by doing so they intend to exclude me from the human realm, which, after all, is exactly the same as the realm of what makes sense. Senselessness is something quite other than humanity: because what seems most lacking in sense is the desperate poverty of someone dying, one through increasing weakness gradually and knowingly losing his senses or his sense outside of himself, that is everything he can see, touch, smell: of the most ordinary good things, light, water, air. He is falling away from the state of possessor, which is the only human state, into that of having nothing, which is bestial, and perhaps even less than bestial.

No more of this sad talk which could lead us astray. To be brief, let's say if you were to call me a mad fool, I would accept that, provided however that this did not infer that I am a stupid beast, incapable of understanding the good things normal healthy men enjoy, things like a pear, an orange and an artichoke: fruit and vegetables, in other words, not to mention more sumptuous treasures like mountains, woods, the banks of rivers and shores of the sea, salty bushes on the coast baked by summer sun, women walking along the water's edge: everything which anyone, however mediocre his attentiveness, can enjoy with the use of good sense, however coarse it may be: in other words, stupid as you please (perhaps it's only fair to call me that!), but not poor in those goods we all share and which seem the unalterable or perhaps most serenely olympic features of the world, through their abundance and repetitiveness.

But perhaps we should put an end also to this pleasant talk of shared and uncontested riches, at least for the time being. On the level of the daily chug-chug and the snatch and grab of every hour, I must say that even this hubbub is somehow shared because if the world is going to ruin, or only this country, through corruption and crimes that are ever more violent and fierce, I'll be going to ruin along with them. These things happen: entire groups of people, differentiated by ethnical features or geography or religion, sometimes distance themselves from common humanity out of pride or some sudden decision, or slow progress or long march towards sunset and night. In this situation, however, you must admit that there is nothing that distinguishes me from others, from those on the brink of ruin who do no think they are madmen or fools. If anything, as things go from bad to worse, I tend to be sociable more spontaneously than most people: I like to chatter cheerfully in taverns, be understanding with whores, good with children and a friend to anyone who comes my way. My silliness is a *stultitia loquax* and belongs in the category of loyalty: it is still a manner of speaking or of meaning that I am in the same boat with others, as one can say even when one is unable to follow my course. One runs adrift instead; a boat on one side, a second boat on the other, and in the middle a deep and silent sea between them. What can be done about this situation? Let's end this talk about being adrift, which offers no promise of getting on sure ground.

Getting back to the whole question of meanings, I should concede that occasionally I find that some meanings are extremely vague, both from what they should or could signify or, as one says, their disposition to signify, and from the possibility they have to be uttered or just said. Let's say, on the one hand, that is objectively, that the presence of the verb 'to mean' is felt to be stirring: in the air, in other words, in the shade, in the light is a sense in which only the word is missing; on the other hand, subjectively, that is in my mind, there are voices stirring desperately which at one point seem lacking sense: exclamations, like, for example, 'In the arse! In the arse!' repeated several times unexpectedly and urgently.

If one pays attention to the tone, the sense of the expression would appear to consist of suggestion and command: action to accomplish immediately in the direction of some arse categorically mentioned like arse here and now. But what action? Which arse? After a certain amount of doubt, in order to ascertain the meaning of these voices, at least tentatively, I decided to kick someone near me in the arse, respecting the categories of time and place which the exhortation 'in the arse!' seemed to contain.

So it is not from madness, as some would have it, that I kick some people in the arse, but quite the contrary, it is my obsession with meaning, which urges me to insist that nothing be lacking in meaning.

Nothing? Well, almost nothing! There is, I have said several times, rather than a sense, the good will of a sense: a will and need to come close to something that could be a sense by dint of kicks in the arse for the first person in sight, but there is also the case in which things are not lacking meaning but merely a word; often what conventionally one means when one says 'nothing' appears to be one of those senses that are silent and present everywhere; in the air, light, shade, swirling around, wrapping and covering everything and everyone like the famous cloak of mercy.

But why talk about cloaks? – I might be asked. If this is no madness, what is this talk about mercy? Religion? Philosophy? The beast is speaking philosophy: throw the jug at him! some will say.

In fact one tried to do it, that is to stand, take the jug by the handle and stretch the arm back for throwing it, but before he could launch it, I jumped him. The truth is that it can be useful, at times, to invent a madman: the madman here is meant to be a phenomenon of nature as opposed to reason, while our accountants, that is the secular and religious authorities which govern the country, are reason against nature. When the reason of these accountants finds it opportune to not recognise a fact as its own work, that is, made out of cunning for short term gain, it invents a madman to take the blame. So it is in the case of murders, which are always facts of short term gain in this country, and which on the contrary, still for short term gain, would like to pass as facts of nature: like mishaps from a thunderbolt or an avalanche, which no one minds.

Well then, I might be asked, is it not a sign of madness to kick an important person in the arse, either because of quantities of money accumulated in the course of rapid and triumphant careers in economics and politics, or for favours gleaned from religious authorities?

That's an exaggeration! – I respond. It is usually modest individuals I tend to slap and kick in the arse, waiters, or third rate civil servants, someone who works in the town hall or the post office (little folk in other words!) towards whom it is customary to spit on the face or piss on the head. If a few slaps or kicks have gone to someone more important it was in a frenzy of excess, perhaps undeserved: in other words by mistake. But *non omnis error stultitia dicenda est.*

But aside from a slap, a strong kick and a feeble kick, what do you say about other strange things generally: tantrums while serving the public, for example? 'Well, well!' I say. Let's examine these strange things one by one. Did I refuse to send on a telegram? What is strange about that? Why shouldn't an employee refuse to serve the public if he feels tired, or suspicious or merely bored?

But let's proceed in an orderly fashion: one autumn day, rather late in autumn, neither cold nor warm: clouds in the sky, but some clear patches: the minutes rolling by, sometimes in the midst of silence, sometimes through the rustlings of various office machines, the stompings of feet, the shadow of moving clouds puffed along by the wind, the shadow of people moving on the other side of a translucent glass office partition. As I mentioned, the minutes are passing quickly; thinking about it again, it is hard to say more than the minutes were passing almost silently, as if on tiptoe: boring, but pleasant in other words. A moment of calm: very few customers and little to do; and suddenly the tranquillity and almost total serenity turned into uproar: people crowding in, rushing, fussing, hateful. These unexpected variations happen in the course of an office day. Among others a certain type appears with a form on which, aside from the address and the name of the sender which are required for every telegram, there is nothing but a cypher or groups of cyphers: numbers in other words but without a shred of a letter.

'What's this?' I ask.

'What do you mean, what is this?' he says. 'Can't you see? A telegram.'

I have an instinctive dislike for anyone who treats me as if I were a friend, for example, calling me 'tu'. The man was tiny, with a miniature face, which was aggressive, verging on the lethal, like the little snout of a stone marten.

'Do you have your identity card?' I ask, trying to stall.

'What? Do you have a high fever?' he says.

I consider how big the service window opening is and calculate how it might be possible to grab him by the head or the neck and pulling him at least part way through, and then I swiftly stretch out my arm. But he dodges me, even more swiftly, and in the meantime gives me a blow on the wrist like a true stone marten, using a ruler someone had left behind on the window ledge as his weapon.

Obviously the man was overdoing it because he felt safe behind the transom that separated the employees from the public and logically, I believe, my first impulse was to leap over to catch up with him. I did jump up on the table and from there, with a leap over the border of the dividing panel calculated to fall at least near the man if not directly on top of him, and therefore be able to grab him. But I made a mistake in my calculation, and I was out of practice, so I ended up straddling the partition with one leg on one side and the other on the other. The man had reached the door and was about to leave when he saw me stuck there, stunned by the bruise on my groin caused by the jump I had failed to make. He retracted his footsteps still holding the ruler and tried to strike me several times until I came to my senses somewhat and flung myself down on his side, managing to land close enough to grab him this time.

I don't want to go on at length: it is a banal episode, like many which occur in dealings with the public, which, as we all know, must be kept at bay with every possible means, kicks and slaps included, when necessary. This is the custom and it certainly cannot be deduced from my behaviour, as it was done, that I am aggressive and violent. Considering my height, anyone might imagine that once I had grabbed hold of him I could have bashed the little man against one of those big office windows, but I did not do that. I limited myself to shredding his clothes and tossing him naked out on the pavement, so everyone would learn that post office employees should be respected. I behaved like a sane and healthy man, intent on instruction rather than any vengeance or rancour. Moreover the director himself, who speaks so much of violence, stood watching the entire scene very closely, including the strip, without saying a word, just like all the others, including the customers.

Why didn't I want to send the little man's telegram? This was the director's question to me, and consequently the main if not the only subject of our conversation. Well, if I haven't already I will now confess that I don't like numbers. I freely admit this, although I realise this will make it easy for some people to deduce that my dislike for numbers shows clearly the weakness of my reason. More clearly or less clearly of my philosophising? This about philosophising is one of those rumours which once put into circulation is difficult to deny, because it's hard to prove any supposition.

I once heard that if someone philosophises, this implies he has syphilis; in another case that he lives off prostitution; I've also heard it indicates that his mother once had spotted fever. Every human condition, in other words, seems to be deducible from philosophy and I think this is why – because of the breadth philosophy seems to have – everyone ends up talking more or less about it at one time or another.

The director, for example: he had already accused me several times before of philosophising: therefore of being crazy. But, I ask myself, when I make statements such as: 'two inches away from my arse I don't give a fuck who fucks whom', isn't this moral philosophy? Well, this sentence was not uttered by me, but by the same person who would make you believe that I am crazy, merely because I chattered about the soul, like most people when they are drunk. In any case, this sentence was part of the conversation about the telegram with the numbers.

I said, 'Just think, these might be war secrets!'

'What war?' he asked. 'Don't be silly!'

I started to tell him about attacks, bombs and such like weapons and the director said that until they put bombs under his arse all was fine; actually, so much the better. 'You should keep in mind that the more the shit flies, the better I like it.'

I didn't want to contradict him. 'Say what you please. What do I care?' I was thinking. But at this point, after having asked me many times why I was causing trouble, came the famous phrase which he attributed to me, against all evidence. He stopped under a light and linking his index fingers and thumbs he said, almost spelling each word and in a cadence that became ever more solemn: 'It comes to pass (I hope you noticed I said "it comes to pass") that in this shitty country, actually in the entire universe and in every other possible universe, there is nothing and no one more worthy, more exalted, or more noble than me myself in person.'

This moral solemnity is certainly typical of our times: everyone thinks this way, but not everyone says these things to the first person they meet. For example, calling the country shitty is more appropriate coming from the pulpit than the street. But since he was the one who started all this, I pretended to go along. 'That's right' – I said to agree with him. 'But then why did you mind about the telegram?' I added.

He thought for a moment, looking at me and then rubbing his eyes; actually, if I remember correctly, rubbing his nostrils with the heel of his hand: 'I don't,' he said, eventually, with unexpected kindness. He turned his back on me and left, moving quickly this time. Certainly I would have been able to go on my own accord, but I didn't feel it was prudent to let him leave so abruptly without saying goodbye. In other words, I didn't want to be accused of rudeness. When there is any hint of a lack of courtesy, those of superior rank always hold this against their inferiors. Many things are done for no particular reason, out of that reverential fear that is instilled in us since childhood through stories of the vengeance of the powerful, whether it is political, ecclesiastical, or bureaucratic power. And the vengeance is terrible and frequently unmotivated.

'But why did you start kicking me in the arse?' I will be asked. In any case this happened only later, and, in my opinion giving someone a kick in the arse doesn't necessarily go against modest and obsequious behaviour. Actually, as far as I am concerned, I must admit that taking my size into account, which is almost twice the size of the director, I have always thought I could kick him as much and as often as I pleased and it was the very thought that made it easy for me to be obsequious. I say this to show the absolute and all but banal normality of my thoughts and behaviour. Basically a director of the post office is not very important, and once the working relationship is over, it is entirely normal to start slapping or kicking him. Who wouldn't do that if they physically could?

In any case, after ten minutes meandering around unfamiliar parts of the old town, he stopped in front of an entrance door and said to me, indicating the impressive building which was covered with scaffolding: 'See, they are restoring it and turning it into a museum.'

'Excellent,' I said.

He looked at me for a moment, shifting his weight from one leg to the other.

'Would you like to go in?' he suddenly asked me.

On the spur of the moment I was perplexed and didn't know what to say. 'Was that an invitation?' I asked myself.

'Make up your mind!' he urged me. So I did, and told him I accepted his invitation.

'Invitation?' he asked me. 'All right. But let's not be too formal!'

I said it was something that would just take a few minutes. In the meantime we had gone into a sort of dark and gloomy corridor, with arches placed high on a long barrel vault. We walked down the entire length of this entrance hall and saw dark masses like trees in the shadows of a courtyard through the last arcade. We found a stairway on the left, actually a majestic stairway with broad steps, which was in semi-darkness, like the entrance.

'There's no lift here,' he said. So we started to climb, I don't know how many floors, but he stopped every two to catch his breath. 'It's good exercise,' he huffed. 'Good for the heart.'

'It certainly is,' I said.

'Fine for keeping fit,' he said. While our conversation went on in fits and starts because he was short of breath and I was imitating him, we suddenly found ourselves in the entrance hall of the director's apartment. It is no exaggeration to say suddenly: both sides of the door at the top of the stairs were wide open. A bulb hanging from a wire fastened to the wall gave dim light so I could see first of all some buckets, ladders, a shovel, a pile of sand, and only then did I notice a woman bending over a large drawer resting on the floor.

'I am having some work done here, these old tiles removed and the floor sanded. Then I am going to have wall to wall carpet, grassy green. It's more modern.'

'What a good idea!' I complimented him.

While he was telling me about the flooring I looked around to show some interest. The woman stood up, scarcely managing to lift the large drawer, which I thought was too big to go through that narrow door so I rushed to give her a hand but she moved aside and said 'Get away!'

I didn't pay any attention to her, and took hold of one side of the drawer and pulled it towards me, yanking it away from her. Some of its contents (old documents and photographs) spilled onto the floor and into the pile of sand.

'You idiot!' the woman grumbled, glaring at me. In the darkness she looked almost beautiful, with green eyes and a nose that was slender but jutting out. The light from the lamp hanging on the wall above her head cast a strong shadow which accentuated its outline.

'Get away,' the director intervened, waving his arms: 'he was only trying to help you! This is Edi,' he then added, winking at me. Since my arms were full, I felt I had to bow, and more stuff spilled out of the drawer.

'Why don't you put it down,' said the director, and I did. In the meantime the girl had disappeared.

We went into a square room, not very large, perhaps five metres by five, with a large sofa and two heavy armchairs; one side had two rather long windows, with the frames painted white, and uncurtained; both the door we entered and one on the opposite wall were also painted white. The walls were pale yellow and the upholstery the same colour, with slightly darker stripes. A pair of frayed Turkish carpets with a red and faded blue design covered the floor.

'The problem with these old apartments is the plumbing,' he told me. 'There is only one lavatory here, while there should be at least three for the number of rooms.'

'Oh,' I said. 'What can you do about that?'

'Exactly,' he replied. 'Do you know what a new waste pipe would cost? And bear in mind there are also the necessary permissions which no one is giving away, and then to deal with all the demands of the people on the lower floors. In other words' he concluded, 'a radical solution is needed.'

'Of course!' I said approvingly.

At this point, after looking at me questioningly, and scratching his head several times, he moved closer to confide in me that he had used the expedient of discharging the waste of the other two lavatories directly into the rain gutter. In other words one could now say that the apartment building was dripping shit. He raised his eyes and gave me a wink.

I naturally praised him for this advice, and as I was being laudatory the beautiful lady of the house came into the room. The director introduced us immediately while, as it seemed to me, she kept nodding her head. She was looking at me, smiling and nodding continuously. I didn't know what to do.

'It must be a nervous tic!' I said to myself.

In any case as soon as the director introduced his wife to me she said, to my astonishment, that she already knew me. 'Don't you recognise me?' she asked. 'I always buy vegetables from your stall.'

I was about to explain that I had never sold vegetables, but the director intervened, saying that it was a cousin of mine who looked very much like me. I didn't think it was appropriate to deny this. I noticed that, aside from the tic which slowed down after a few minutes, she had a beautiful smile, calm and reassuring. I thought she must be about forty: her face was fresh and young, but there was some of that almost dry fineness around her eyes and features that comes with age.

'Don't you ever help your cousin?' she asked me, and without waiting for an answer, went on to say that the vegetables were beautiful, and fresh, and she would be happy to grow them. She spoke eagerly, looking around and tugging at the fringe of her scarf: a black scarf, I remember, of shiny silk, with red and yellow flowers. Only when she stopped talking did she scrutinise me closely with her still fleeting gaze for half a minute at least and then exclaimed: 'This is certainly not the same man – he doesn't have a bump on his nose!'

I was reassured and nodded.

'Do you like my new house?' she asked. 'Yes? I don't manage to feel at home here. I go around and around, morning to evening and then, even looking out the windows the bulge of the gutters blocks my view of the street.'

'Oh, the gutters!' I said, laughing.

In the meantime the director had handed me a big glass three quarters full of whisky. It must have been at least a quarter of a litre and I hesitated to take a sip, because it seemed too much to drink on an empty stomach.

'That's right!' she explained. 'There are at least two metres of roof between the windows and the gutters: the apartment doesn't take up the entire width of the building.'

'You could plant cabbages in the gutters!' I said, intending to be amusing.

The lady looked at me with surprise.

'I don't understand what you mean about cabbages!' she said

hesitantly, as if she were talking to herself. 'But my husband is certainly right when he says I am stupid.'

The director came near me and took the glass from my hands before I had started to drink. 'Don't pay any attention to her,' he told me brusquely, shoving his elbow into my side.

'But if the gutters are well fertilised . . .' I said, pretending I hadn't heard the last phrase about being stupid, 'cabbages should do well.' She did not seem to be appreciating the spirit of what I was saying, so I changed the subject. 'Could I have just a taste of that?' I asked, indicating the big glass the director still kept in his hand. He gave it back to me, rudely this time, splashing a few drops on my sleeve. To spite him I started to drink.

'Have you seen Edi?' the lady asked me, drawing up a chair next to mine and sitting down. 'Edi comes here often. There are times, entire weeks, in which she almost lives with us. We have a dead father in common.'

I was watching the director who had moved away and turned his back, apparently busy with bottles and glasses on a piece of furniture under the window. I could see his reflection in the glass scowling, almost grim. What's bothering him? I wondered. I couldn't see how I was to blame and tried to reassure myself that the expression on his face was perhaps only an effect of the reflection.

In the meantime she was talking, it seemed to me, about this relationship she had with the girl I had seen in the entrance hall, and how they shared everything. 'Everything,' she emphasised. 'Do you understand me?'

I said I understood: 'And she's you half-sister?' I asked.

She seemed confused: 'Half sister? Why do you ask? Oh, no!' she then said. 'We both lost our fathers last year, each lost her own father. They barely knew each other. Do you like her?' she asked me after a silent series of nods that seemed almost to be alluding to something, but I didn't know what.

'Well,' I said. 'I barely saw her.'

She stood up suddenly. 'Then I'll bring her here now,' she said. She had no sooner left the room than the director moved away from the bottles and glasses and circled my chair; he shifted the chair his wife had placed close to mine: 'She thinks Edi is my mistress!' he said to my back. 'Then he moved around and looked at me, even more glum. 'Do you go along with that?'

'Go along?' I repeated dumbfounded. Then I started to laugh. The idea of the director having a mistress made me laugh. As you know he is fat, almost rotund, with short arms; but this is nothing compared to his face and head. He has two levels of baldness; that is his forehead slides up over a plane of red skin, then a protuberance rises above it which is the dome of his skull. His eyes are tiny, almost invisible: dark little holes in the midst of scruffy eyebrows. His nostrils faced outwards, and were much larger than his eyes. He pointed them like two gun barrels when he spoke, so one felt watched by his nose, or perhaps more sniffed rather than watched.

I couldn't see him as a lover. I thought he was making up everything. I don't pretend to know what a woman sees in a man. Women can stomach a great deal, but how could anyone bear to let such a snout get close to them? 'How ridiculous!' I said, trying to brush it all off as a joke, but this seemed to make him more angry.

'You don't know how to behave,' he said, as he turned away snorting and puffing disdainfully.

At first I stayed calm but his noises of disdain were sometimes as loud as sneezing and showed no sign of stopping. I started to get cross: 'What do I know about your affairs? After all you were the one to invite me,' I said.

This seemed to calm him. 'Why were you following me? He asked me almost kindly. Why are you always following me?'

I tried to smile. 'Out of respect?' I asked; but then I went on, saying there were rumours in the office that some people would be fired and I was worried about my job.

'You have nothing to worry about,' he told me. 'Let me tell you now that you have been promoted to secretary.' He still stood with his back to me, but from the tone of his voice I felt he was laughing, or rather suppressing a laugh. What's more I knew that there was no job of secretary in the office, and although I thought he was mocking me, I hoped he was talking about some sort of a symbolic promotion: a confirmation of faith that the office had in me. If that weren't the case why would the director have made up such a stupid joke?

I was really surprised: 'But are you sure?' I asked several times. Stupidity always takes people by surprise.

At that moment his wife returned, preceded by Edi. I stood up and offered her my hand. Although she took it, I felt she was brushing it off, rather than shaking it, more because she was in a bad mood than because she was rude.

So be it, I said to myself, and started to look closely at her, almost to examine her. Her body was much more beautiful than her face. It was almost sturdy and delicate, with exquisitely feminine contrasts: of strength, in the hips and thighs especially, and almost fragility in her waist and shoulders. Her neck was long and sturdy as a column. Her head seemed almost too small in comparison, at least that was my first impression. Later I realised her features were fine and her eyes pale green, but all was slightly spoiled by her eyebrows, which were angled down towards the outside like a conventional tragic mask, in which the eyes, beautiful as they might be, seemed empty. In other words a melancholic type that seemed strangely vulgar in contrast with the joyful opulence of her body.

'Have you noticed how beautiful she is?' The signora sat down next to me again, and leaned towards me, resting an arm on my chair as she spoke.

I nodded. In that moment the director took the empty glass from my hands and gave me another, which was just a little bit smaller. I started to sip it automatically, and discovered – after I had gulped some of it – that it was not whisky but some mixture flavoured with anise.

'Oh,' I said puzzled, looking at him.

'One of my concoctions,' he explained with an authoritative wave of his hand. 'Enjoy it. Besides, there's no more whisky.'

'Maybe I shouldn't . . .'

'Why not? Don't you want to celebrate your promotion?'

Perhaps I was already drunk, because certain things bothered me and others pleased me inordinately. When I am sober I am equanimous, sometimes to the point of being boring. I liked the director's wife better every minute, so I started to talk with her about philosophy; actually theology, it was said. Even if you want to call the chit-chat I had with her philosophy, I don't find philosophy important: certain subjects such as good or evil, sin, salvation, have no value in themselves but only indicate our humour or state of mind. In my case I should say that religious things have always helped me get my hands on a woman, that is place them in any position whatsoever on a woman's body and then move them to a better position. But aside from the strictly tactical and not at all philosophical function of speaking of the soul to get close to a reticent woman (although there are not many of them), there is also often a psychological function, because often, speaking of the soul, an amorous whim which lived on nothing is able to gain ground and assert itself as a plausible feeling.

So be it! I was probably drunk, and therefore unabashedly lost in contemplation of the lady's hazelnut eyes, the fine nose, the lips that had a pleasing fullness without being coarse or thick. All these things she held just a few inches from my eyes if not on offer at least on display, and I kept talking to keep them from going away.

In the meantime the director probably gave me more glasses of his concoction, because at a certain point he remarked I was drinking like a fish. He was drinking too, as I recall. His bulk betrayed a habitual drinker, if not an alcoholic. Edi was drinking as well, but not the signora because I tried to drink from her glass once, pretending a mistake, and discovered it was soda water.

'We have blended our thoughts!' she said. I was amazed, but in the meantime, perhaps to distract myself, I told myself I could place my hand on her, and take hold of her knee, for example. I was about to do that several times, but restrained myself: the director was continuously moving around us, watching me. He seemed suspicious and I didn't want to provoke him because I was afraid I'd lose my job. Naturally I no longer believed in the so-called promotion, if indeed I had ever believed in it.

NIGHT II

I remember a story I was told when I was a child, about some of our neighbours. It seems that the wife was in her forties, when she was persuaded by some of her religious friends that there was nothing more disgusting then the sexual act between people who are too old to have children. They urged her to not deny her husband his conjugal rights but to try to urge him to be chaste, provoking a reasonable repugnance in him, through suitable speeches. She did not have a discursive turn of mind, and could think of nothing better to do than ask him a question after the act of love, and it was always the same questions for at least a couple of years: 'Bartolomeo' – this was the man's name – 'why do you do such filthy things?' And he would answer: 'The flesh is weak!' Or when he was in a good mood, sing part of a love song from some opera.

Then one day, one Saturday, they both dressed after their afternoon siesta and went to the kitchen to prepare supper while they waited for their children to return. She was tending the stove and he stood at the other end of the kitchen by the window, chopping onions. At the usual question, Bartolomeo why do you do such filthy things? he meant to reply that the flesh was weak, but he couldn't say the words. This time the weakness of the flesh seemed to have worn out, and become thin, almost transparent, because of all the repetitions. It was May and he was watching the trees in the courtyard already thick with leaves; the sky stretched bright blue above the houses, as if through the dusty perforated curtain of the weakness of the flesh. He tried to sing something, but couldn't get started. No words, not a single syllable or sound came to his lips, and he wondered if he could even grunt. Then he realised silence had installed itself as ruler of his conscience.

'Why do you do such filthy things?' his wife repeated, while she stirred the sauce without even bothering to look at him.

He was then lost in the vastness of an interior silence which he now felt definitive, and taking the knife he was using on the onions stabbed himself in the throat with such violence that he died within two minutes, before his wife took any interest in his silence and turned to look at him.

Now this story from my childhood says two things to me: in the first place, perhaps it is better not to cause trouble to humanity in the same way all the time: even if you want to cause trouble, it's best to use variations from time to time; it is more kind, I mean. In the second place, it would be naive to think that all questions need answers. Some words pronounced in the form of queries, addressed to others and even to ourselves, aren't questions at all, but movements of feeling: anger, fear, compassion: either compassion for others or for oneself or rather self-sympathy. In any case when one is seized with these movements of feeling, it is best to pick up a rosary and to count all the intrusive details of the invading stupor with the beads, using the fingers. When you count to a hundred, or in certain milder cases only to fifty, usually your mood has changed. Everything is seen more clearly, without querying: an entrance door, for example, and an alley; and not an entrance door? An alley? But it is not easy to escape these feelings and often there are intermediate states in which the urge for questioning may appear to vanish but actually be lurking in darker and more distant corners of our conscience, and sometimes hop forward, making its appearance with unexpected and vengeful violence.

Fortunately that night, as soon as I had left the entrance door of the director's house I wasn't the only one to question myself, but to save form also Edi was at my disposition, so I could share my anxious doubts with her.

'Did she really say that we were exchanging thoughts?' I asked.

'Yes, I definitely heard her say that.'

'What does it mean? What if she had talked about exchanging saliva?'

'She didn't,' Edi said unrelenting. 'I am sure she used the word "thoughts".'

'Oh, the crazy whore!' I wailed, holding my head.

'Stop it,' said Edi grasping my elbow. 'Don't take it so hard!'

I was glad she was sympathetic and silently followed her down some steps that linked two alleys on different levels in the old part of town. It was not actually raining, but the stone steps seemed slimy in the ruddy light offered by two or three lamps. We found the lower road much more brightly lit and full of people. Many shops were still open. People were coming and going doing some late shopping with a bearing that seemed familiar and intimate to me. In these streets, reserved for pedestrians, even the stinginess of the municipal lighting seemed adequate, given that the main areas in shadow didn't appear to conceal any danger or hazard.

I pointed this out to Edi, but my words were confused and vague, if not prolix. I spoke, apparently at random, backed by a strong and precise feeling for the things around me, shadows, yellow and red lights, dampness, the clatter of footsteps and especially the intimacy with which Edi was holding on to my arm.

'What did you want me to get for dinner?' I asked at a certain point.

'A cooked chicken, two onions,' Edi began, 'two ounces of prosciutto, unboiled, three eggs . . . But . . . let's start with chicken. I'll think of the rest later.'

I have always abhorred chicken, for their smell, the puffed-up look they have when cooked, and when they are raw and alive I hate the glum, sideways, doubtful way they examine and re-examine the world before taking a step. Even the large oven and the chickens rotating on a spit could not remove the chill from the cold bluish light inside the poultry shop.

'Among other things,' I said at the entrance, holding on to Edi's arm, 'I now realise I don't have any money.'

'Oh!' she said, stopping. We walked away from the shop, and then she said, 'Perhaps it's better that way.'

I shook my head. 'Don't be upset. In the office,' I explained, 'there is talk about redundancies and I want to keep my job.'

'Well,' she asked. 'What would you like me to do? Should I pay?'

I resolutely refused. 'You could lend me money. I would pay it back tomorrow.'

We stopped for a while at the corner of another street, apparently to think things over.

'Forget it,' she said. 'The shops close in ten minutes. But it's not a question of money, believe me. I could give you everything in my purse, if you want. I think you shouldn't think so much about losing you job. At the door, when you were already half way down the stairs he told me he'd get rid of you. He didn't like the way you put your hands on his wife's arse.'

'On her hip,' I corrected her. 'Only her hip. There was no way he could have seen me. He had already left.'

'He saw it, just as I saw it myself, through the door, in the mirror,' she explained. 'He was standing next to me.'

I hung my head in silence, convinced by Edi's words: 'And yet,' I said, smiling almost to myself, 'he should have realised what might happen to him the moment they fire me . . .'

We had stopped at the corner and many people walking along the street bumped into us. I put out both hands to shove two of them back, more to protect Edi than myself. At a certain point a dozen children arrived running, shouting and sliding, with their heads down, not looking. I suddenly found myself with two children in my arms, one for each arm, kicking, shouting and spitting. Edi was knocked over by the others and when I stood up again, after I had put down the two children I could no longer see her. 'How could that be?' I asked myself. I thought I saw her across the street in the group of children, as if she were being pushed or swept along by them; but now, looking from one side to the other I could only see walls in the shadows, broken by light from the shops, which were now starting to go out, one by one. Fewer people were walking in the street, one after the other vanished inside the entrance doors, which the darkness of the walls concealed. I could see one straight in front of me, between two barred windows; a rather tall and narrow door, built into one of the windows, lowered down to the level of the street. I had already noticed how these enormous old houses had many shop windows, also tall and narrow, cut from the old windows. Anyway the door (or entrance door if that's what it was) looked closed and I gave it a push, and entered a dark space, which opened out on the opposite side towards a paler darkness of fresh air and night. I moved in that direction and entered an interior garden, not very large, with four or five trees and abundant shrubbery.

Some light filtered through from the first-floor window and, higher, the grey from clouds illuminated by reflections from the city allowed me to discern the rectangle of the courtyard and when my eyes became accustomed to the dark I could also detect a portico on my right which ran along that entire side.

As soon as I reached the portico I heard a rustling sound coming from the back, where I could see the beginning of a stairway. It was all completely dark and this explained how I thought I had entered into one of those monasteries or convents I knew still existed in that part of the city. 'If there are monks,' I thought, 'they might even invite me to supper. Otherwise I will tell them I am lost and ask them to show me how to get out.' I no longer thought about Edi or the director, or at least I wasn't worried about them. My drunkenness, if that's what it was, had subsided to a squabbly but tranquil mood: a sort of dim curiosity about anything that might happen in the world, however banal.

When I bumped into an enormous empty drum, which fell over with a great crash (which I felt was immediately reabsorbed by the silence of the garden) I was not alarmed, but remember I stood still for a few minutes looking at what I thought was the shape of the overturned drum in the dark, and talking out loud to myself: 'Look at that!' as if this was a great wonder. The fact was that probably I was already drunk without realising it, and therefore like many drunkards I saw everything that happened as something very special, unique, floating in the air and not mingled and jostling with many other things happening, as normally occurs. At this point someone ran up to me with a raised broom: actually I saw a shadow come at me and felt a broom in my face. I deduced that someone wanted to cast me out of that place as if I were an ordinary dog, in spite of my stature.

'This is not something monks would do!' I said. I grabbed the broom with both hands, and started whacking until the handle broke. I was whacking at random, though, and I often hit the hard stone, the pilasters I believe. The shadow faded, and I proceeded almost blindly, with no hope of finding my assailant, who had remained silent and invisible after two or three oaths in the rage of the attack. I bumped into a door, which must have been barely closed by a single hook, I'd say, because it opened as soon as I shoved it with my shoulder. That is how I found myself in a room that was large and dark, cluttered with shelves, stepladders, barrels, and crates of bottles and some iron containers I thought were for beer.

I have always detested what's called cabaret, at least the form it takes where I live; most often in bars with two or three people telling a story, usually obscene, intending to arouse mirth, at the expense of someone else, summoning nods of complicity from the audience.

There was a platform in the midst of the tables in this place, where two actors were taking turns to laugh, speaking about the way their wives looked, until a third rushed in to make some urgent statement about a whore. I thought, what if I stepped in at the sound of a kick up the arse? But looking around I realised the huge room was almost empty, except for a few waiters lined up against a wall and a dozen whores at various tables all on the right hand side of the room; and all so clearly bored that I thought it wasn't worth the effort to take any trouble over them. The left side of the room near me was entirely empty.

The comedians disappeared and a singer with a large guitar started to sing an old song about a life of crime, full of memories of prison, in quite a sweet voice. Then she also left and there was profound silence, exaggerated by a few squeaking chairs or whispers and made more vast and almost more shadowy, although the indirect lighting of the room was bright and left no shadows.

In the meantime I'd ordered a cognac and when the waiter arrived, bringing a tray with a bottle and a glass, I asked him to leave them on the table. Perhaps I no longer remembered I had no money, perhaps I was still drunk and wasn't thinking about money. What interested me was the acoustic space of the room, which seemed to be occupied by such a dark silence. I attempted a definition of it: it was formal, it was a silence which, in its general darkness, had shape and even colour or tone and which shifted, however, according to the small sounds or noises that interrupted it occasionally. The shape of the silence was different every time and, I felt, came out of the different proportions between the smallness of the sound and the largeness of the space: form by analogy. So I was in the midst of analogical shapes, and started to think about the shape of the director's wife, which I felt resembled Celestial Aida, a shape that was divine and in inverse relationship with the distaste, actually the disgust I felt for him.

Is she truly crazy? I asked myself. The inverse proportion, or rather the disproportion between what one could undoubtedly call her physical beauty and the obscure ugliness of her husband justified the loss of her reason. I remembered the inverse case of an attractive fellow who married someone we all agreed was the ugliest woman on earth. He went completely mad within two years and took his own life a year later. At the funeral his mother went up to her daughter-in-law, took off her shoe and gave her face such a thrashing she had to go to hospital, and had an operation which eventually healed and left her looking almost pretty.

Who knows, I thought, if they fire me, I could kick him in the face. But I immediately realised this was not a serious thought. The sense of pleasure the place gave me, and especially the amount of cognac I had drunk, encouraged lazy and inconsequential thoughts: feeble thoughts not worth mentioning, which I sometimes abandoned halfway. But I can say that even these stubs or tail ends of thoughts weren't entirely insignificant.

For example, I thought a phrase such as: 'You can't have everything you want' and at the same time something like I want or I don't want? and others even less articulate, and yet significant, at least if they are taken all together. I think this belongs with those sentences that on the one hand tend to the simple negation and devaluation of the will, and on the other shows simple listlessness or indifference as a positive choice: a new virtue, barely emerging out of vagueness. Thinking about it again, the 'virtue' of letting everything happen as it may, seemed to me both dignified and seductive, turning everything golden and fluid, like the cognac I was sipping. I discovered this golden fluidity in each of the things I saw and this marvel led me to repeat half out loud: 'How magnificently unintentional this world is!' After this exclamation I tried to formulate in a rather weak or even vague way, a theory about the lack of finality in the universe which permitted one, perhaps only me, to see any moment in my personal life as the point or purpose of the entire universe.

While I was busy with these thoughts, making the chair squeak with the vibrations of my silent laughter, I saw Edi. Or rather Edi saw me, put her hand on my shoulder and asked in a voice I didn't recognise at first: 'How did you manage this? Didn't you say you had no money!' Only then did I turn to see her, scrutinising her from head to toe. This inspection revealed she was even more beautiful than before at the director's house. In this light her face seemed more radiant and less made up; her eyes showed a less mournful sadness, or a more gentle melancholy. But above all her body seen at close range made me see how fragile and at the same time strong she was, with these qualities reinforcing rather than contradicting each other.

'Do you realise how slender you are?' I said, putting my arm around her waist.

'Do you realise how much cognac costs here?' she replied without losing her composure, and put her hand on mine, which was wrapped around her body and rested on her stomach.

'Please sit down,' I said, withdrawing my hand and making a belated gesture of standing up.

She sat next to me, continuing to smile strangely.

'I'll ask them to bring you a glass,' I said, raising my arm to summon the waiter.

'And who is going to pay?' she asked. I dismissed her question by shrugging my shoulders, and saying something like: 'I would like to see the face of anyone who refuses me credit in this brothel.' I said nothing menacing though: in fact the waiter standing behind me could hear what I said and by my meek voice thought he could tell me that he didn't serve beggars and tried to take the bottle which was still half-full from the table. I stopped this by putting a hand on his face, lightly, almost gently, to protect the bottle without making a sound. But Edi disappeared during this scene with the arrogant waiter.

I don't want to make a point about the correctness of my account of such insignificant events. Perhaps I gave him more of a clobber than I intended, and the waiter was really rolling on the floor between the tables. I don't really remember because I have never paid much attention to waiters. What is important about a waiter? What is important is that waiters, not this one or that, but all of them began to treat me with great haughtiness and to ignore my orders so I had to help myself to whatever I could find on other tables. Even a chicken. As I have said, I don't like chicken, but I got one in the dark, taking it and its cover from a tray the moment it arrived at the next table. I immediately realised I had my hands on something like a capon, or a partridge or pheasant, and put it back on my neighbour's plate, where it was supposed to be. I wiped my hands on a corner of the tablecloth and urged him to eat it. 'It's not something I really like!' I added, while he looked at me without saying anything, but with manifest interest.

I admit that my manners, perhaps a bit too casual, might interest or surprise someone and even irritate someone else. I didn't give it another thought and continued to take food wherever I found it, until satiated, or rather, fed up with some of the screeching I heard, I returned to my table, and a delegation of three waiters came up to me.

'You have done a lot of damage,' said the tallest and most authoritative of the three. 'It is best for you to pay and leave this place immediately.'

'Best? Why best?' I asked; but I wanted to be conciliating and agreed to pay. 'If you will bring me a blank piece of paper I'll sign it,' I said.

'What do you mean, blank piece of paper?'

I explained I did not have a chequebook on me; actually when they inquired I told them, for the sake of peace, I did not have a bank account and had never had one, but was certainly willing to honour any financial obligations I had incurred in the course of the evening. I wanted to compliment them then and told them how much I liked the place and how I would have been pleased to stay longer, and then, I concluded, 'I will put black on white to whatever papyrus you please.'

'No,' said the most authoritative waiter, with a honeyed smile leaning towards me and whispering. 'Of course we'll give you the papyrus, but up your arse!'

As I have already said, I don't like people to speak to me in a familiar way unless I have specifically asked them to use 'tu'. I also think it is offensive to talk about arses and arseholes. 'Whose arse?' I shouted, grabbing one by the jacket and pulling him to the ground. The other two moved away. The third started to crawl under and around the tables, but I grabbed him, and put my question to him again.

'Now be good,' said the man at the adjoining table whose chicken I had snatched by mistake. 'Give the gentleman an answer!'

'I am just working,' the waiter sobbed, still on all fours. 'What do you want from me?'

'You should be ashamed,' the man at the next table commented. 'Proper people don't work.'

I looked at him askance: 'But I myself work.' I released my grip on the waiter and he escaped.

'There is work and there is work,' the other man said. 'What sort of work do you do?'

I told him I worked in the post office, and in spite of his protests added I knew perfectly well that my work was worth little and therefore as lowly as the waiter's job, if not worse, so much so that some customers and even their wives spit at a few of my colleagues. Fortunately I have always managed to get everyone to praise the postal service and even the people who work in the post office whenever I asked. All I had to do was to slap them around a bit first.

'That's an excellent method,' he approved. I liked his special kind of good manners, although I didn't really think his appearance was pleasing. He wore spectacles with black frames,

too big for his face, with such thick lenses that his small nose
seemed barely able to support them. He looked about fifty: his
hair might have been white but it was so dirty that it looked
yellow and so long and straight that it slid around his head
every time he moved. When it fell over his face he shoved it
back, using his fingers like a comb, and then I could smell his
reeking lotion. Yet the naturalness of his gestures made even this
smell seem natural: his perfume was probably expensive but
certainly disgusting.

'I find that gesture of yours very elegant,' I said referring to
the fact that after I deposited the partridge on his plate he, with
equanimity, had let it fall on the ground. The waiter was furious.
'Do you think he should pay for the partridge?'

'Don't give it another thought,' he replied, moving his chair
around slightly closer to me. 'You know,' he explained, 'after
picking it up from the ground, he will just add a few extra
mushrooms and take it to someone else ... One mustn't be
fastidious in restaurants!'

'Then why did you throw it away?'

'Hygiene had nothing to do with it,' he explained. 'At the time
it seemed like an amusing thing to do!'

I complimented him, saying it was really amusing and then he
praised my deeds: 'It is always hard to know how to kill time!'
he sighed. 'What a world! They should pay someone like you!'

I nodded: 'It is called being an animator: one who gets paid to
make a scene,' I said.

'Are they paying you?' he asked, after a minute of silence.

I began to protest, saying that my spontaneity and my
detachment were universally known, but he interrupted,
apologising. 'As I've told you, it is rare to start off the evening in
such an amusing way.'

'Shall we put our two tables together?' I asked.

He didn't seem to want to: 'Not because I'm stingy,' he
explained, 'but since you are not part of this establishment I
don't want to be forced to pay for the damage they will want to
add to your bill.'

'Don't talk about paying,' I became indignant. 'I am inviting
you.'

He smiled to show his appreciation: 'Thank you,' he said, 'but
I must refuse.' He went on to explain that in that place they

would not have understood my generous intentions: actually, since I seemed to be so hard to handle, they would have used every opportunity to convince someone else to answer for me.

'What do you mean, convince?' I asked.

'Kicking and punching,' he said. 'But given your build, I suppose that doesn't worry you much.'

'Are there many of them?' I asked, laughing. 'Two's company, three's a crowd, they say.'

'Well,' he said, 'one starts, this paid for that; then others come in in a big group, or even a few at a time, one with a bottle, another with a knife: waiters, errand boys, whores and even a few customers who take advantage of the opportunity.'

I didn't answer: the conversation didn't appeal to me in general; then I started to worry, thinking I was imprudent to not have knocked the three of them out, when they were close at hand. That was really silly! Now there would be minus three, I told myself bitterly. I was starting to feel dejected. In fact there is nothing more depressing than the discovery of one's own stupidity.

The room was again filled with people, confusion and sounds, and I looked around, feeling uncomfortable, and not thinking about anything. At least nothing that I can remember.

NIGHT III

'I want to tell you a story,' said the man with the glasses. I agreed to listen to him, even thanking him, because I didn't want to displease him although I was in a bad mood. But while he told his story I was thinking of other things, especially my bad mood. Was I worried about the gang at the bar? I don't think so: in fact if I had been threatened or even assailed I certainly would have been happy to demolish the place. Usually I would have found this a euphoric prospect to me, exciting and even edifying, but now it seemed hollow, actually decadent. Even the talk from this man near me sounded hollow and limp. I gave an occasional nod, without paying much attention, until I suddenly realised he was talking about Edi and the director; actually that he had been talking about them the whole time, in an indirect and allusive way.

At this discovery my bad mood vanished, or became clear,

and tedious banality rather than confused and irresolute feeling was soon replaced by intense and impatient curiosity. Certainly feelings either last or change inexplicably; in certain cases, this incalculability of feelings can be reduced to a problem of nomenclature; one indulges in a vague or confused sentiment only because it takes time to find a name for it to enable it to be relegated to the past or put it in an archive, so to speak. First one tries to define it with an appropriate name, and then out of boredom or distaste opts for any name just because at the time it seems vaguely evocative. In my case tedium was the word that came to mind, only because someone who happened to be standing behind me was talking to someone else about the rain that was pouring down on the city at the moment. The feeling echoing this fortuitous rain vanished with its title, to leave place for another, not yet named.

I say this because, gentlemen, I don't want to conceal from you that in certain cases, when I seem to be' talking about what happened, I am really talking about what vanished and about the moment in which it vanished to find a place, so to say, in the archives of nomenclature: in other words, I am only talking about words. The present on the contrary, being pre-verbal, is only an indistinct gurgle of consciousness, in which, at least for me, the impulse to agitation prevails without speaking of the impulse to search for words. Sometimes in the course of the evening this agitation was expressed, as you know, directly and immediately, in a frenzy of slapping and kicking in the arse: unintentional slapping and kicking however and eminently impulsive, as I have already explained.

But returning to my sudden interest, permit me to describe it now in terms of agitation. I realised, I think, I had lost much of the confidence of the man with spectacles, because my mind was busy hunting for some word like tedium. But I was thinking I could reconstruct part of what he had been saying about Edi, entrusting myself to the echo of the sounds he had made when he spoke, which sometimes lingers in the ear of the inattentive people for some time after the words have been spoken. Yet I was thinking that this same sort of phonic retrieval, which on the one hand could distract me from listening to what was being said at the time, was an effort I could avoid if I merely asked him to repeat what he had said. So I did. But such was the urgency and even impetus of my request that the man with spectacles shrugged his shoulders: 'I mind my own business,' he said evasively.

I realised he was alarmed. So I reassured him by saying that he had used a particularly amusing turn of phrase which now I had forgotten: 'Perhaps I am drunk,' I explained. 'The loss of recent memory is a symptom of drunkenness, I believe.'

'And also dementia! No,' he added, 'don't worry. What's more, *relata refero* (I only refer to what I heard)'.

I said he was right. In fact although I didn't remember precisely what he had said, I admitted that my boredom and lack of attention were due to the fact that I already knew what he was saying, because it was in the public domain: the usual tale about recycled money, in which obviously our post office plays its part, like any other government body. Probably I knew more about this than he did, so I told him: 'Did you realise that a small post office like the one on Market Street where I work has the same cash flow as the biggest banks?'

'Of course,' he said and we both started to laugh, I think to show that our misunderstandings were over and he could speak frankly again. But of what?

I wanted to take the initiative and told him the story of my employment, which is after all the banal story of all employees, that is how I had to give up a fifth of my salary, which after taxes was taken from the gross to repay the debt contracted with the person who found my job for me.

He looked at me, clearly astonished.

'Excuse me,' he asked with hesitation. 'What do you mean? Don't you want to pay?'

'I am certainly no anarchist,' I assured him, 'but as I have just finished paying after five years I am afraid I'll lose my job! I need to buy another one! But it is hard to get credit these days. There are people prepared to sell their house to get a job. If I only knew someone,' I hazarded, 'someone with civic or religious authority of some sort . . .' He nodded agreement. 'You were saying the lady who was with me probably has good connections.'

He shook his head: 'She knows lots of things, perhaps too many. Perhaps she could even be blackmailing someone. But it seems today that everyone could be blackmailed and everyone is a potential blackmailer: there is no longer any force in blackmail:

it's become a society game.'

'Ah!' I laughed. 'It's like wearing a paper nose to go out to shoot someone!'

'That still works,' he replied. 'You have finally said something serious.'

I was silent for a while. He dug a cigar out of his pocket, lit it, pushed away his plate and settled himself against the back of the chair. Each gesture he made showed me how much at ease he was and how he intended to calmly enjoy this ease. Instead I was seized by my usual impatient boredom again: 'Did you say there are rooms reserved on the first floor?' I asked, and stood up without waiting for his answer. 'I'll go and see,' I decided, turning towards the stairway at the back of the room, which I could faintly see on my right.

'Good for you!' he called out at me, as if saying goodbye. 'That's right!'

I passed close to the central platform and the chanteuse in the midst of one of her melancholy songs, and after I had crossed the room started to climb the stairs.

Everything was lost in shadows, both menacing and inviting. I am not speaking of the greenish shadows on the stairs, but the sense of extraneousness and confusion of place. Occasionally, but not very often, one bumps into places like this which open new possibilities and promise a new chapter of existence: the unexpected is there and the logic of normal expectations falls away. One gets the feeling of being an *ingenue* there, ignorant, awkward. 'What is above the next floor? What will I do after the next floor?' I asked myself, scratching my head. The double question was doubly rhetorical, but was firmly based on my doubt of having lived up to that moment in vain. I remember, as I climbed the stone steps, so broad, I believe, to allow horses easy access to the rooms on the first floor or *piano nobile*, which was customary in grand houses until the eighteenth century, of having rapidly reviewed my modest understanding of Latin. I was dwelling on brief phrases in that language, which had not been useful in my work at the post office until that moment, but just because they were useless in the course of normal life perhaps could help me in exceptional circumstances like this. '*Quantum mortalia pectora caecae noctis habent!*' I repeated several times, whispering, in the belief that this phrase somehow interpreted the empty vastness of the space, even more than its darkness, and could render it familiar to me. The ceiling was lost in a solemn and indecipherable darkness, after a large semi-circular window that shimmered like magic, partly because of the internal reflections and partly, it seemed, because a certain nocturnal light managed to penetrate the glass. It was quite cold and the sounds from the bar were not only faint, but had different and unexpected tones.

'What if the man with the glasses has sent me to the devil?' I wondered, still climbing. I looked around and could see no connection between the place I had left and the place in which I found myself, which looked like the entrance to a library, or even worse, a dormitory for nuns. Should I be acquainted with some Latin patrology, in case I met some wicked nuns? This uncertainty explains my relief when I entered a corridor or rather a gallery, no less solemn than the staircase, and saw a man approaching who could only be a waiter, judging from his tail-coat.

'Well, well!' I exclaimed, going up to him joyfully. He was one of those men who hold their necks twisted, that is slightly leaning to the side with an attitude of deference mixed with questioning. He was rather tall: the peak of his skull, thin and almost fragile, I thought, came up to my eyes. He had the smile of a strolling player and black hair, shiny and glued to his head, which one would expect to see on a waiter. He stood in front of me smiling and looked at me in this lateral way without saying a word.

'Where does one drink?' I asked, just to say something. The question, I immediately realised, was incongruous, also because still having at least half of my bottle of cognac, I had brought it with me, putting it in the pocket of my jacket, and it stuck out in plain sight.

The waiter's smile, in the meantime, without changing any lines or folds of his mouth, shifted more clearly away from deference towards insolence. 'Where did you come from?' he asked in a whisper.

'Sir!' I shouted, 'one always says sir!'

'Have you an invitation, sir?'

I brushed him aside and walked down the gallery.

'I am looking for friends,' I said, without looking at him.

At this point I realised a second person was behind me, and

turning around I saw the new arrival, stopped a few steps from me, talking to the waiter. He was a big fellow, almost as tall as I am, with a double breasted blue suit, short reddish hair and a heavy nose, with a thin slice of mouth barely showing below it. Also his eyes looked half hidden by his short forehead, which dropped down almost to cover them. More relevant though was his flat disproportionate chin and his almost unarticulated bulk, which made him look like a cube.

Sent away with a nod of the head, the waiter moved towards me: 'You've got to get out,' he said making a gesture with his hands without moving his arms, which were by his side slightly forward. I saw his mouth form a round hole when he spoke and it all seemed so extraordinary that I started to laugh.

While I was still laughing, the waiter leapt on me and grabbed the lapel of my jacket which began to rip. To get free I did the only thing I could, and punched him in the temple as hard as I could. After I had stunned him, I hauled him on my shoulders. I had worked for the general meat market, hauling carcasses for a year before I got my job at the post office, and had acquired great skill in balancing a quarter of beef on my shoulders. But this fellow weighed as much as half a beef, and while I intended at first to take him all the way to the stairs and let him roll down I realised as soon as I had picked him up that I couldn't haul him the ten or twelve metres to the stairs. In the meantime I was afraid he would return to his senses.

So I went up to the first big window in the gallery, which was closed and dumped him, almost without giving it a thought, just because I couldn't manage to take him any further. Under that weight perhaps also because of the desperate heave I gave him with my last effort to free myself, the window broke into fragments, snapping off its central frame. The old wood was fragile because it had been drying out for hundreds of years, and exploded like a shot. Strangely enough, I hadn't expected any of this; I actually was thinking about something else. Two steps from the window and almost dragging myself along, exhausted by the effort, I remember looking out the window, into the black of night, and noticing something like a sparkle of stars. Impossible! I told myself. It's raining. As soon as the window vanished, so to speak, I was suddenly face to face with the serenity of night. And there really were stars.

There's no need to think I didn't realise what was going on. Aside from the shattering of the demolished window, there was the thud of the body landing on something that sounded like a roof, judging from the rattle of shifting tiles that broke, and then a series of other sounds more difficult to interpret, accompanied by emphatic curses.

I leaned out to look, having first removed a few dangerous fragments of glass that were hanging in the broken frame, but without seeing more than what looked to me like a tile roof, a metre or so below the window, and in the distance, trees still thick with foliage although it was autumn. If he can curse, I thought, that means he's all right. So much the better! I decided like a fool, without foreseeing what was going to happen to me.

In the meantime the outburst of cursing that I attributed to the man who'd gone through the window had subsided; there was a sound of rustling branches and then silence, except for the sound of leaves and other vegetables sounds in the perfectly still air: in other words those sounds attributed to night in general, rather than to a specific source. But I was especially enchanted by the stars, at first unexpected and now firmly present, intangible from anything that has ever happened or is about to happen in the world; aside from those gentle sounds that seem to come from the breathing of the night. For all one could say in general that the night was calm, the true calm came from the stars: serenity and peace came from them. Nothing up to that point seemed more persuasive than this thought about the serenity of the stars, which I considered at the time as a triumph of intelligence. I was content with myself.

It was becoming so cold next to the broken window that I pulled the half bottle of cognac out of my pocket and took two big gulps. 'What should I do now?' I wondered, as soon as the cognac had strengthened and warmed me. I was no longer intimidated by the place; the broken window and some slivers on the marble floor had taken away that chill of the tomb or the nunnery that I had detected before, and even the architectural rigour, which remained undeniable, assumed in my eyes a haughtiness that became familiar as the once grand hotel that has grown old. So, when I looked around the place at my ease, I realised there was a series of doors, four altogether, on the wall opposite the four windows that looked out on the garden. The windows were disproportionately tall and wide with respect to the doors of normal dimensions, painted the same pale brown as the walls, and set into the wall, so at first they escaped my attention. If I realized they were there at all it was because I saw one, which corresponded to the second window in the gallery, half open itself for an instant, towards the outside, which seemed unusual, that is open towards the gallery and not towards the room, to which I thought it should offer access.

This door opened slightly and then immediately closed again. 'Why, look at that!' I said to myself, greatly curious, and somewhat suspicious, after I realized what was going on. I moved away from the window towards it. I took hold of the handle, banged the door open and found myself in front of a very tiny man with a paunch whose eyes were round with surprise; before the door could swing back again because of the workings of gravity, I realized he was someone I had seen before in the local papers. I opened the door again, but the man had vanished. Then I realized that this was a double door and that this man had remained in the room between the two doors to spy through the slight opening, probably since the time the waiter had gone through the window. I tried to open the second door, but this resisted me.

Perhaps, I thought, it was locked, but now I was so curious about the man I had seen that I tried to open it: 'Now, sir, don't be afraid!' I started to speak to the closed door. 'I'll explain as soon as you open the door.'

I shook the door, but it resisted like a wall; I even gave it a few shoves, but the other door, the exterior one, fell in and landed on my shoulder, leaving me little room to manoeuvre. I ought to hold it fast, I thought; and then I remembered I could use some fragments from the window frame to wedge between the floor and the bottom of the exterior door, to hold it open. That's what I did, and then when I looked more closely at this second door, I realized that it was even more stout than the first: thick natural wood, very hard. So I made a running start from the window in the gallery and gave it a real heave with my shoulder. The door resisted, but with relief I noticed a crack opening by the handle. I was now sure that a second good heave would be enough to open the door, when someone turned the key, and silently, slowly, the door began to open by itself.

I went into the room, and on the side by the window saw that a round table had been prepared for a meal. Two women were sat at the table, and three men were standing as if they were waiting for me. I saw the little man with the paunch and the round eyes I had caught spying on me previously, and among them I immediately recognised my director. 'Well, well!' I exclaimed, joyfully moving towards him, 'we meet again!' As I spoke I went to shake his hand, but he withdrew it, and held it behind his back: 'You bastard!' he said, looking straight at me.

I wanted to think of his word for me as a joke, and at the same time I didn't know what to say: 'What do you mean?' I asked, laughing.

'You complete bastard!' he repeated without taking his eyes off me. One of the women I hadn't really seen tried to laugh, or rather to cackle. Then everything started to seem irremediably stupid to me. With my arms hanging (the right arm hurt a little after all the heaving I'd done with my shoulder) and an attempt at a smile, I tried to find some spirited saying sufficiently intelligent to let me out of the situation honourably. At this point I remembered the serenity of the stars, the dark masses of trees against the pale air of the night and the peace that elsewhere, just beyond this room, was intangible from the human stupidity.

'Leave the room!' said the man with round eyes in a voice unexpectedly authoritarian. The third man, even fatter, dressed in grey with a yellow tie, bald, without moustache, collar-like beard, repeated the order to get out, but in a subordinate tone. I looked more closely at the little man with spectacles who now seemed to be the most important man in the group, and whose photograph I had seen in some newspaper. 'If my job is compromised,' I thought, 'perhaps I could turn to him.' But the little man turned his back on me, when he realized I was looking at him closely. He had a roll of fat below his bald neck, I noticed, that was the same shiny pink colour. This layer of fat, which is not rare in men of authority, presents a sartorial dilemma: the tailor must either make the collar of the jacket above this roll of fat and therefore practically half way up his neck; or decides to keep it below, enlarging the circumference of the collar so it forms the border of the roll of fat, which remains in plain sight. This was the alternative chosen by the tailor for the man with spectacles, and now this sartorial attention I found quite touching, so that I started to laugh. I noticed, in this case and in others, how certain ideas, to which one attributes an intellectual or emotive value, mistakenly or correctly, tend to remain tinged with thoughts which may be entirely extraneous, for quite some time. This happens to me often: for example, seeing the little cushion of fat below the neck of the bespectacled and authoritative little man I felt more like laughing than cursing because the idea of the serenity of the stars continued within me. Come to think of it, I wasn't laughing about his roll of fat, but his authority, which in comparison with the so-called stellar serenity seemed laughable. I said laughable and not ridiculous, because there was no rancour in my laughter. I was aware it was joyful laughter, because I find cosmic comparisons always produce a disinterested and benevolent happiness. In spite of the insults the director continued to level at me, calling me among other things a 'shitty beast', I wasn't the least bit sad, nor annoyed with these men. If I gave the director a few kicks in the arse it was only because I realised from his behaviour that I had not the slightest hope of keeping my job. In this situation who would have abstained from giving him a kick or two? I am trying to say my reaction was a normal one: human, very human, because I was more amused than vengeful. But neither these episodes nor these characters are important in the overall picture of the night's events.

When I entered the room, Edi was not there; I am absolutely certain because I would have not only seen her, I would have seen only her and not wasted my time with any of the others. I was hoping to see Edi again even as I climbed the stairs. Of course this hope was unexpressed and oscillated between different degrees of probability. In general, I can say that every time the ambience or the people seemed strange or even hostile to me, my feeling of hope became more faint, so that the hope of seeing her again became less probable, entirely improbable or even hopeless. But at a certain point, while I was about to give another kick in the arse to the director who was running around the table, trying to escape me, I looked up and saw her.

'Oh!' I said, and felt surprised at being discovered almost with my foot up aiming at the director's arse, in an attitude undoubtedly amusing, and jocular but also decisively vulgar. I remember I began to smile apologetically, even half bowing. She returned my bow and started to laugh, or rather smile silently, but so openly that in effect her smile seemed like laughter to me. She was almost leaning against the wall, close to the mirror mounted above an elaborate rose-marble fireplace. The mirror was important, because it let me see the room, which reflected darkness and naturally reduced all the characters in the room, including me, to an ambience that was dark, even perhaps evil, but of minor importance to her, who appeared luminous and splendid. These ancient mirrors, as one knows, harbour a blackish depth which filters the scene they reflect, removing any urgency or real immediacy. When I saw in the mirror the man who'd gone through the window walking behind me, limping, but with a crossbar in his hand, at first I paid no attention, or rather I did, but didn't believe what I saw, because this sort of mirror removes so much reality from images.

Fortunately my incredulity towards the reflected image lasted only a second or even less, but that second lost before turning to face my adversary was enough to let the crossbar fall on my skull. I just managed to move my head to the side, and the blow, after almost detaching my ear, landed on my right shoulder close to my neck, fracturing, or at least cracking my clavicle. The gravity of the blow I had endured certainly did not escape me, nor the danger of the situation, with an arm clearly out of use; so without losing any more time I gave him a big kick in the stomach, sending him some metres away against a sofa.

It is strange how certain men, however big they may be, start whimpering once they are out of combat. I tried to pay no attention; I realized that a kick in the stomach was enough and I didn't need to give him any more, but his wail, and its interminable rhythm saddened me. Only at this point did I realize we were alone and this made me feel an anguished solidarity with him. I went up to get a better look at him: his rough face, leaning against the back of the sofa upholstered in red and green stripes looked extraordinarily pale and shiny as wax.

'Would you like me to bring you anything?' I asked with the gentlest tone I could manage; but he showed no signs of hearing, and continued to moan with a sort of implacable and progressive faintness: his wails became more feeble and infrequent, but this didn't give me the impression of a diminuendo, but more like a crescendo which was a crescendo of anxiety, at least in me. I was not much better off. Fierce pain spread all the way to my stomach and kidneys. My head was spinning, and my vision was blurry. It took a great effort not to lie flat on the floor. I thought of refreshing myself with some cognac, but realised that the bottle, which I unfortunately had put in my left pocket, was broken. I tried to get rid of it without cutting myself. Now what shall I do? I asked myself.

Strange as it may seem, the idea of leaving, *futtre le champ*, quitting the field, as they say, didn't occur to me. I think I was wanting to look out for the man who'd gone through the window: I felt a confused obligation of loyalty for him; I actually thought, 'But how stupid!' I applied the adjective to both of us.

In any case, since I had no cognac left, I moved toward the table which was set with plates still full of food and several bottles of wine, one still three-quarters full. I finished it off in short gulps without losing sight of the waxy face of the man who'd gone through the window. It seems now a very long time, but how much time actually passed while I was drinking and watching him? Five minutes? Ten? In any case when I finished drinking he had stopped moaning, put his head down gently and closed his eyes. Today they told me that he is out of danger and will be released from hospital in less than a month, almost back to his old self. I'm glad. I probably wouldn't have gotten over a clobbering like that. In other words: all honour to the deserving. I say this with sincere relief. But then I was convinced he was dying an interminable death in which I felt involved.

What can I do? I kept repeating to myself when I looked around and saw Edi at the door, which had been open the whole time. She beckoned and said, 'Come on, let's go.'

I was undecided. 'But what about the man who went through the window?'

'Went through the window?' she asked. 'Let's go!' Her voice was peremptory and she took hold of my broken arm. I started to curse for the pain, but she beckoned me to be silent. I gave her my other hand and followed her. I vaguely remember that after going through the gallery we went down some narrow wooden stairs, we passed a sort of long balcony above the garden and from there, after another set of stairs and a corridor, we were on the main street going through a door next to the Central Pharmacy.

NIGHT IV

I realise that while I am writing things seem comprehensible, sensible, orderly; but this is merely the effect of grammar; I am seized by the process of writing and the fact of its rules, so to speak. What I know, what as a writer I need to know about grammar and syntax, appears to be an understanding of facts, and how these facts took place and why. Actually I didn't know what was going on: it all befell as if I were part of an incomprehensible game of fate or fortune and had no way of foreseeing or reflecting on anything. Even my awareness of what was going on while it was going on was somewhat confused and fragmentary, because thoughts often go their own way, entirely different from the sequence of events. But someone reading me might well think: 'Here is the reason for this and that as well!' It is a common error and widespread. This extension, actually this transfer of logic from writing to fact is due to the fact that nearly everyone writes today: prisoners, whores, priests, horse trainers and everyone of consequence knows how to write, even someone like me who can barely do arithmetic. Nothing is more widespread than the ability to write and nothing is more deceptive because what distinguishes actual events and makes them radically different from writing, at least for some people, is the ignorance of what is going on. There are naturally other criteria for realizing what is actually taking place when it is happening in the present. I think the most useful and ordinary of those criteria is by comparison. In fact there is nothing that does not somehow resemble something else: even if this comparison does not explain or describe anything, it gets over the immediate singularity of phenomena, bringing something else to mind that is different or merely set in a different time or place. The problem with similes is that they are always ambiguous: an ambiguity, I believe, due to the variability of the approximation with which one thing resembles another. For example, I have often seen men that anyone at first sight would define as phallic headed, but they don't all behave in the same way or appear to have the qualities one might expect from the shape of their heads. Nature or accident have placed the basis of the likeness, one might say; but then something else intervened to make the likeness more or less persuasive. There is an art, with all the deliberation that term bears, with which one progressively approaches a likeness that destiny has barely sketched out: so, while many men could be said to be phallosimilar, only a few fully attain this resemblance: in this case one could say that their being almost coincides with what they resemble, point for point and in a deliberate and knowing way.

Enough of that! If I have gone on this way it is merely to explain how I, without knowing anything about what was going on during the night, managed to orient myself somehow, following or discarding likenesses. Now, for example, when I speak to Edi I realise I was fascinated by her not only because I thought she looked like a rose, in the vague sense in which one occasionally says of a woman 'she is a rose', but for the growing perfection of this resemblance. I saw in her signs that were only vaguely allusive at the beginning but became ever more closely conforming to her actual being, so that in her these two terms 'appearance and reality' coincided in what is commonly understood to be the nature of the rose. In other words, without ceasing to be a woman, Edi became, at least in my eyes, ever more a rose: from the pale beginnings in the director's apartment, when she turned to me the first time and called me an idiot, to the moment when she took my hand, and drew me, semi-unconscious because of the pain in my shoulder, through narrow streets and alleyways, urging me on from time to time with a peremptory 'Keep moving, you idiot', that increasing and confirming of roseness became more immediately perceptible. For example, at the beginning I had not noticed any fragrance, while now, while she was dragging me, each tug released an increasingly strong whiff of rose. 'She sprinkles herself with rosewater,' I thought and at a certain point I asked her. 'Rosewater?' she replied. 'This scent cost a fortune!'

Finally we came to a doorway, and in the dark and in silence climbed some stairs, and after she opened a door, Edi pushed me into a place with two big windows which, in the dark of the space, were shiny with the faint brightness of night with their outlines clearly shown. I kept looking at them, when Edi turned on the light: 'Don't worry,' she said, 'the windows look out over rooftops. The light will not show from the street.'

I let myself collapse into the nearest chair: 'I feel dreadful!'

She came up to me: 'We must clean the blood off your neck,' she decided, taking my good arm as if to pull me to my feet. 'He came close to decapitating you!' she added shaking her head.

I explained there was nothing wrong with my neck; just a bit of blood from my ear, where it had brushed against the bolt, but I was afraid my shoulder was broken. She didn't listen to me but pulled me into the bathroom and began to daub cotton wool and alcohol around my ear. I let her do that; I actually closed my eyes for a minute while I was sitting on the edge of the bathtub, comforted by the touch of her fingers. 'She has light and clever fingers!' I started to think, but the pain interrupted every thought before it got started.

'Your shirt is dirty, and so is your jacket. Take them off!'

I managed to slip out of my shirt and jacket, without too much pain, thanks to her help and a few curses, despite my inert arm. Now my chest was bare.

When she had finished, she took two steps back and rested against the washbasin while she looked at me in silence for an entire minute.

Then she said, 'But you've turned blue! Your whole chest is blue and so is your arm!'

I couldn't manage to turn my head to look in the mirror, and could only see part of my face reflected in the mirror above the sink. In any case I said: 'Am I? I have a ferocious pain. Is there something for me to drink?'

She shook her head: 'You don't need a drink! You need a hospital.'

I shook my head; I told her a few glasses of cognac would get me on my feet again so she wouldn't have to bother.

She agreed. It was not a good idea to go to the hospital. *They* would have found me immediately. And perhaps the shoulder wasn't so bad, since no wound was showing. We thought for awhile about the meaning of all that blueness and swelling and she appeared reassured at the end. 'You haven't broken anything inside,' she concluded. 'Otherwise your arm would be out of position, while in comparison with your good arm it only looks slightly swollen. You have very thick arms.'

I agreed. 'Yes, that's true.'

'Thicker than my thighs!' she declared after a minute of silence. 'I could give you an injection: in that arm it would be as easy as in a buttock.'

'No one touches my arm,' I protested. 'It's bad enough as it is. And then, what is the point? There are no wounds, as you said.'

'For the pain,' she explained. 'It is morphine: good stuff from the pharmacy.'

After some discussion I concurred it was a good idea, but the injection should go into my good arm, because morphine travelled around the body and, even if there was some delay, would eventually reach the source of pain.

'Why do you think they would arrest me in the hospital?' I asked, while she gave me the injection. 'You saw yourself it was a question of legitimate defence.'

'I saw nothing,' she declared calmly, replacing the syringe. 'There is no point in getting me involved. And who said the police would arrest you? The police only do what they're told and no one would want you arrested. On the contrary! Don't be an idiot!'

I protested I wasn't being an idiot, but perhaps I was, as she had repeatedly claimed. I didn't understand who would have found me in the hospital, if the police weren't searching for me, and if someone else were searching for me, I didn't understand what harm there would be if they found me in the hospital or someplace else.

She said she was sorry to have called me an idiot. She explained that she did it out of sympathy, because she had called her brother an idiot when she was a child. She loved him a great deal, and he had died. 'The sad thing is,' she added, 'that now they suspect you know possibly much more than you actually do.'

'How could I know more than I do?' I asked. The pain was fading and I started to feel weary, but not unpleasantly so. In spite of my tiredness I felt that thinking and speaking were now easier for me.

She took my hand again, pulling me away from the bathroom towards the entrance hall: 'You can sleep here, if you like,' she said. 'I have a folding bed for myself; I'll leave you the big bed: you need it.'

I thanked her: 'I would really like to sleep with you, that is under the same roof. I see that you want to protect me, but I don't see why I should be afraid of them. Who are these people you call "them"? The man whose photograph I've seen in the paper? And the one with the beard, like a collar and the voice of a sacristan? And the director? If those are the men, I could give them a kick in the arse any time I pleased.'

She nodded, smiling: 'But let's see,' she said. 'What do you really know?'

'Arms trade?' I proposed. 'Drugs? Both? How should I know? I am the most ignorant man in the world. The man whose photograph I saw in the paper could be a politician and from that I infer that there are some shady doings somewhere. But these are mere inferences. Isn't it rather,' I asked, 'that they have given you the task of finding out whether I know what they think I know?'

She turned her back on me abruptly: 'Now you are a real idiot!' she said. 'Don't you realize that they would kill me, if they discovered I have helped you?'

I tried to appease her and change the subject: 'You are a rose,' I said. 'You have the fragrance of roses, the health and delicacy of roses, and your voice is also rosy, even when you get angry.' I knew I was speaking foolishly but I didn't care.

She laughed and asked me what voice roses had, and I told her a story, largely true, and perhaps a bit made up as well, under the impulse of the moment. I said when I was ten years old there was another house with a garden near the house where I lived; there was no park or anything grand, but just a little garden next to the house, a square ten metres wide. In one corner of this garden were two trees, perhaps linden and there were rose bushes near the fence. As soon as it was dark, some evenings in the month of May I would climb over the fence and sit on the ground near the roses in bloom. Although it was dark, every time the little girl who lived in the house discovered me and stood next to me watching me, without saying a word. I furtively watched her shift her weight from one leg to the other until she ran away ten minutes or so later, as silently as she had come. Her presence disturbed me, but I was resigned to it. The disturbance the silent little girl provoked was different from my happiness for the roses; I felt that irritation and a certain kind of joy can stay together very well without mingling.

While I was telling this story she laughed several times. She asked me how tall I was when I was ten, and if I liked that little girl, and other such things. 'Why did you quarrel?' she asked at the end.

'With the little girl? I never did!'

'What do you mean, little girl!' she was irritated. 'I am talking about the director.'

I explained that a few slaps was certainly not a quarrel, but more like a joke, or at the worst, a misunderstanding. I was speaking fluently but also somewhat automatically, without thinking about what I was saying. I had some ideas that were hard to define, ideas that were more like effects or even phenomena, like, for example, summer when the storms come, with wind in the clear sky: a turbine in the midst of a thicket of trees and shrubs in full sunlight, twenty metres from the observer. Aside from the turbine in the isolated thicket, everything is calm and silent so that the rustle of the branches seems to be caused by the stirrings of a beast on some joyful rampage. The same turning of the dark green and shiny leaves to the unexpected paleness on the reverse side that by contrast looks almost white, makes one think of the instant variations in a laugh; but this laughing joy has just taken shape when suddenly the wind falls, and, perhaps following a wandering shadow, nostalgia and sadness arrive. Perhaps it is the fragrance of the plants, abused by the wind, that changes the sentiment and with it the ideas and words; but perhaps there are moments, points, boundaries, in which the universe turns and changes; in which without warning one moves from happiness to sadness and back again to happiness; or rather forwards and backwards and forwards again.

This last idea of forwards – backwards and forwards – backwards seemed important and I wanted to share it with her: 'There is a rhythm,' I began, 'a sort of pendulum, but without that mechanical rigidity of a clock.' I didn't find enough words. 'Do you understand me?' I asked.

'Yes,' she said. 'What is it?'

I didn't know what else to say except that I had suddenly had a profound idea and that she must believe in my words, because profound ideas are often the most vague as well: 'If an idea is sufficiently profound,' I said, 'it doesn't need to be precisely defined. Its profundity is sufficient in itself. In other words it is sufficient, but indefinable.'

'Right!' she said, clapping her hands; and I was aware that whatever she had understood or not understood from my chatter, I felt envy for her intelligence, or rather a desire without hope, a great nostalgia for her thoughts and not only her thoughts but her hands which applauded mockingly, and for the speck of light that glinted in her mocking eye. I also envied her past, what she remembered or had forgotten, in a word, I envied her existence which I wished had been mine instead of my own, perhaps by eroding or destroying mine.

'Very well!' I said, standing up. 'You have amused yourself enough. Now can I use the toilet?'

She made a face of mocking supplication: 'Go on!' she said. 'Don't be angry. If I sometimes smile at what you say or do, it's out of sympathy.' She held onto my hands again, but this time with both her hands, bearing the weight close to her chest, almost to her throat. 'And affection,' she said. 'I am doing many things for you out of affection.'

I was aware that the hand she held and pulled was part of my injured arm, but this no longer hurt me, or rather, although it hurt, I didn't care.

'I still have to use the toilet,' I said.

This is a crucial moment, because it is probable that if I had not gone to the toilet, she would still be alive. Or indeed at a certain point I might have lost consciousness anyway, leaving the way open for the killer or killers. Who can say? What seems most unreasonable to me in any case is the argument of the prosecution according to which I would have been the one who opened the window at a certain moment of the night and threw Edi onto the rooftop and from there to the street, and naturally, closed the window again. Only after these actions did I retreat to fall asleep in the lavatory, where the police naively said they found me.

Has anyone ever heard or read of a killer who falls asleep in the lavatory after the crime? And then isn't this care to open and close the window absurd! If it is true that I pushed someone through a window (and that was an accident and not a habit as now they would have it) I certainly was not concerned about opening the window first: in fact, any human body even if small, thrown with a certain energy, acquires sufficient weight to pass through a closed window and afterwards there is nothing left to close.

In any case, they say that the behaviour of madmen is always atypical, that is absurd; or rather that it comes into the typology of the absurd. I don't want to waste any time defending myself. If it suits you to judge me guilty of murder, you, sirs, will be the judges and there is nothing I can do or say to change your judgement. If I am writing now, in the first place it is because I have been given paper to do so, and in the second place because I don't have anything better to do. What is there to do in prison, aside from kicking other prisoners?

And, as time passes, it becomes ever more difficult to plant those kicks, because experienced fellow prisoners acquire enough agility to take their arses away from the natural trajectory of my foot. So writing soon becomes the only way to pass time which, when one is shut up, seems to become immeasurably long, containing an entire day and sometimes even an entire month of the past within a single hour.

So writing restores a slower movement to the passing of the past, taking the slowness from the passing of the present and making it more tolerable. Writing, the more one practices it, seems to me to be an ever more skilful and profitable hunt for a certain happiness that has passed by me in certain moments, fleeting and quick, leaving me in doubt as to its actual existence.

Was this happiness really there? I now ask myself and try to reply with as much accuracy and detail as possible. For example, while I was sitting on the lavatory and thinking about Edi's declarations of affection, uncertain whether to consider them mocking or sincere, I lingered over this uncertainty as if I were in good company. I could feel the proximity of sleep, but this time I didn't badger myself, as I usually do, with tortuous and difficult thoughts. Usually just before I fall asleep I have the impression of trying to find a way for myself amidst the meanderings of incomplete thought, expressed in propositions like, for example: 'He bent over to polish his shoes with a handkerchief' (certainly a very silly thing to do); and every time the stupidity of this or that gesture made me sad.

But that night, as I have already said, sitting on the pot, anything that came into my mind seemed like a good version of existence, easy and fluent, that is. Therefore, I asked myself using the familiar form of 'tu', are you happy? Honestly I could not have answered yes, and yet happiness, or a certain festive feeling kept on in my mind, even with regard to silliness like 'polishing my shoes with an handkerchief'. Then suddenly I realized that what had saddened me up to that time in the incomplete thoughts was not so much the stupidity of the actions they represented as the absence of subjects. These actions which present themselves to the imagination without anyone making them or having ever made them, have something funereal about them, a flavour of mourning and lamentation, and I even believe they bring bad luck. On the contrary, I was decisively happy that night sitting on the pot because I also believed I had just discovered the secret of sadness, not only that which comes at the beginning of sleep, but of universal sadness. Perhaps there is some exaggeration in the importance I attributed at that time to this discovery, but everything, in a certain sense, was exaggerated and jumbled. In fact, I believe that rather than distinct ideas as I now expound them, I had double or even triple ideas at the time. Certainly in contrast with the sadness I discovered in actions that had lost their protagonist, I now had the sense of a triumphing protagonist in the person of Edi, now extensive and inexhaustible. There was a quality of spectacle, I thought, in her tiniest finger movement, in the most fleeting movement of her lip, in every phrase she pronounced, however uncertain the intention appeared of what she was doing or saying, that made Edi a star and made me feel like someone drawn into the theatre by the sight of a glorious name on the poster. I was actually about to fall asleep, but this time I prepared myself with a peaceful and serene spirit, and probably was already asleep. To simplify things, I will say that in part I was thinking, in part sleeping and the part of me that was sleeping lent a background of silence, and a stately slowness to every thought I had, however banal. Quite naturally I also suspected that perhaps I wouldn't manage to get up from the pot and leave the bathroom. When I finally admitted to myself that I could no longer stand up, my thinking came to a halt. The last memory I now have of this final moment strangely has nothing to do with the night: I felt there was a great and peaceful light, like a cloudy day, and in that light the endless rustle of a forest of yellow leaves.

PASO DOBLE (1980)

Sharrock is a contraction used as a family name referring simply and precisely to a family story widely dispersed in the south. Such stories in some respects exemplify and are symptomatic of those racial and tribal characteristics which are held as proper to the people of that region. Well, this name is matronymic and has been attributed to the matron of the line, mother of many generations, who was found dead on a heap of dung, for all the world like a rug caked in shit. Hence 'Sharrock', shit-rug, by elision of the 't'.

It may be that the name implied some kind of evaluation in the sense that this woman of about twenty-five years had been extensively employed in a great number of rapes and fornications, and when worn out no one could object to her being cast off. Priests and the judiciary found such an interpretation acceptable and insisted on its legal ratification by extending this name to all those who took their origin from her. Moreover they devolved upon her descendants certain actual obligations having to do with shit, cesspits, and drains in general.

Consequently this event had none of the sense of futility often attendant upon accidents. On the contrary, officialdom considered her history memorable and worthy of being commemorated in marble or stone, possibly as a frieze on some great cistern. In the establishment of obligations they discerned that in the fate of the progenitrix all should be understood as having happened through necessity in an exemplary manner, rather than by chance and accidentally.

As an aftermath of one of the many rapes to which she had submitted there was a living son, who, when his mother was found dead in the manure, was seven years old. A few days after his mother's passing the child was put on board a Greek boat as a bumboy.

The story at this point could have been lost with our heir heading out to an unspeakable destiny beyond the limits of confused horizons towards the polyvalent possibilities of fortune. Who could have foreseen in which harbour (or dung heap) this son could have been discharged, alive, or maybe even dead, like his mother? Every peripathesis is an attempt on the coherence of history.

Instead three years after, in 1810, a discovery occurred, which has been meticulously documented in the diary of the parish priest of Lumezia. A note appended to the pages devoted to the month of June 1810, may be roughly translated as follows: *Half way through this month a youth was seen aboard an Egyptian boat and was immediately recognised as the very same one that the female known as Shit-rug gave birth to. Should he have been left to go with the Turks? Instead he was reclaimed and taken in as one of us. Since he was almost 10 years old, many wished to have him baptized as a Christian and so it was done as they desired. He was given the name Rosario because such a name gives us hope that if this baptism caused any offence to holy religion the Queen of Heaven will intercede for us.*

Without question in this discovery may be perceived features of the popular will as an institutional authority. Not in vain is it said 'Vox populi, vox dei'. In any case it is evident that if this child had been lost among people ignorant of the mother and of what had happened to her (her flight from the convent; her sojourn in the woods; her acquaintance with caves and grots and the shadows of dangerous beasts; her being, as people said, something between a sow and a woman), all would have been lost, like any other accident, in the painful marasmus of the universe.

Instead, in reclaiming the child the villagers had made out of an accident a beginning, out of the fate of the mother an exemplum, and indeed almost a norm for future events. One could say that they had referred the effect back to the cause, and that, as in every discovery, they had seen and recognised the continuation of the mother in the son, and had extracted the facts of her case from estranging fortune and consigned them to the stability of history as a species of destiny.

The pious villagers thought that the child could not inherit the ferocity of the adult mother because such an inheritance, feral rather than human, would be inconvenient, not to say dangerous. However, taking into account (somewhat jocularly if you will) her available femininity, they thought that her name Sharrock (Shit-rug), by which she was known from the first period of extensive rapes, should be visited on him. In the first phase, when she was about eleven years old, she would hide in the village chicken sheds; then, running, she would skirt the hedges and fences, cut across the scrub and brush, until, felled by a length of rough wood, she'd be done by her pursuers – youths of the village, at times more mature men, quite often old men who by chance found themselves in the vicinity.

Nothing could seem more casual than this. But looking more closely, her being done near the chicken sheds, shows notable characteristics of moral certitude. Certitude (according to Plato) is given by what is commonly accepted and known, like for example the son who should honour the father and the mother and suchlike propositions.

Well, what could be better known than that orphans, who lack the sustained penetration of paternal authority, when they remove themselves from the jurisdiction of the convent (to which they have been entrusted, in order to lead a life of penance, thereby improving the quality of their own death) should become the prey and vessel of sin?

This is an instance of primary certitude. A characteristic or sign of secondary certitude can be discerned if the mode of her being done is considered. Filthy nooks near the chicken sheds; dirty scrub strewn with crap on the edge of the village gardens, just out of sight of the housewives (but not so concealed that she could not be taken in by a searching glance) – these were her arbours. These good women then, pondering the holes in their lower regions and, analogically, the Pauline dictum *'inter feces et urinas'* (by which the apostle refers not only to birth, but to conception, and to any copulation, even between married couples, and not just to those disgraceful couplings, *contubernia*, with those who have forsaken repentance); these good women, then comprehended, in these fornications in the garbage, not just a secondary certitude, but an exemplary manifestation of the universal certitude of sin.

Sometimes, though, hearing the weak cries and sobs of the orphan from her stunted little voice, resembling mewling rather than full lament, they remembered her tender age and the straitness of those orifices which cannot be forced without pain. These cries opened even in them a certain distress or anguish. In this kind of instance, they would immediately elevate eyes and thoughts to heaven, mumbling '*Miserere mei, miserere mei.*' Considering too how it is necessary to take care of one's own sins, rather than the sins of the other, and how it is right to be in fear and trembling for them, they disentangled their thoughts from any temptation of succour, knowing also how old men, when drunk, can be dangerous when interrupted in their amusements.

Well then, all these events were certain, certainly effects or phenomena deriving from necessary causes, like thunder in a storm or like trachoma in the eyes of children, which latter, as everyone knows, is the fruit in the children of the sins of the fathers. These things were certain, and being so, true, therefore significant. In fact just as one says that the trachoma is the certain consequence of sin, so it is possible to say that it signifies sin. In sum, certitude, truth, and meaning are no more than modes of restoring effects to their causes, and phenomena and appearance to reality.

Now, since it was necessary to restore the son to the mother, the name Sharrock seemed kinder than 'sin', which, in her case, comprised all her fornications with young and old men and at times with a big dog which someone had excited over her for diversion. 'How is it possible to tell these things of his mother to a son?', the matrons would ask themselves.

But the son must know; to know it is not necessary to know all particulars, just a few details selected and therefore easily referred to general meanings. An example would be that, having found the mother dead on the dung heap, some people pissed on her, or details such as this, which conveyed the general idea of piss and shit. Which idea, though not itself essential, contained essentiality, with ease and a certain pragmatic elegance.

Pure essentiality is difficult to convey, and this difficulty cannot be overcome through the encumbrance of detail, but on the contrary, through some discretion of signs. Just as one does not need to enclose a field of potatoes with walls for it to be recognised as such (a few indicative stakes being sufficient for this purpose); so the name Sharrock (shit-rug) had this discrete indicativeness when considered as a composite emblem, in which 'rug' by virtue of its juxtaposition with 'shit', would gather to itself associations of dishevelment, filth, tatters and tears, and this was appropriate because the mother as a penitent orphan indeed 'tore' herself from the nunnery. 'Shit' on the other hand, conveyed not only an image of her evacuation from the convent, but of her proper origin; because, of course, one says that sinners are excreted by the devil, as if coming into the world from the original locus of shit rather than from the other more immediate orifice.

Be that as it may, between the boundaries established by these or other stakes on emblematic limits stands the norm or the locus or the special field, which in its entirety the son will regard as destiny in the sense of his own proper prescribed destiny, and on this account it will preclude all that is causal and fortuitous, and, consequently, all fortune for himself and his own descendants. Fortune is the faculty of evasion, of inclination towards whatever is other, a material possibility inhering in things rather than men, like the faculty a tree possesses of becoming a roof beam, or kindling.

Fortune for Rosario would have meant any digression out of his own name, in practise any estrangement from the shit, which, although understandably alluring, would have meant a reduction from the significance and truth of his own origin. Indeed it is said that Rosario had some fancy or aspiration to become a stone mason, but since none of those engaged in that particular trade in his village wanted him to be near them, no alternative was left to him, save that of traffic in dung.

In the parochial papers there is advanced some kind of mechanical investigation, in Lucretian terms, of the fancy of the young man. In there we find mention of some kind of individual clinamen or inclination which external pressures would conspire to reduce and control. Rosario, it is said, although constrained to work in dung, used it in such a way as to make barriers, and even complete walls of shit, so perfect that they could contain the viscid slurry in an extraordinary and admirable way.

The argument about the clinamen in the venerable notes of the priest is, of course, involved with a parallel argument about destiny, and in a more jocular vein with considerations about social control, where society is seen as answering to the totalitarian authority of the church. Here, in brief, was how the reasoning went. Clinamen, then, and, in the specific case of Sharrock's son, in the tendency to wall-making is a purely material thing, that is, a tract of matter, quantitatively individual and fragmentary, a capricious and insubstantial ambition of the particle to coalesce, conserving its oneness, and maybe even its sameness and presence. This could be seen as a vindication of *haecceitas* (that indifference to the universal, and to the particular, in the sense of particular destiny). The intrinsic instinct of its own weight or animality can be said to be fortune for a stone or an animal. In men, however, only incidentally can instinct be construed in a benign ordinance; it remains always true that in the great majority of cases instinct infers perdition.

To this, too, one must add (wrote the priest) that at the level of instinct the object of one's proclivity in the arena of what is not yet attained, cannot be considered intrinsic to the particle, the singular, but exterior and therefore common. Indeed, the saintly theologian has forewarned us: *Non habet homo res exteriores ut proprias sed ut communes*; therefore the particle cannot even pronounce its being in differentiation from the common. Again, the saint says in another part of the *Summa: Res ad invicem non distinguuntur secundum quod habent esse quia in hoc omnia conveniunt.*

Nobody therefore can legitimately think of coming into being as a distinct entity, and at once, but all come into reality as to an undifferentiated place. The distinctions begin elsewhere. They apparently begin in history, but in truth it is providence that initiates distinctions in the immense totality of existent beings with its genders and species, and in the bestial tumult of humanity it imposes order and category – the grace of the commandment. In other words the commonplaces of ethic and praxis are given to men by providence for their salvation, because prior to the categories of being, for creaturely individuals, notwithstanding any inherent clinamen or inclination, there can be no proper being, only a confused tumult, an abstract and savage potentiality without beginning or end. Only in the *ought* does the insubstantial possibility of being become concrete and certain for each individual. All things therefore for men proceed from the *ought* like a gift from God. Giving to each one his own, the church, minister of providence, gives certitude, goodness, justice, and virtually all the characteristics of perfect reality. Shit, then is what is conceded to Rosario Sharrock, not cement; and shit will be his *ought*, his destiny.

Of course, if all goodness, certitude and justice are reduced to shit for Rosario some futile wits might ask: will he be happy? The answer is: happy in the material sense, perhaps not, but he will certainly be spiritually content, even joyous and certainly proud. Collaborating with his own destiny (namely shit), being proud of being like shit, almost, indeed metaphorically shit, Rosario grasps his own true reality, and, in so doing appeases God and his own soul. These aforementioned futile wits might laugh at somebody proud to be a turd, of being an individual particle of the gender shit, but, on the other hand, mother, son and their descendents contribute to the integrity and stability of the family.

In any case no happiness or joy is implicit in the singularity of the self, but proceeds out of the generosity of the *ought*, and this is true not just for the individual but for the entire church. In saying that the church is happy, one must not understand this to mean that ecclesiastical happiness is inherent in what the word 'church' denotes, but as somehow belonging to the connotation, significance, and value of the church as a total reality. In fact the church is said to be happy because it ought to be happy, in the same sense as it is said to be good because it ought to be good, and holy because it ought to be holy. In other words, when we speak truly of the distinctively real we cannot constrain ourselves to say its being, but we must digress to what it ought to be. In a superficial sense, therefore, it does not seem as if the church has choices. Nevertheless, at the level of the single individual, for the single ecclesiastic, a choice is there, or, at least, there is the tragedy of a protracted almost interminable moment of unconfined liberty, at which point is chosen the ecclesiastical or necessary good, against any individual inclination which remains a simple possibility. The tragedy of choosing is only there for the individual and it resides in the difficulty of the triumph of ecclesiastical good, a triumph that is necessary, even inevitable, as the difficulty in every case in no way oppresses or confuses the church, only the individual, whose difficulty is in the participation with *ought*, the order and the law of God.

The papers of the old clergyman went on in a prolix and

confused manner about the priesthood, and the abstract reasoning often went astray amidst casuistical hypotheses. For instance he asked: it is possible (if one considers a specific case in point) is it possible to baptize with piss? Apart from such incidental questioning and reasoning, it was concluded that penance expressed the dilemma of the individual in this difficulty or tragedy. Tragedy here may be understood as exemplary punishment or penance, which is the only destiny open to the individual and therefore a difficult and dutiful unhappiness in the single individual within the happiness and ease of the church. A happy church cannot but be tragic at the individual level; moreover the truly happy church must force this tragedy into the resisting jaws of individuals, one by one. Above all the outlaw, the fugitive, the solitary, must be circumscribed within the iron palisades of the most humble destiny, the most miserable version of penance, like a sheep stripped of all its fleecy offerings to the wind.

Certainly there are those who seem at first sight happy as individuals: the Pope, the bishops, other divines; princes to a lesser extent, who discharge something of an ecclesiastical responsibility; generals, colonels; captains maybe; hangmen too, who in their daily humility may be considered to attain liberty in the good, because their actions immediately contribute to the good of the church. In this limited sense, then, their individual existence may be said to be easy and happy. Their individual penance, in fact, is all joy and festivity, but if this is so, it is either because of some complicity or, better, some fundamental coherence between their singular nature and that of the church; or because their penance by virtue of a singular grace, comes to coincidence with that of huge purgatories of the dead, issuing immediately in the beyond. In this last instance one may allow oneself to contemplate an indulgence of the dead towards the living.

But how can it be possible to think of such an indulgence operating on the son of the Sharrock woman, who, in the ferocity of wild death must have been confronted with, not the christian dead, but a limitless purgatory of pigs, shadows of innumerable sows, honking ghosts, all lost in the perdition of gorges of shit?

Needless to say, the presuppositions for legitimising the extension of her name to the entire family were argued exhaustively in the ecclesiastical records. But a century after these events another Rosario Sharrock was reading and rereading the notes of the good old parish priest without being entirely convinced. Well (this was how the modern Rosario was reasoning) – it is true that this ancestor of mine was violated on all the village dung heaps, evidently embodying an emblem of beastly fornication, but this had happened only at the outset of her life, and for a relatively short time, for four or five years at the most, when, having fled the nunnery, weakened by fasts and penitential vigils, almost undone by the beatings of the holy nuns, the debility of her bones disabled any resistance to sin.

When she came to woman's state, living wildly in the woods, needing to win food for herself and her tender offspring, she began to kill wild beasts, at first starting with the smallest, such as rabbits and cats, then progressing to larger and ever larger animals – sheep, rams, dogs, and at last calves and bullocks – and later becoming so swift and strong that she could strangle a big dog with one hand or bring down a bull with the blow of her axe.

So then, why search in the dung or in the shit (with which certainly she had some frequent habituation) for a model, type or species of her life, rather than in the forest and among those wild animals that were equally if not more familiar to her? Why concede this priority to shit and see in it the *ubi consistam* for her people, almost if it were *palpitans in ovo*, a distinct excremental salient?

However, alas, the fundamental problem escaped Rosario; that is the repugnance of Holy Church towards the natural and spontaneous life, which is considered wild in that it implies no restraint, unlike those silent gatherings of the desert fathers in their hermitages, and is typified as the sleazy foetid den of a she-wolf and her brood.

We heard, the pious villagers would say, the squalling and howling and the most awful clamour when that sow and her bastard prowled the mountains.

'This child speaks a great deal of sense,' the doctor was saying to the priest. 'No need of that' – the priest replied. 'His job is to empty the chamber pot.'

This conversation repeated itself, almost without variation, at each visitation of the doctor, but nevertheless, each time, the discourse acquired a different significance. On one occasion the child saw in this exchange a terrible example of frailty in human destiny, in that the parish priest, once all-powerful and feared, was now reduced to the management of infantile hands and discourses, those of Rosario Sharrock, who in 1912, at the age of ten, in no way enjoyed a better social and intellectual status than did the Rosario of 1812. On another occasion, however, the expression *'No need of that'*, sounded like an imperious call to silence, not a silent silence, because the priest would speak, especially when, the soothing effect of opium having subsided, with dilated eyes he would ask himself: 'Where can I turn? Where shall I go? Where can I go?'

All the same he would not move an inch. As his questioning did not expect an answer, his hypothetical going and turning had no destination. The very nature of his speech was belied by his horizontal and unproductive immobility, a quality pertaining more to silence than to words.

Unless – little Sharrock was thinking in his infantile way – unless it may be that words instead of being a species of action (as is commonly believed), things that move and happen, are nothing but decoration, things added or appended to what really occurs, as if to close or render unproductive the facts that derive from their motion. To what end was the old man asking 'Where shall I go?', when in fact it was common knowledge that he was going to die a bad death? The pain that he felt, if left to its own motion, would have conveyed him to death, whereas his saying 'Awful, awful, awful' seemed to halt this effect, or at least to produce the impression that the pain, proper cause of necessary and imminent death, could revolve on its own, or resolve itself entirely by flowing into the magic stillness of words.

These words – he would like to have said – were there only to fill up that little time between cause and effect, but there was no way in which they could become the partition he desired. Instead he kept quiet, allowing himself just to look at him, thinking: 'Look, old man, I am waiting in silence that your death may come.' And in truth the waiting for the cause to effect itself is, properly, silence. Words are no more than the falsifications of silence, or, perhaps, if daughters of silence, bastards.

Now, there is first of all destiny, that is the mutation of fortune, not a great transformation, but the smallest possible step from one thing to whatever, like from the parish priest being a great authority to being nothing but a stomach digesting itself, producing shit, not from fried chicken, that he had gorged himself on before in enormous quantities, but directly from his own priestly carcass; or, more simply, a transformation from life to death.

In any case, this mutation, from one thing to another so different as to be considered an opposite, was in fact such a brief shift, a movement so infinitesimally contracted, a distance so straitened, that it could not be protracted by vicissitudes worth discussing, but subtly demarcated by a fine shadowy dividing line, such as obtained between water and air, those radically different elements.

This fine thread could not but be silence and destiny, that is, the necessary process from cause to effect, without will or possibility – the unique itinerary without incident or variation. If this destiny is not the same thing as silence (which, though it may last, cannot be said to be truly a fact, because to say 'silence' involves negation of other facts, such as singing, dancing and so on) it is very similar to it. Therefore, what is the point of speech or of words?

If one says death there is nothing more to add. So also if one says life or silence, because such expressions are, internally, inside themselves, everywhere equal, containing nothing but themselves. They may be concepts, or mental elaborations, but if so, they remain inarticulate; they cannot be extended, flattened, or spun; they cannot be coerced into an orderly progression with an intervening variety between what they are at one moment and what they are at the next. Although they may come suddenly (in that death would come without warning to the priest through his internal rot, just as life was thrust upon him through a fuck), neither his life nor his death can be said to be the fact of fuck or rot. These words then, death, life, or silence, are mere addenda.

Now, once an addendum of this kind has been uttered what follows is a full stop. If, however, something enters such an addendum it does not come out the same thing as before. Now is it possible to be dead and to be distinguishable from death? So, if someone is alive, he cannot be said to be distinct from life, and if someone is silent, it is not possible to distinguish him from silence. But since the priest used to talk or, rather, used to question himself, and seeing that this was an activity he could well have done without, one could say that for him talk had the same value as silence, or that it was a variety of silence, and that this possible equivalence of silence and talk could be considered as his actual concrete groupings of words, questions, declarations, or whatever. Each utterance then, may be considered separately and distinctly, but at the moment, for the sake of the discourse, they all may be thought of as belonging to the gender of silence, just as Rosario himself belonged to the gender of child.

Having set up things thus, one may say that those priestly questions annunciated themselves as the contents of silence (like the voices or cries of his own ancestors which the peasants used to hear in the woods one century before), things discrete and indecipherable, in that they did not express, unlike thought, possibility, which tends towards another thing. However, they were directly and actually something in themselves, feeling or thinking perhaps, some kind of impetuous fury, like he had seen in a decapitated chicken, scurrying in the yard: a brief agitation between a laying hen and a cooking bird.

How could it be maintained – thought the child – that such agitation was an expression of chicken-possibility, rather than just a state of things real in itself? So, if some critical distinction could be posited, it could only be between the general class of chickens or priests and a particular chicken or priest in a particular state. And again, that distinction is simply silence, because only silence is capable of creating the split between what may be in the general and what necessarily is in the particular. In this chicken, clinically dead, but running, there were no possible remnants of the gender chicken. Supposing that deprived of her head, and therefore of her eyes, not seeing where to go, she could have legitimately asked of herself, 'Where can I turn? Where shall I go? Where can I go?' – no answer could have been possible, save '*Siste furiale impetum*, chicken,' or some other appropriate admonition.

In reality the chicken in this case, no longer of the chicken gender, was, in her discrete particularity, totally at one with her scurry. Whatever is actual has no need to be the expression of anything else: it is necessarily itself in its own particularity. Only the general or the materially possible clothes itself in expression, presenting itself accoutred in thought out of a nostalgia of being which at the same time is intrinsically opposed to such masquings.

Well – thought little Rosario – the priest's questions were at one with his death and there was no need to answer them, so he just enjoyed them, quietly and peacefully, in the interval between one bout of diarrhoea and another and the emptying of the chamber pot which was his charge, as he subsided into the calm and lucid quiet of the September evening.

So then it is only the possible and the general that require or go towards thought, not the actual and the particular. But maybe it would be more correct to say the opposite. If thought is a species of activity, it is, so to speak, the thought that moves, and seeks some kind of gender of the possible and not the contrary. For instance, enjoying the quiet of the evening the child could think a panoramic extension into the expanse of the countryside, with its small towns and orchards way beyond that which the tiny window of the priest's room disclosed. Through the half-open window he could see a fig tree, its leaves shining in the sun, and beyond that a fragment of a hazel on the slope of the mountain, yet could visualise the flat land beyond the mountain, and through it towards Battipaglia, and the straightness of the wires and poles of the new telegraph. Of such things one can think and talk, saying, for instance, that such a direct reification as the wires added to the expanse of the plain, gave it depth and clarity, which, although deepened in this way, was always of the gender of landscape and orchard. Was this, perhaps, the 'good sense' that the doctor mentioned, making itself plain.

If he had voiced these thoughts in the doctor's presence, it was just for infantile diversion. Perhaps the remote emptiness of some class of the possible elaborated itself with verbal festoons, just as present reality, for the priest, elaborates itself with the futility of interrogation. For the boy himself, reality was elaborated by the foliage outside the window, by two ripe figs ready to hand, and by the related problem: 'Do I eat them? Do I not?' This is the question, every time we consider the gender of the countryside or of that which can be eaten.

This possibility of gender was no more than redundant chat imposed on the immediate reality of silence, but in itself chat cannot be said to be. In sum, if one regards things from the aspect of reality there is nothing but the particular, and, by interior implication, destiny. In the domain of the particular there is, perhaps, a vocal, but essentially silent, waiting. If, however, one regards things from the aspect of chat there is nothing, a nothingness of nothing, only an artificial effect which is thought, reason, even good sense, reconciling diverse things with the most convenient or ready-made gender, for diversion in the void of waiting.

Returning then to Battipaglia, the telegraph and the priest. Priests telegraph to Battipaglia the death of the priest. That's good sense. Which priest telegraphs which priest? This is reason. It would be more diverting, however, to think of the subtile, linear rigidity of the telegraph wires with pendant priests looped by their necks. Perhaps without any great mechanical difficulty one could pull the wires to form loops, and then release them with the priest's necks caught in the snares. The wires would then, through natural elasticity and tautness, return to a harsh rigidity. Anyway this subtile and tense straightness of the wires, hardly visible by itself, would have been given substance to by such an aerial procession of clergy, black and silent and solemn.

Good sense? Certainly not. Reason? No. Perhaps what we are talking of is simply thought without specific purpose. The devil, it is often said, only appears to say 'Boo' and to scare dogs and children. Perhaps he appears only for decoration, and so, even thought, which is pure and simple and without purpose, appears as decoration and evidence. It disposes random and disconnected things in any gender or class of possibilities and because of this disposition seems to possess a certain certitude. What could seem more certain than this procession of pendant priests, rigid and straight like a sword in a vagina silentii?

Sometimes when the silence took over, priest and child would look at each other through the curtain of opium as if through a window, one on one side, the other on the other side, both mindless, vacant, in a great quietness.

A similar thing used to happen between chickens and scorpions. As he had seen many times, the chicken would watch the scorpion, swivelling the left eye towards him, and the scorpion perhaps would watch the chicken above him, raising his little tail and his tiny trembling pincers towards the great shadow. So they would stand, still, or they would move relative to one another, each matching the other, in a *paso doble*, until with a sudden decision, *furore accensus et ira terribilis*, the chicken snaps the scorpion's little tail with an exact lunge of the beak. One could see the little black tail fly, and then from the most distant nooks and corners of the yard two or three chickens, in an intense flurry of excitement, scurry to surround the maimed little creature and together they contemplate him from above.

Why then did this rage of the chicken so suddenly enter into the manic quiet of the *paso doble* with the scorpion, and why did the scorpion become the object of such fierce regard by the chickens? Sometimes he would find himself looking at his priest with a sudden access of rage when the old man, soporifically, with mouth agape, would release long monotonous farts. Violent emotions – Quintillan said – are usually brief and momentary. Perhaps, thought little Rosario, they do not occur or mature within the individual organism, psyche or person, but happen to the person unexpectedly and suddenly like lightnings out of the blue.

If this is so, perhaps such emotions are not in men, in their inner selves, but out there, in some part of the external world, behind an angle of a wall or a window pane, or like the ideas, in the empyrean. Having therefore their own being, they may intervene from their hidden space into the explicit location of men or of chickens, striking them in their instantaneous appearance.

If this is the case, his obsessed contemplation about the hanging priests along the telegraph wire, the tranquil clarity and certitude of his imaginary landscape, was but a quieter and more detached acknowledgement of that same idea which all of a sudden moved the chicken to maim the scorpion, and that, at times, moved him, with a start of agitated mania, to search for a piece of rope to strangle his farting charge, forgetting that his own childish energy would not be capable of accomplishing this.

Anyway this scenario of pendant priests that he used to call pure non-calculative thought was nothing more than a rather slow and prolix theatrical translation of that external incursion from above, that manifestation of the idea, which, although presenting itself, flesh and bone, in its naked necessity, had not as yet fully come into collision with him. Passing near him or maybe winging him it fell outside the ambit of his existence, somewhere beyond the window, the fig and the mountain, in the plain of Battipaglia, as lightning falls in the wood rather than in the village, retaining an indifference to both.

Ideas then are perhaps as indifferent to men as they are to chickens or scorpions, to priests and to little emptiers of chamber pots, whereas the various thoughts these ideas suggest are nothing but dilations upon or versions of the fugitive appearance (not entirely held) of some passing idea, fallen just beyond the horizon. So, an idea, coming from the west, from the sunset, even from the sun itself, having probably tranversed a distance of sky, had somehow come to stop on the plain of Battipaglia. That was all that was possible to say.

If one had spoken of such a thing to another, he would ask: 'Which idea? What is its name? How much does it weigh?' How else can it be possible for a discourse to define an idea? Or better, some discourse is possible provided that one speaks of the way, the when, and the situation of the idea and of whatever refers to the activity or phenomenology of the idea at the moment of its showing forth. Ideas do not exist for man but in their disclosure as events.

But apart from this discourse or event, an idea must be said to be continuously known, so that it is possible to say: 'I know what it is, provided you do not ask me what it is.' Are there not things that are known, so to speak, in silence? Darkness is a sufficiently obvious case, and so too is time. If one must speak 'about them', one may approximately say that they are things that envelop and comprehend the human subjects, rather than being enveloped and comprehended by the subjects. Therefore they are not objects, but themselves subjects, and may be stronger than men. What is relevant is that there is no sensible negotiation with ideas; darkness, for instance, although it is a thing proper to the sight, cannot be seen. Moreover it can be said that ideas are not things in the concluded, tangible and manoeuvrable way that things are. There is no action to be imposed on them. They inflict their action on all. It is futile to consider them as entities; it is useless to speak of them as if they were entities, because, among other things *entia non sunt multiplicanda praeter necessitatem*. However, since they are, they must be in such a manner, that nothing said thought or done could effect any change on them. It may be said that they are, *motu proprio*, whatever pleases them to intervene; as the chicken pleases to intervene with the scorpion. So, in the last analysis, if there really are ideas, they cannot be, in any other mode than that of a chicken. In short, without question, one can say ideas are chickens.

'If only your worship would tell me how many ideas there are,' exclaimed the child.

Sometimes his priest possessed, as if behind a veil of irremediable extraneousness, something like a calm that could be questioned; or, to put it in a better way, in this rapport between them, if to the evidence of extraneousness were added the appearance of a watchful and circumspect prudence, the priest's face, although undone in an abyss of internal biological decadence and beaten by waves of torture, at the same time could be seen as an object of inquiry. The questioning about ideas, or whatever, was nothing but a way of formalising such an inquiry.

In the formality of inquiry the child could look at the old man for hours, scrutinising his hairy and mucous nose. The eyes, now unquiet, now fixed, always too big for the face – once very large, but now the fullness had relaxed into folds on the skull, and the rich flesh shrunk into wrinkles – had assumed now an immense disproportion in that contracted visage. If he wished, he could clean the priest's nose with a wet rag or shave him without paying any attention to the old man's fear at the sight of a razor. In any case, although the old man could be said to be the object of his scrutiny, neither he nor his response (usually exclamatory, 'son of a bitch' or suchlike) were of much importance.

The inquiry of which he was speaking was grounded in itself: a bridge of reason which, although it did have something like supports in himself and in the priest, and from another point of view in the fig tree, or even in the razor, and in the basin of soap with which he shaved his companion's face, it is not possible to say that it was a bridge between the two of them or between any of the aforementioned things.

Why then say bridge of reason? For example, to the question about the number of ideas the priest's reply was: 'The broken arse of your mother.' But this story of his mother's arse was not sufficiently clear and simply to be considered in any way related to any idea, not appearing with the suddenness of lightning in the way that the 'idea' of cutting the throat of the priest with a razor showed itself to the boy. It seemed, rather, a tired discourse, endlessly repeated, in its own way reasoning maybe, but otiose, and possible only in that both of them seemed stationary objects at a distance one from another. Of each one, from a distance, it was possible to say anything, just as one can say 'it rains', seeing, from a distance, somebody walking around with an umbrella.

With regard to the idea of cutting the priest's throat, things happened this way, more or less: he was holding the razor, looking at the priest and smiling. The priest was looking at the razor, and at him and snorting through his nose. The story of the razor cutting the throat was a vesture of the idea, appearing in the room not individually to the priest or to him and perhaps not even to either of them. It would be better to think that he himself, the razor, the idea, and the priest, although disparate and extraneous from each other, were present at the same time and approximate, whereas the maternal arse, on which the priest insisted so much, was attached to the mother somewhere else, in the chicken shed, the stable, and so could in no way intrude. It could not touch or be sensible to the idea, or approach near the point where the partners of the idea and the arse could interchange. With regard to the razor, himself, and the idea, such was the closeness that one could speak of the child feeling the fury of the idea in the handle of the razor. It must have been the same for the priest as he looked at the blade.

Nevertheless if this is how things are, then why say 'it rains' while somebody walks out on his own? Or more generally, why say such a thing as 'arse', 'shit', 'maternal cunt', or what else, remote from that finding of nearness in ideas, things and people, an intimate nearness, independent of anything which can countenance one, and only one action, one, and only one necessity?

Given this necessity, this self-sufficiency of truth (if not the whole truth, naked and simple), reasoning, however considered, cannot be but evasion.

The bridge of reason, then, and the whole situation of inquiry, were other than the idea; whatever the idea might be was other than whatever had the status of truth and necessity, which is nothing but the dignity accorded to ideas. On the other hand not only were reasons, inquiries and thoughts lacking such a status, but even facts and action were lacking it; and yet beyond action and thought, the idea implacably remained suspended over its objects, over him, the razor, the old man, as the chicken's beak remains suspended over the scorpion.

If dignity then, was near the idea, there, though silent, was true thought, and here or below subsists merely the verbal appearance of thought. How then to define such difference? If no authentic definition be possible is it not possible to think of such thinking or doing, below, as an alternative of precisely the same value as the very idea itself?

There was no doubt that while shaving the old man, or cleaning his nose, or emptying his chamber pot, in reality he did nothing. This doing of his was a not-doing, spoken of as action in the way that one says that the leaves move, such moving not being a doing proper to leaves, which is rather a growing to greater darkness, than a drying, than a withering.

The idea in the leaves' case is a growth to withering death. The idea in the case of the priest, of himself, and of the room – apart from the instance of inquiry or bridging of which he had spoken before – remained, firmly, 'to kill' the old man. Even if in the meantime the leaves moved, he cleaned the priest's nose, and even perhaps his mother acquired a broken arse (a probability, this last, even if untrue, but such as could be accepted to disencumber the field of futile arguments).

In conclusion then there are facts about maternal arses, the moving of leaves, the cleaning of a nose which may be taken as being true or false *ad libitum*. Done or not done, because they are as indifferent to truth as to reality. Other actions are true without doubt, because to cut an old man's throat, at least as far as the idea is concerned, is true action, the truest. Nevertheless, even such an action could be done or not done, at least for a moment. In other words, although certain acts, with regard to ideas, emanating without deviation from ideas, are undoubtedly true, it is possible that provisionally they are indifferent to reality, or have no immediate pressure for performance.

'Tell me, your Worship, how can something be true and nevertheless, for some time at least, unreal?'

'Your father is a sodomite,' the old man spelled out with

authority, who, having been shaved discovered a new loquacity.

This lack of doing in accord with the idea, and therefore with truth and necessity, seemed at times like certain quiet evenings in September. While the light diminishes in the vacant sky, one is brought to think on the consolation of the heavens, with the hopefulness that people expressed when they used to say that if one could, even for a moment, be sure of a better state after death, then suicide would be a perfect option.

But such consolations, or the temptation to refuse to do what is necessary, are not just provisional but unstable also; therefore everyone, sooner or later, persuades himself into the action that the idea dictates. The protraction of inaction, its freedom in absence and vacancy, as in a post mortem, is not of such a substance as allows a prolonged, indefinite pursuance. Lacking any solid substance, it is something pertinent only to a circumscribed condition of waiting, similar to silence, but different in having quantity and duration, considering the little time or space it occupies in the dimension of thought, not a concrete, but a negative space, containing only what may be because it is not, signifying only an incidence in the texture or concrete necessity of doing.

'Is it then possible, your Worship, that freedom is no more than an incident, something like the possibility of not doing what is necessary, leading to an incident of reason, something like a provisional reasoning of what it is possible to do? Prudently, of course. What do you think, your Worship?'

But his priest was seized by a violent attack of the shaking runs, and so eclipsing all other questions the instance that insisted was: 'What am I to do? Will the pot in the commode hold this abundance, or will it overflow?' Anyway even this question was a vagrancy, because as soon as the diarrhoea spent itself, circumscribed by the lid of the pot, all the questions about the amount of shit and the capacity of the pot that at first seemed so intrinsic to the imperative of doing, showed themselves incidental. It was an incident within the larger necessity of doing, at face value within the incident of reason he had declared to be inquiry, which now revealed itself ampler than the momentary inertia which the mechanism of necessity would casually concede. While the passing over of this shitty episode did not require, in the child's view, any logical punctiliousness, merely a simple nexus between the anticipation of a fact and the fact itself (such were those considerations of quantity and capacity), reason, however, always traversed this not-doing or vacancy, with its long bridges through the empty consolation of the heavens. These were no coarse planks for unsteady crossings, but constructions of immense proportion and complexity, not so much for passing over, but for staying right in the middle of the gulf. Under this construction it would be better to say that the nature of reason could be seen as a bridge in itself with no function or purpose other than that. Being so, it was equivalent, by analogy, to the paso doble of the scorpion and the chicken, and to their inquiry and reciprocal observation, keeping their distances, firm and steady.

By virtue of analogy again, it could be said that between the priest and him the relation of mutual extraneousness was precisely the interstice of a fixed and unalterable distance, as there is between two pillars of a bridge, which are, of course, other than the bridge itself. Although the supports allow its existence to the bridge, it cannot be maintained that the bridge is there for them, rather it is there for the distance. However one wishes to manipulate this story of the pillars and the bridge, it is clear that it is the distance that enables inquiry, not pillars, bridges, or whatever.

In another way it could be thought that it is the essentially static character of reason which allows its incidental insertion into the tissues of necessity; establishing, in so doing, some of these necessities as monumental firmness, pillars. Only in this way can reified necessity be seen to stand, or, in other words, the necessity itself, although apparently traversed by the incidental bridge of reason, like a vindictive idol or an eternal deity, is in attendance at the edge of thought's lagoon in flesh and blood, its standing never to be circumvented, ignored or misconceived.

Again, the chicken, as well as the scorpion, or if you like, himself as well as the priest knew of the necessity of killing. This knowing was the only certitude that could be said to surface in the incidental emptiness of thought. As all is enveloped by the universe, so, thinking is enveloped by obviousness, by slogan, whose burden is a necessity of such inalterable indifference that it is not worth attempting to talk about it. Nevertheless, as everything that is derives its singularity as an incident in the

universal being, so every particular thought, every structure of
the reason, derives its specific peculiarity from this horizon of
knowing, this circle of silence, that at every point shows itself as
the inalterable figure of necessity. Such necessities are true
aspects of the universe revealed to the singular man, which he
calls idols, but which, in reality, are nothing but paradigms of
essential actions, that is to kill, to kill, to kill, to kill; or other
similar ideas and divinities. In fact, if one piously accepts this
circle of monstrously severe chickens around one's own
thinking, then one's reason, the bridge from edge to edge of
one's existential lagoon, would be elaborate, ornate, splendid in
nouns, verbs, figures, rhetorical occasions, verbal incidents such
as are capable of enriching silence, or of making dumb knowing
a copiose loquens sapientia.

Well, in the empty clarity of the heavens the consolation was
in such ornate tissues of words, such verbal play; now silken,
mutable, like a fig leaf in the evening breeze; now rigid and
vibrant like laurel leaves in the grove's shadow; but always
gracious, captivating, amusing.

If the universe can pay homage to the alienating wishes of the
singular man, this will not happen through prayer, exhortation,
or command, but only through some kind of obsequiousness,
through some gracious and genuine gesture, some decorous
attempt which the animal universe, without caring to read the
signal properly, sniffs, almost, in a pause of its own agony, in the
miasmus of its own damnation, so that sniffing, it distinguishes
itself from its own torment.

In this way a molecule can regale the ocean with the shivering
of its own different splendour. In the curve of waves, infinitely
grey, travelling over ancient wrecks beneath, the molecule, in its
clinamen, pirouettes, and suddenly, then, ends in silence. The
same universal silence; and . . . but . . . instead . . . meanwhile . . .
meanwhile. . . .

Meanwhile everybody craves his part, his locus, his useless
space or his splendid scene in the night of the universe. But
perhaps only those who are wise, pious, those who know how to
bow down to the divinities which from all sides press down
upon us, can wrest for themselves a longer dance, a longer
interval, a more divergent parenthesis between the glance of the
severe goddess and her fierce beak.

In this interval the most pressing question is not *quae verba dicere possent*, but how, in the verbal selection, an alternative to reality may be mirrored.

If one desires the singular incident to be of some duration, and coherence, so that one can say it is one and the same, this cannot happen but through trafficking and exchange between accident in reality and the necessity of reality, between one in the sense of sameness, and one thought of as true: a tangle, then or a fraudulent attempt on the indifference of the universe. Nevertheless *hic labor, hoc opus est*. This then is the real thing, the real act, not like his brother's reiterated febrile gesture of strangling cat after cat, rat after rat, or cat after rat.

'Would it not be better to hang kings, viceroys, or generals at least?' he asked his brother.

In answer to this question, wonder and joy appeared in his brother's big toothless mouth: a sign of real happiness, as it appears in the mutes, who, lacking words, arrange their desires for immediate enjoyment and contemplation, and who look from the material present always to a slightly remote one, perhaps seeing too how the hypothetical general or the profile of such, could inhere in the profile of a cat.

His brother's seeing was more than just ordinary seeing, raising the cat vertically, with the tail grasped in one hand, the noose around the neck in the other, he elevated it against the quiet light of sunset, as if considering it more attentively. His attention now implied a further engagement in the immediate sense which makes it possible to say that the reality of the cat, its small teeth grinding in its little distorted mouth, had become in itself richer and more engaging.

'In every case, this much is certain,' he said to show his sympathy to his brother. 'The thingness of things does not stay with things.'

Of course many other ideas came to his mind, the general sense of which was as follows: reality does not reveal itself in its entirety in things, but strays from them; or, reality is what, even at the smallest point, almost imperceptibly in its unique occasions begins to inhere in whatever occurs. When we have the beginning of an inherence, immediately we have reality. Reality has a tenuous beginning in the material presence of the cat or of the rat, but it grows from this small and fragile opening, becoming stronger and more differentiated, becoming more real; that is, it improves its own reality. If that were not so, why would we say on some occasions: 'That's not it'; or on others 'That's it'.

In this case, then, the hung cat was 'it' in the strongest sense of the word, that is a growing 'it', an improving 'it', and therefore by this improvement coherent to its own inherent, immanent principle. What the brother was seeing was the immanence of the more real, which, although beyond the physical evidence of the cat, against the light, was in the cat itself. To disregard the cat would have been to disregard the stronger reality; and, vice versa, to renounce this other force would have been to throw away the cat, saying 'that is not it', which could have been done only in a futile change of mind, but never in the serious, engaged domain of thought that remains steady, seeking sameness.

A general, or a king, then, could be said to be the metaphysical immanence in the physical profile of the cat, but considering only the essential as all children do, Rosario concluded with sufficient certitude that the elation in his brother's expression derived from the fact that he was looking at one and the same time at his physical cat and at a metaphysical general, as in immanence or confrontation between the better and the not yet better.

One can even say that in this engagement of serious thought the bridge of reason is nothing but the confrontation between the metaphysical and the brutally empirical version of the same reality, which nevertheless is always immediate to both versions, or the commonplace of the immanence of the better to the less better. If there were no immanence in both versions, how could it be possible to hold this confrontation between the two? What sense would there be in saying 'better a hanged king than a hanged cat'?

So: even if the idea is one, and one the norm and commandment that cannot be evaded (unless it were possible to relinquish all pity, thereby in fact incurring divine wrath) then in this order, norm, or commandment it is possible to compare empirical and metaphysical aspects of things, acts, and other minutiae, in themselves trivial or useless; and in this comparison delay for a time.

This delay then, this extended duration of incidental reason, this time gained for the singular man, is what makes the difference, not words or actions. Considering this, a difference can be found within the steadiness of homage or pietas, and with it the choice in which consists the arbitrariness of the singular man.

This very choice, then, may be said to be between a wild virtue, in which is expressed a spontaneous and passionate obedience to necessity; and a virtue cultivated, astute, fraudulent, but meditated and capable of reducing, or at least attempting to reduce, universal necessity to singular destiny.

'What do you think of it, your Worship,' he asked, shaking the old priest; his large head collapsed on his shoulder was trembling lightly now and then like a leaf in the breeze, more and more delicate and cool, that comes in the late evening.

'Uh-um. Uh-um. Uh-um,' said the priest, suddenly opening his eyes, his head still reclining on his shoulder. 'What?' he asked.

'Nothing,' the child reassured him. 'Your Worship, is only shitting. Should I light the lamp?'

While he was going towards the lamp, like every other evening, the old man, stretching his arm out across the table, tried stealthily, but not without scrabbling, to reach for the bottle of laudanum that the child always put well in sight, but at a safe distance, no more than a centimetre beyond the reach of the stretched arm and extended fingers of the priest. It was like every other evening.

'Leave that bottle alone, your Worship', warned the boy as usual.

All was equal then: the lamp, the paraffin, the slight humidity of the evening impregnated with the smoke of burnt stubble. The same moon, still pallid, although it had slightly shifted its position in the sky, and become fuller, could not be said to be very different. Or could it? How different? A little? Very different? How different was the priest's reach in trying to steal the laudanum, or was it identical? Absolutely identical? And at the same time absolutely different?

'Your Worship should not drink the laudanum now. You know very well the bottle should last through the night. Only tomorrow can we start on a new one.'

This slow, tranquil explanation, this, yes, was a novelty, because the child never gave explanations, only warnings. This explanation was a prolix extension of what was necessary, a disentanglement of a totality, which, although contracted in that one single moment of the evening, comprehended much else; just as the room comprehended many pieces of furniture, books, the commode, the old man's long table – always the same things in the same room. Apart from their original concentration or contraction, these things now belonged together in a different manner, more relaxed and calm, with a greater distance and without those hateful interferences which made of the room and the hour an oppressive totality of time and place. Now, for instance, to go from the table to the lamp, obeying the prolix tempo of the explanation, was like the first strolling out for its own sake, so extensive as to include (hypothetically at least) the courtyard, and passing under its porch the garden, and then the lovely laurel grove, which, in the evening, beneath the rising moon, he knew to be thick with rigid leaves, dense with the nests of spiders with their swart clots of dried flies. And then, following allurement after allurement (obeying the same steadiness of mood) – one could go beyond the minute attractions of the world and the ample skies of the effulgent moon towards other settlements, other countries.

This much is certain. The variety of the world invites; nevertheless there is always one particular thing that is a good invitation, or a discrete proposal, such as when the mayor of this village asks the Piedmontese lieutenant: 'Sir, would you like to taste my wine?' Another kind of invitation is when he says 'Eat, you sow', to his mother, because her milk is needed to suckle the mayor's son, where the lieutenant's sampling of wine has no end but to please and delight.

There are two manners in which things may be proposed: one gracious and gentle, the other imposed in fret, as when the mayor shouts at his mother: 'Go and get figs,' and so saying propels her into the courtyard with a kick in the arse.

When he gave the old man this lengthy explanation about the laudanum he had, so to say, emphasised the brutal necessity that the old man should not drink the laudanum, but at the same time this explaining opened into a space of free talk, which could itself open into something else. In fact why not invite the old man to drink while engaged in talk? For instance, 'Would your Worship care for a little laudanum?'

Having lit the lamp, he brought it to the table and sitting, started to look at the old man with a different curiosity.

'Tell me', he asked. 'What if what has to be done were done with complaisance and decorum? Wouldn't it be so much better?'

This is the point. Would it be possible for all things done to have been done with decorum? For example: the mayor kicking his mother, the offering of wine to the officer; the mayor shooting his brother in the mouth? Even worse, if someone discharges a blunderbuss into someone's belly, like someone once did to his ancient grandmother, can this be done with complaisance? To tell the truth the mayor shot his brother with salt, not lead. His intention, according to himself, was only to ruin his teeth, not the whole mouth and tongue.

At least in the mayor's case a certain decorum may be discerned, a certain discriminating intentional accuracy. Even here perhaps it ought not be out of place to speak of complaisance. Maybe the problem is other: the shooting of both his ancestor and his brother were retributive and secondary acts: in the first case because her life was lived contrary to repentance; in the second his brother ate the mayor's fried chicken.

These last acts derived smoothly from other facts in a more or less direct and responsive manner, whereas his mother's kick in the arse or the proffering of wine can be considered original, primary actions, emerging out of an impulsive vagariousness in doing them that the mayor had. This same vagariousness issued in the ball of phlegm that the mayor projected onto his father's head. 'It is nothing,' his mother declared, considering her husband's bald pate encrusted with the mayoral phlegm: 'It is amusement.'

Amusement, evasion almost, can be seen to inhere in such acts, in which case they resemble the evasiveness pure thought and useless reason, which presents things in themselves, gratuitous, isolated. To take pleasure then in a hung priest was independent of anything, referred to nothing, was secondary to nothing. If somebody asked his brother, 'Why are you hanging the cat?' he would have replied: 'It was a fancy.' And indeed this phrase was the one most frequently used by his brother before the mayor had made him dumb.

The imagination inheres not just in words but in actions too.

Out of imagination in fact, and not just for the purpose of amusing the Piedmontese, both his brother and he had asperged the procession of the patron saint with pig's piss. The fact that the Piedmontese and the locals or other people delighted in this did not detract from the primary and imaginative character of the action. Instead it confirmed it because imagination and delight are correlative characteristics of arbitrary doing, pure thought and pure action, as opposed to thinking and doing correctly, which relates to other thoughts and actions. In this sense imagination can be likened to freedom and fortune, to strolling out for the strolling's sake, now regarding one thing, now another, with complaisance, not for any external reason or cause, but for the delight in the appearance of these very things, their being offered, as the mayor offered a drink to the lieutenant.

Offered by whom? This is the problem. But before the problem of the subjective agent in its more immediate sense, there was the problem of what was being offered, which was opened into discursively. For instance: 'Would your Worship like a little laudanum, or would you prefer a kick in the belly, or a knife in the throat?'

The difference among these alternatives consisted in the fact that he would certainly have accepted the first and refused the others. Further, would not the mother and father have refused to be kicked on the arse or spat upon? Unfortunately the kick and the spit were an immediate and undeniable bringing home of reality as reality, whereas the spoon of laudanum and the glass of wine could be considered as gifts brought home by a reality as it should be. Or rather, in both cases, these immediate and primary gifts occurred as gratuitous or fortuitous events, but whereas with regard to the kick and the spit one must speak of a brutal accidentality, which would be refused rather than accepted. One may, with regard to the offering of wine or laudanum, invoke something like grace or fortune.

'Well then, your Worship, would you care for a spoon of laudanum? Should I put it in the wine?'

'Eh-yes,' said the old man with gluttonous assent. 'Eh-yes, eh-yes' he continued to repeat, while the child poured the laudanum into the spoon, which he then, with pharmaceutical care, tilted into the glass, without spilling a drop. 'Eh-yes,' said the priest, watching the straw-coloured wine clouding with amber tones, as it mingled with the maroon of the laudanum.

In this series of actions every minute detail was enjoyed, making it such that it could not conclude with the brutal finality of a kick in the arse. It proceeded slowly and with decorum, taking a certain length of time, that was a centre of attention to all those involved. Moreover, it could be added that between the old man and the child there obtained deliberate conjuration in the action, setting it apart from all else, enacting a selection from among the things of the world, setting aside all that is not utile, delegating them to exclusion beyond the space of the action, and drawing into that space the lamp for its light, the table for its level expanse, the spoon for its concave holding, the wine for its dispersions.

Everything then was happily ordained, part by part. Things that might interfere – books, old sausages, crusts of bread and bits of chicken – although all over the place, were held at bay by a magical circle, so that in the domain of the act, and the time and place in which it was enacted there was no superfluity.

In this gracious offering, the gratuitous and the necessary, fortune and what ought to be, imaginative freedom and technical discipline, were reconciled in a balance so difficult as to be a delight. It was just as it had been when he and his brother, balancing on a narrow lip of a wall, their brushes already immersed in the bucket of pig's piss, measured the advance of the procession by the growth in distinction and clarity of the recited litanies, second by second. In the air lightened by the evening dew, they could see the growing celestial reflection of the candles: even their increasing anticipation, before the aspersion of piss, was an integral part of their freedom when they had dispersed their blessing. Before belonging to after; after belonging to before. Although he shouted, 'Come on, run,' to his brother, the calm accuracy with which he moved along the top of the wall, balancing the bucket in his hand, saying 'The whole lot on the priest's head', endured, increased or evolved according to a necessity and rule of its own, exceptional to everything else, totally selective. It happened then that while the parish priest was agitating the standard and shouting and swearing at those who had broken rank, the brother, taking account of his movements and those of everybody else, found him on his own, at a point near the wall, and drenched him with the full bucket of piss all at once, so that the priest abruptly stopped, and was silent. In an instant the confused and vocal consternation of the crowd changed into a deep silence of calm and wonder.

'Does your Worship remember last year's procession?' asked the child. This was not properly a question, rather a consolatory insinuation. He wanted to suggest that the flat ferocious logic of the universe had incidents such as those described which were objectively happy, and that they were not few.

Not all that is out there then is grey and indifferent, but maybe there is something (in natural history, in botany, in mineralogy, in the tribology of materials), a moment, a passage, which can be extrapolated from the universal context, and enjoyed for a length of time as a thing in itself. This was now happening, possibly, in the biology of the priest. His drinking of laudanum and his feeling happy was as if unconnected with his huge intestinal disorder. It was a closed moment ordained under rules of lucid calm, an episode of quiet, or maybe quiet itself.

Perhaps then in such moments of extravagance, in some uniqueness inexplicably inherent in the facts, there is an ingredient which refers to individual destiny, the ought no longer necessity in the total, indifferent and unmediated sense of the universal and the infinite, but reconciled with the particular and the singular. Through this, the singular comes to be complete in itself: a self-reflexive totality, extending or expansive within a time of its own, and sufficiently durable. So perhaps, even in the case of his ancestor, destiny, instead of being defined and imposed directly from the external world through the implications of the emblematic title 'Sharrock' (as the church maintained), defined itself, with slow deliberateness, from the interior, through a kind of continuous interchangeability between every moment and any other moment. The beginning, the middle and the end of her whole life were interchangeable, in at least as many combinations as can be mathematically derived from three terms. When sequential order is eschewed a repetitive calculus is entered into, continually rehearsing sameness after sameness.

This combination series, where end and beginning are alike and interchangeable, could be said to comprise the calculus in which all his family could be thought to have the same destiny.

One fact or whatever other element in that destiny is mirrored in another fact or element, and this second one in yet another, beyond the first, itself now other. So through such likeness, extended throughout all their alternatives during a century or more, he could recognise in himself and in his progenitrix, common likeness, but a difference also in the way in which a mirror can be said to be different from the object reflected and the reflection.

Apart from all this, there is a likeness in the characters and moral determinations of all those who take part in this destiny. In fact his determination to hang the priest, and his brother's to strangle generals were alike, maybe just in imagination, or possibly in that they both referred to the same fantasy. Nevertheless, their determinations were alike certainly in this aspect – they both had referents in historical facts: the fact that the brother hanged cats; and that the progenitrix used to strangle dogs.

Therefore, this bridge of reason, this tissue of relations among the contents of pure thought was nothing but an acknowledgement of likeness, a mirroring, a recognition of characters, almost a silent embrace of them, in which he, the child, now could embrace and recognise his ancestor of a century before. Like her own son, he would have clipped in the circle of his infantile arms the great woman's ponderous bum, burying his face between the cheeks of the buttocks, and would have said: 'I too, I too will strangle dogs and priests and nuns; I too will strangle bishops, cardinals, popes.' And although these latter are more difficult to get your hands on, and in reality rarer to come by than dogs, nevertheless, in the ambition of determination, they *are* as huge immense dogs, or, they could be said to be dogs. By the same token, in the brother's thought, generals were equivalent to cats, could be said to be cats, and cats could be spoken of as cat-generals.

Destiny, therefore, could be said to be the correspondence of like moral determinations of intentional meanings, even if those meanings are referred to a variety of facts, or attributed to things in themselves insignificant and occasional. This version of destiny seems more thinkable and therefore truer than destiny conceived as an emblematic confluence of piss and shit. Even if shit and urine were not lacking in the family's story, these ought to be considered gifts of mundane fortune; or if you like, salient features of that reality most present to his family, an inventory of the family, a sequence, like the litany of the saints. What does it matter which saint comes first in the litany? Equally, which comes first, piss or shit? So it is with everything in the heavens and on the earth. There is no order in the sequence of individual things, so that they may be cited as denotations with no connotations whatsoever. To say 'Rosario' means nothing, just as to say 'turd' means nothing, although someone may amuse himself by gesturing to one turd among many, or toward a saint among many. Of course, if, as seems probable, every likeness between things may be established through the ostensible gesture, with its commanding gratuitousness, many things may be made to come to immanence in some emblem or sign, provided that the gesture which puts such an emblem into being is an intentional action, like when you hang cats for generals, giving cats general connotations.

Of course reality for his ancestor could be said to have been mainly shit, but the nunnery also, the forest, the wolves, dogs, rifles, the hunts, and the church. It is true all these flow together into one unique immanence, shit, but the assumption of this, the most proven likeness to himself, was as futile as saying that his brother was like a general.

But wishing, however, to insist on this emblem, the only thing that can be said is that the whole world was like shit for the woman: the stones were shit, the water, the dogs, the nuns, the old men, houses, chicken-sheds, churches. But then what power could have imputed this immanence of shit to the universe? No, no power, rather the shit itself, in person, discharged itself from the heavens to the earth – a unique connotation, a great idea – which like a generous shadow from above accompanied the process of experience, fact after fact. Something was looking attentively and silently from above and attentively and silently was being looked at from below, from birth to death, or, more simply through the duration of this reciprocal looking, this reciprocated consciousness, in the process of facts, fact after fact, indifferent to birth and death, and to all individuating limits. Although things are intrinsically different, they move together, their exclusive characters without meaning. There is no birth, no death, no killing, no being killed, only otherness, extraneousness, and in that the bridge of reason's incidental peace, the thinking of likenesses, which everywhere and at all times is the only possible peace.

This is how it was between himself and the priest. Between his pouring of the laudanum and the other's drinking of it, there was only a proceeding in accord, an arrangement, a specular going, from two remote points of a separate distance. Now the bottles were empty, the old man was sleeping and the boy was awake. But from both remotenesses they were going in a *paso doble*, perhaps not even looking at each other, having no need any longer, but looking instead at the sameness of another thing, that sameness containing the sameness of all other things, and, as well, their own likeness. Just as the boy, awake, could see, calmly, the same things: the books, the chairs, the lamp, the table, all the other small unnumerable objects; so in that nerveless sleep, perhaps the old man was seeing everything in tranquillity, the elegant successions from thing to thing without agitation and internal dissension. In quiet, in great quiet, in the luxury of interminable time, he could have counted all the stars in the heavens, all the leaves in the world, all the same leaves and stars and ideas, without fret, giving himself up to the slight rhythm of the child's embrace, as he was rocked to and fro in those small arms, that frail circle.

POSTFACE

It is customary for the critic who attempts to characterize the work of an author to start indicating what appears to be the literary tradition in which such an author find his place. But it would not be possible to indicate specific meaningful antecedents for the present collection of short stories. Pirandello? Svevo? Joyce? Proust? Kafka? Perhaps all of these rolled in one, and yet the essence of Spina's creative work would still elude any attempt at a convincing definition. Though to a certain extent reminiscent of Pirandello's argumentativeness, of Svevo's ironical psychoanalytic attitudes, of Joyce's shocking flow of conscience, of Proust's elegant psychological narrative, of Kafka's nightmarish representations, the narrative of Spina could hardly be linked *tout court* to any of these literary manners. Like Dante's panther, it spreads its scent everywhere and yet does not reside anywhere.

The overall impression is that the narrator is prisoner within his own mind, unable and unwilling to emerge from it or to escape from the intricacies of a world in which past and present, reality and phantasy seem to have lost their connotations. The result is a fascinating maze in which the reader, once having penetrated, will proceed deeper and deeper, unwilling to extricate himself. The intelligent originality of the author's mind as revealed by his written word attracts even more than his starry skies, his clever reflections, his unexpected burst of (black) humour and the combination of the narrator's adventures.

A 'new' author, a new classic.

Giovanni Aquilecchia
University College
London